It’s [illegible]

It’s you

It's Not Me It's You

Charlotte Bigland

embla books

First published in Great Britain in 2022 by

embla books

Bonnier Books UK Limited
4th Floor, Victoria House, Bloomsbury Square, London, WC1B 4DA
Owned by Bonnier Books
Sveavägen 56, Stockholm, Sweden

A CIP catalogue record for this book is available from the British Library.

eBook ISBN: 9781471412554

This book is typeset using Atomik ePublisher

Embla Books is an imprint of Bonnier Books UK
www.bonnierbooks.co.uk

Dedicated to everyone who slogged their way through the stories I wrote as a teenager. You're the reason I kept writing. (And hopefully improving said writing!)

PROLOGUE

Saturday 5th November

There's a knock at the door. With a cold clogging up my sinuses and making my nose run, I open up to a foggy London afternoon with a drizzle of rain in the air. Two police officers stand opposite me. One is pretty, curvy, female. The other, a gangly male. I grit my teeth, hoping that they're here to arrest Bob, my live-in-landlord.

No such luck.

Obviously.

"Jennifer Beeny?" asks the woman. Her voice is soft but serious.

My chest jolts.

"Jennifer Beeny?" she asks again.

"Y-yes?"

My hand, still on the door handle, slips. Whether from drizzle or my own sweat, I can't tell. My mouth is dry, my palms are wet and my heart is racing as I wait for the police officer to continue.

"I'm DC Powell and this is Inspector Grantham." She motions to her colleague, who nods. "We need you to come to the station and answer a couple of questions."

Oh. Oh my God. I try to form words, try to spit out a sentence, but the traffic blocking the road ahead splutters to a start, drowning out my croaking attempts.

I nod.

Passers-by stare when I'm led into the police car and again, fifteen minutes later, when I'm escorted out. If I wasn't so shell-shocked, I'd probably think I look badass – a fierce London gangster. Although I'd need bigger boobs, better hair and less snot dribbling down my face.

No one stares in Hammersmith Police Station. I'm led to a small room off the main corridor, that looks roughly as I'd have imagined, given my limited consumption of detective shows: dark walls, a wooden table with two chairs on one side and one chair on the other, a recording device on the edge of the table. I look for a two-way mirror, but there's not one to be found.

"Not what I expected," I mumble.

Oh God, I shouldn't have said that; they'll think I *expected* to end up in a police station.

"I mean, exactly what I expected. No – nothing like, because I've never . . . expected anything," I trail off, cheeks burning. DC Powell's brows furrow in either amusement or concern. She pushes a braid behind her ear and sits down.

"Okay, take a seat, Jennifer," she says as the officers settle into their own. They place folders, notepads and pens on the table. DC Powell presses a button on the recorder and states today's date and everyone's names. It all feels rather like a film, and I have to remind myself this is very much real life.

"Jennifer, it's your legal right not to answer the questions we ask, but not answering may be held against you in a court of law," says Inspector Grantham as he rifles through his notepad. It's the first time I've heard him speak. His voice is deep, a little posh. His Adam's apple moves up and down his long neck as he speaks, and whenever he coughs or swallows. He has the most pathetic moustache I've ever seen, fine and thin, like the first attempt of a fifteen-year-old boy.

"Oh okay," I say, the word "court" clattering around my skull, launching from one swollen sinus to another. But I won't end up in court. Impossible. Still, there's a lump in my throat I can't swallow.

"So, a bit about you," he says, eyes still fixed on his notepad. "You're twenty-three years old, grew up in Redcar, you've spent the past ten months in London, currently lodging with a man named Bob Knight. Jennifer, interrupt me if any of this is incorrect." He pauses and I nod. "And you're a receptionist at OnIt Insurance."

They've found out a lot about me. I wriggle on the hard plastic seat, an attempt to loosen a body I fear I'll lose control of. Sweat tickles my brow. My hands shake against the table.

"Yes, all correct. All true about me, all true, yes. Sorry, which . . . why am I here?" I ask for what feels like the thousandth time. The reticence of the two officers is frustrating, and it seems to amplify every clumsy mumble I make. A confession to an act I don't even know has been committed seems on the tip of my salty tongue.

"Jennifer, take a breath," says DC Powell. She gives me a small smile.

Good cop. Just like the shows.

On the table, Inspector Grantham lays down five photographs. Each photo shows a person.

I recognise all of them.

"Liam Garcia, Daniel Brown, Jamal Shaw, Sebastian Matthews, Scarlet Smith," Inspector Grantham says, Adam's apple bobbing away. "Know them?"

"Uh. Uh, a little."

"Know why we're asking you this?"

"N-no."

Inspector Grantham pauses. His hazel eyes scan my face, looking for something. Looking for lies. I swallow.

"Well. Know what's happened to them?"

"Err. No."

Inspector Grantham narrows his eyes, sceptical. Bad cop. My palms grow sweaty again, and I attempt to cool them by placing each atop the table. This doesn't work; I just feel stuck, glued to the place I wish I could get away from. I don't want to continue this conversation. There's a ringing in my ears which grows louder as every fibre in my body fights the urge to dash for the exit.

"All five are either dead or missing."

The ringing in my ears ceases.

"What?"

"All five are either dead or missing. And we don't just think you knew them. We think you *dated* them. Even Scarlet, am I right?"

I'm caught on the verge of laughing and crying, horrified by the situation and surprised by his decision to single out the girl.

"I'm . . . I'm bisexual," I say, and watch as Inspector Grantham raises his eyebrows (a similar consistency to his moustache) and scribbles into his notepad.

DC Powell, meanwhile, lays out five more photographs. Each shows a CCTV still, and dread overwhelms me.

The CCTV pictures are of *me*. My year in dates, scattered across London, with my expression simultaneously giddy and absent in each – my brain dizzied by alcohol, by nerves, by expectations and disappointment. My long mousey hair. My fringe, more often than not stuck against a sweaty forehead. The quality isn't good enough to see the smattering of freckles across my nose, but a double chin I didn't even realise I had is unfortunately on full show.

"You dated everyone in these pictures," says DC Powell, her voice sterner than before. "And all of them are now dead or presumed dead."

"Oh wow. Christ," I say, only narrowly managing to avoid letting my thoughts slip: *when you put it like that, it seems more than coincidence.*

Panic rising, I look down at the images again. Wipe my damp forehead. I scan the pictures, moving from left to right: Seb and I propping up the bar in Tank and Paddle. Liam and I meandering about the Tate Modern. Daniel and I lunching at One Lombard. Scarlet and I parting ways in Waterloo station. Jam with his hand on my waist at the Lamb Tavern.

Five different partners yet the same white blouse in every photo. Fuck me, my wardrobe needs an update.

"We're hoping you might be able to help us fill in some gaps. So, what we need from you, Jennifer, is very simple," says DC Powell. "We just need to know when you last saw these five people."

I nod, keeping my eyes wide, my lips parted, attempting to make myself look as innocent as possible.

"So, working chronologically, when did you last see Liam Garcia?" asks DC Powell as Inspector Grantham makes furious notes – presumably, though I couldn't say for certain, not just the word 'bisexual' over and over.

I let out a lungful of air and shrug my shoulders. This is ludicrous – something you watch on television but never envisage actually happening. My eyes close and I rub my fingers over my eyelids. I pull my hands away and open my eyes; my fingertips are smudged black from three-day-old mascara. I need a face routine. One with the cleansing, the toning, the eye cream and serum and whatever else.

New blouse, something to disguise my double chin, a load of face shit. I'm using a police interview to create a shopping list. Jesus, it's like I *want* to go to jail.

"End of February," I finally say, a little too loud. "We went to look round an art gallery, the one in the CCTV image. He hated it."

"Uh-huh. And you didn't see him at all in March?"

I pause, torn. I grip the table hard, squeezing the wood between my fingertips. "No. I didn't. He went skiing quite soon after the Tate date. Maybe he never came back." My voice wobbles. I don't sound convincing. I don't sound convincing at all.

"Oh, he came back alright," says Inspector Grantham, with an accusatory raise of one sparse eyebrow.

The interview continues, with the officers asking about Daniel, Jamal and Sebastian in turn. I answer as earnestly as possible, trawling through awkward dates, inappropriate comments and questionable sex. Speculating on the mental health of each of the men when asked, confirming that none had spoken of plans to run away.

"Okay, finally, Scarlet Smith. When did you last see her?" asks DC Powell.

"Early July. We only went on one date. She knew I liked art so we went and looked at this graffiti tunnel, I can't remember what it's called. Near Waterloo."

"Leake Street Tunnel?" DC Powell asks, a small smile flitting about her plump lips.

"Yes."

"It's a cool place," she adds, and I'm briefly reminded that there are humans beneath the police garb.

"Yeah. And she seemed . . . Well I really didn't know her well at all, but she seemed normal. And fine. And—"

"And yet she disappeared three days ago," Inspector Grantham interrupts. "Mind letting us know what you were up to three days ago?"

"I . . ." I'm caught off guard by the fresh blast of ice in his voice. "I was in bed with a cold all day. And the days after, and for most of today. My landlord can confirm, but just look at my nose!" I point at my moist, red nostrils.

"Noted. Thanks for co-operating with us, Jennifer," says DC Powell. She gathers the pieces of paper up and taps them into order against the table. Tap-a-tap-tap.

"Do I . . . Should I . . ." I pause, struggling to articulate the question on the tip of my tongue. "Do I need a lawyer?"

"Are we going to find out things that make you look guilty?" Inspector Grantham asks, a twisted smile spreading across his face: *gotcha*.

My face grows hot. I paw at my nose.

"No. No, of course not," I mumble.

"We'll talk you through everything as and when it's necessary, Jennifer. I'm sure you'll be absolutely fine." DC Powell pauses her paper-shuffling to focus her brown eyes on mine. Good cop.

"Provided you're not hiding anything, of course," Inspector Grantham adds, with yet another accusatory eyebrow raise.

Bad. Cop.

They let me leave after they've finished reeling off statements about my rights and the law and confidentiality.

I decline their offer of a lift home and step out into the cool, loud air, alone for the first time in over an hour. I breathe in London; the air is thick with traffic pollution and smoke from distant firework displays. A real treat for the lungs.

My first instinct is to head to the river. I follow Hammersmith Bridge Road and veer left as soon as it approaches the Thames, ducking down to the quieter part of the river path, away from the Blue Anchor, which is just beginning to fill with customers as night draws close. I lean against the wall and look out across the water, watch the reflection of the sun disappear.

Breathe.

My second instinct is to check my most recent messages from Liam, Daniel, Jam, Seb and Scarlet. There are no surprises here, of course, no ominous pleas for help I'd managed to overlook. The single common denominator is that I'm the most recent message sender, left on read by them all. I would find this suspicious, if it wasn't so typical of my life.

My third instinct is to phone someone. I dial Mum's number first. I grow nervous as it rings, only half-wanting her to answer. There's a solitary rower heading west, stirring the water into circular eddies as he passes under Hammersmith Bridge. A bulb at the front of his boat lights his way across the river. Mum hasn't answered yet. There's a light at the back of his boat too, illuminating the water he's just disturbed.

I wait for nine more rings before hanging up. I blink back tears. I don't know why I thought she'd be able to offer advice or comfort. It's after five on a Saturday, she's probably a bottle or two down by now.

I scroll listlessly through my phone, finally settling on Saz's number, overcome by the urge to hear her chirpy, familiar babble. I clear my throat, wipe the tears away with my scarf and press dial.

"Jen! OMG, hi! I thought you were ill? Work has been *so* boring – apart from the fittest guy ever at reception yesterday."

"I've just been questioned by the police," I interrupt her, desperate to get the words out.

Saz is silent. In all the time I've known her – admittedly, not too long – she's never been lost for words. But apparently a police interview is the way to shut her up.

So I take a deep breath, and then I tell her everything. Or almost everything. Everything I told the police, at least.

Lying is coming naturally to me now.

TEN MONTHS EARLIER

CHAPTER ONE

Friday 21st January

Two weeks in London, and I'm already a cliché: one of those dull people who detests the tube. The crowds, the heat, body after body pressed into carriages like cattle. The cancellations, the constant delays. The line closures and shit rail replacement buses, which crawl through London traffic at two miles an hour. The sunken, filthy seats on the Piccadilly line. The arguments. The smell of vomit. The tourists and their suitcases – a constant trip hazard. All of it. It brings out a side to me which didn't exist up north.

Oh well. It's not quite the glamorous new life I had envisioned. But it's new, nevertheless. That's what matters.

Naturally, the Waterloo and City line doesn't behave when I need it to. One of the trains has broken down. Commuters are backed up along the walkway. It takes me fifteen minutes to squeeze onto the crowded platform. And it's another ten minutes before I'm on one of the trains, pressed between three people's armpits and a fourth person's backpack.

I'm sweaty and pissed off by the time I reach 42 Lime Street, a small (or 'boutique', according to their website) recruitment office in the heart of the city. Jamal Shaw is waiting for me in reception, smartly dressed in a navy suit.

"Jennifer Beeny," he says, tilting his thick-framed glasses.

"Hi."

"Good news. Great news, in fact. You got the job."

"Oh, perfect." My heart leaps; Lord knows, being a receptionist is hardly most people's dream, but it's always flattering to be chosen. And a relief that I won't have to scurry straight back up north, cash-strapped tail between my legs.

"Yep. OnIt Insurance rang me up today and said they loved you. There's a contract to sign and all that jazz, but – long story short – you start Monday."

He grabs my hand, gives it a vice-like handshake. He's the same height as me but he's strong. The same age as me but his shit is sorted. I suspect his turn-ons include crisp white shirts, new ties and getting other people jobs.

"Well, that is great news, thanks, Jamal. Although, you could have just phoned me?" I try to make this sound as non-accusatory as possible, but my blouse is still sticking to my back and I had been planning an evening of unpacking the last of my bags.

A smile spreads across his face.

"Two things. One: you can call me Jam now, not Jamal – too formal. And I'll be calling you Jenson. Jennifer isn't right, and we can't be having a Jam and a Jen, can we? Madness."

"Jenny is the traditional alternative."

Jam rolls his eyes. "*Boring*. You need something fresh, something laddy."

"It might shock you to hear I've never been called a lad before."

"That does shock me," he says, tilting his glasses and adopting an expression which makes it impossible to ascertain how serious he's being.

"I'm, uh . . ." I'm a little taken aback by his unexpected (and slightly unhinged) friendliness.

Jam cracks a smile. "And the second thing, Jenson: I asked you to come into the city because you're new to London? You don't have any friends here, right?"

I don't have any friends, period. Pushed them all away back when my dad . . . I stop the thought before it can finish.

"You just became a city receptionist," Jam continues, "so you need to celebrate. *We* need to celebrate."

I shake my head, drawn to the safe option: heading home to spend the evening with chocolate, reality television and – most likely – a guilty eye on the last bag, which will doubtless remain packed until I move again.

"Nah, nah, nah. Come on, Jenson. You're coming out? You're

coming out, out right?" Jam asks. I shake my head. New as I am to London and short as I am on friends, I know there's something inherently tragic about hanging out with your recruiter. But heck – I am here to meet new people, too. Even via unconventional methods. And Jam is persistent, he keeps asking until I nod.

"Good girl. Come on then, some of my mates are out too. I'll introduce you to the lads."

Trying not to cringe at his enthusiasm, I let him lead me back outside, into the night, past skyscrapers and gothic buildings. I pull my coat tight, shielding myself from the January drizzle. I can smell my dad amongst the thick fur, the faint scent of fire in various forms: cigars, matches, burnt toast. It's ugly as fuck – brown, tatty and enormous – but it was his before it was mine, and that means something.

Jam ducks into a bar called Tank and Paddle, and I follow. It's big. Brown. Long wooden tables and a wooden floor and long wooden shuffleboards and a long wooden bar. Wood, wood, wood – the smell of pine pushes itself up my nostrils. And it's busy: people ordering beer, eating pizza, playing beer pong. All in the first stages of undress – ties off, jackets off, top buttons undone. Jam loosens his tie and leads me to the bar.

"A few celebratory shots?" he asks.

"Ahh. No. I shouldn't really drink."

"You shouldn't drink on a *Monday*. Any other day is fair game, and don't try to tell me otherwise."

He orders us three shots each and lines them up on the bar in front of me. I can't help myself; I pick one up, holding the sticky glass tight between my fingers and peering at the clear, innocent-looking liquid within. There's a spec of lint or fluff floating about. Bobbing up and down and swaying as I tip the glass. A body, caught up in the water. I blink the image away and turn to Jam.

"I can sell ice to the Inuits, milk to a cow, alcohol to a teetotaller," he says, clinking his shot glass against mine. He downs the liquid and I do the same. Burning. A satisfying burning. Repeated two more times.

"Nice, Jenson, you're a trouper. OnIt Insurance made a good choice in hiring you, a very good choice indeed."

"Why did they decide to hire me?" I ask, fishing for info, despite the fact that professional Jam has quite clearly clocked off.

"Usual garble. Loved your reference from the Stray Café owners. Thought you were simultaneously friendly and professional. Clocked on to your decent school grades. But, anyway, that's in the past. And in the future, admittedly. But not – *not* – in the present! Now, follow me."

He shrugs the last of his working persona away as he leads me through the crowd of giddy drinkers, to a circle of men.

"Lads," he says, and they turn. "Lads, this is my good friend Jenson."

I push my fingers onto the table behind me. Sticky.

"Jenson, this is Pete, he works with me. And this is Filipe, I got him a job last year. And this is another Pete, got him a job a couple of months ago."

I nod. There's a glasses guy. A guy with curly hair. A guy who keeps vaping. Older and more corporate than my usual crowd. I stand up a little straighter, push my fingers harder into the table, worried that I look like a child.

"And this," says Jam, "is Sebastian. An insurance broker. Big dog, head of his company's property team. He's hired plenty of my candidates. And you might see him around, Jenson – you work with OnIt, don't you, mate?"

"Sometimes," says the man. "And it's Seb, by the way." I nod, and then I look up. I properly look at him.

"Holy shit," I say. He might have heard that. I don't care, I just stare at him. Oh wow. Handsome but soft. Not rugged – grown-up but still boyish. Brown hair, brown eyes. A small mole on his cheek, another on his neck. And a wide smile which doesn't falter. I watch, watch and watch. He doesn't stop smiling. This could make him look like a maniac, a deranged serial killer, but it doesn't. The smiling makes his eyes sparkle, indents itself into his skin. Lines appear at the corners of his eyes and lips. Happy lines.

"Another drink, Jenson?" Jam asks, snapping me out of my Seb daze.

"No. I'm drank. Drunk. Tipsy." And distracted by the god a metre in front of me.

"I'll ask you one more time, Jenson. Drink?"

Jam's keen for everyone to have a good time, and this seems to involve getting us all pissed. Truth be told, I'm happy to go along with it. I shouldn't. Lord knows, there are a million and one family-shaped reasons why I shouldn't. But I follow Jam back to the bar. Once there, I twist my head and look back through the crowd at Seb. He's still smiling. He turns his head a fraction to the left and our eyes meet. I flinch.

"Wow."

"Sorry, what?" asks Jam.

I must stop narrating my life.

"Nothing."

"What you drinking?"

"Just lemonade, please," I say, a feeble attempt to be good, to stay off the same track as my mother.

"Nah, nah, nah, nah, behave," Jam replies, before ordering me a double vodka lemonade.

Noise escapes my lips. A weak protestation. But I drink what I'm given. Drink and think about whether I should be letting a guy I barely know get me so plastered. Whether there are sinister intentions beneath the wide smile and glinting glasses. I take a nervous sip. Jam grabs my arm and I jump, but he manoeuvres me towards a basket of garlic bread batons.

"Eat," he says. "Got to keep your stomach lined."

"And my breath fresh." I roll my eyes but stuff a baton into my mouth.

We each chomp down a baton or two and then head back to the circle of men. I drink and watch. It's all blurred: indie music muted by laughter and shouting. The cheese and pepperoni smell of pizza, occasionally disrupted by the strawberry scent of one of the Petes' vapes. The brown of the floor and tables, the grey of the suits, the redness of people's flesh, cheeks made pink from the cold outside and pinker from the sweat in here. Everything into one. Apart from Seb. Keep sneaking glances at his smiling face.

The circle shifts: Jam and one of the Petes leave to get more drinks. I'm next to Seb. Look at him. Look down. Drink my drink dry, nothing but ice cubes left. I open and shut my mouth half a dozen times, not knowing quite how to start a conversation with him, and silently curse Jam for making me eat garlic.

"How old are you?" This question is out of my mouth before I've a chance to double-check it.

He looks at me, still smiling. "Thirty. Thirty-one in June."

"You look so much younger," I can't help but say.

"Well, thanks, I guess," he says, half laughing, the lines at the corners of his eyes deepening. He's well spoken. Posh but not ridiculous. Posh in a nice way, I think. One of those people who even *smells* posh; he smells of whisky and some kind of tree. Oak, perhaps?

I look down. Look at him again.

"You're never thirsty . . . Mean thirty," I say, a broken record, my cheeks reddening at my stumble. "Must be lying."

"Honestly, I am."

Jam returns, pressing another drink into my hand. And then it's not just the noise and colours and smells that blur, it's the entire world. My drink is gone, I don't know how. Tank and Paddle gets emptier – slowly and then all at once. I find myself leaning on the bar, staring at Seb, who stands opposite me. And Jam? Jam and all the Petes? Can't see them, nowhere to be found. I chat shit, a variety of shit, mainly about school. We did similar subjects – Art and Maths and English. He did Further Maths, too. And he likes paintings, tells me his parents own a Monet, but that he prefers Tracey Emin, or Banksy. I try to tell him about my dad, my dad and all his doodles, but my tongue seems to trip, incapable of getting the right words out.

Seb leans in, or maybe I lean in, and we kiss. One elbow on the bar, and the barman just metres away, and our lips glued to each other. I pull away. Push my fingers into the sticky bar. Think about lunging towards his lips again. Think about taking things further. That would be silly, reckless. Or would it? Isn't sleeping around exactly what you should be doing in your twenties?

There's a tap on my shoulder. I spin around and see Jam.

"We're off, Jenson. Have a good night with Seb, he's a top lad. Got a tonne of women obsessed with him, though, so watch out for those," Jam says, grinning. "And text me later to let me know you're safe, yeah? Seb, nice seeing you, mate. In a bit."

Jam waves and walks off, leaving us in the empty bar. Seb takes my hand and I let him lead me out, up onto the dark street and into the night. He hails a taxi and I protest, or maybe I don't. We get in the back and he tells the cabby where to go. More shit chat as it speeds west through eerie streets.

And then I'm not in the taxi, I'm in his flat, then in his bedroom. In his arms, arms moving up and down my body, taking off my white blouse, my skirt. My fingers fumble on his shirt buttons.

I'm in my underwear and he says things, nice things.

"Wow, you've got a good body. Good skin."

I grin, shake my head. I am grabbed and he is on me, lips and hands and chest, pushing himself onto me, pushing himself into me.

Saturday 22nd January

I wake up in a strange bed, my stomach churning and my throat sandpaper dry. A man has his arm around me, an unfamiliar sensation. I open my eyes to see if the room, half-lit by a slither of light, can offer any clues. A guitar, a bookshelf, a cabinet topped by trophies. An upright piano, like the one my mum owns. I like what I see, I just don't recognise it.

I prop myself up. Bad idea, I instantly feel like I'm going to be sick. I lie back down and turn to look at the man I've been curled into all night. Yes. Brown hair and thick eyebrows and moles, starting on his cheek and running down his neck, his chest. I remember. Pete? Not Pete. A three-letter name: Tom or Ben. He opens his eyes. He smiles, and three lines appear at the outer creases of his eyes.

Seb.

"Hey," he says, sheepish.

"Hey," I echo.

He pulls me towards him and our lips lock onto one another. I taste beer and vodka. And I can smell him, or maybe it's just me I can smell, sweat and spirits. My skin is sticky, as if the alcohol is seeping out of my pores. And my stomach churns. Ugh.

But Seb's fit, fit to the touch. I run my fingers over him, over his chest and arms. He's more chiselled, more defined than I realised last night. And he pushes his fingers into my flesh too, greedy. My stomach, my thighs. And all the while he kisses me, my neck, cheeks, mouth. I inhale him: the sweaty stench of last night.

He pulls me onto my hands and knees and moves behind me. There's the rubber smell of a condom, the feel of his hand in my hair, his fingers stroking my neck. He pulls me up so that I'm facing the wall ahead. Except it's not a wall, it's a mirror. He has a giant mirror above his headboard. And Christ, I do not want to see my sweaty, naked self be fucked in it. In other circumstances – when I don't have mascara smudged down my cheeks and a greasy fringe stuck to my forehead and sweat on my top lip – this could be erotic. I wonder how many girls he's watched in this mirror.

He finishes, pulls out and then lies down, bringing me close. I'm sticky between my legs, sticky on my forehead, sticky under my armpits. Sticky and nauseous.

"I need to go," I tell him.

"Oh. Am I that bad?" he jokes; I can hear the smile in his voice.

"I've just got a busy day, things to do!"

"I've got a morning in bed. Then an afternoon with the sofa. What're you doing?"

Scrubbing last night from my body and sleeping my hangover off. But I need to tell him something more interesting, more sophisticated, more *London*. I need a lie. Need a lie fast.

"Going up Big Ben," I say, and instantly cringe at my own lameness.

"Oh, quirky. I didn't actually know that was possible. But okay, I'll let you out. Then I'm getting right back into bed."

I unstick myself from him and hunt around for my clothes. Turns out I was wearing my biggest pants and granny bra. Excellent.

"Literally my worst knickers," I say as he watches me put them on.

He laughs. "Always the case. You still look hot."

Eventually, I locate everything, and we head out of his room, down a corridor and to the front door. We pass his living room – a stylish but decidedly masculine space. His chairs and sofas are a navy leather, whilst tables and bookshelves are cold, shiny metal.

It's like the inside of a Porsche's engine. Well, I should imagine. A bike propped up against the far wall adds a welcome splash of red.

"You cycle?" I ask, as he unlocks the door.

He shrugs. "I do triathlons. So yeah, sometimes. Roughly a third of the time."

"I love cycling," I say, thinking of Redcar dunes, my mum racing alongside me, steering round the waves, pedalling under the setting sun.

The door is opened, and I head out onto a communal staircase. We kiss a few more times and then he lets me go. I dither, wishing I could stay with him for longer, but not trusting myself not to vomit. Seb tells me to enjoy Big Ben and then closes the door.

I take out my phone, hardly surviving on two per cent. I have three messages. One is from Jam, asking whether I'm okay. I reply with a thumbs-up, before moving on to the remaining messages. They're both from Bob, the middle-aged landlord I accidentally moved in with a couple of weeks ago. One says:

> Jen? It's late and you're not home. All okay?

And then, a few hours after:

> Jen. Reply ASAP. Do I need to come help you?

Superficially sweet, but I can't help shuddering. My phone dies before I have a chance to reply.

CHAPTER TWO

Monday 24th January

My first impression of OnIt Insurance was that it's aggressively lime green: lime green logo, lime green sofas, grey-and-lime-green carpet. Like the whole office lives in fear of getting run over by one of the buses that zip past along Gracechurch Street.

My second impression of OnIt Insurance is that Saz, my fellow receptionist, is full-on. Everything about her is bold: tightly curled, bottle-blonde hair, a manic, over-friendly smile and limbs doused in a shop's worth of St Tropez.

Lime green, yellow and orange. I predict a migraine by lunch.

Saz is friendly, though. She greets me enthusiastically, all hugs and air kisses and cries of, "OMG, you got this job through Jam? Same! He's one of the best recruiters, honestly. Not that I'd tell him that – one more compliment and his head will explode! And you're twenty-three? Shut up! Same! What are the chances?"

This sort of chit-chat continues throughout the morning, with breaks only to tell me in a decidedly less enthusiastic manner about how the computer system works, or what we should say when we answer the phone. She's showing me how to book meeting rooms when a gaggle of men pass by reception and into the office.

"So fit," she says, staring after them. "Honestly – looking at hot men in suits all day, can you think of a better job?"

"Aha, no, I guess not. You're single then?"

"Single AF, that's me. I was seeing someone on and off for a year or so, but . . . it's problematic. He's a great person to know, just not to date. Anyway . . . what about you?"

"Oh. Pretty non-existent, honestly," I say. A boring reply. I jazz it up. "Actually, I did meet someone on Friday. Want to hear about him?"

She does, of course, far more than she wants to reply to emails or order office furniture. An instant icebreaker. I don't know Seb's surname, but Saz finds him through Jam's LinkedIn almost immediately, and we stalk all of his other profiles too. His Facebook is barren and he only posts pictures of places and objects on Instagram, but he's been tagged in a few photos, and he looks fit in each, whether at a wedding, on a golf course or shirtless at a stag do.

"He has his mouth open in every pic," Saz says.

I nod. "Yeah, he's very smiley. Very open-mouth smiley, apparently."

"Well, that was a good pull from you, Jen. He looks like a Madonas."

"Adonis?"

"What? You been messaging this weekend?"

"No," I say, putting my phone down and adjusting my chair: seat lower, arms higher. "I thought he might ask Jam for my number."

"But nothing?"

"Nothing. So now I feel like he's not interested. Which makes me more interested."

"Typical. Well, don't message him on Facebook – it's too tragic, you'll just look like a stalker. Get Jam to give you his number, and then work your magic."

"Maybe. Though I reckon I have a *bit* more pride than that."

In fact, I have no pride; that much becomes obvious as I'm boarding the train from Waterloo to Barnes at the end of the day. I've still had no contact from Seb, so I text Jam:

> I've cracked. If you've got Seb's number, please can I have it?

He texts back laughing emojis, a complete one-eighty on our previous formal correspondence – all interview tips and contract details. And then he continues:

> I'm going to make you wait, could be funny.

Just need to think about the power I currently hold, how I could utilise it.

I sigh and reply:

Annoying. You're a bad Cupid.

Jam takes longer to reply this time, and the train trundles between Vauxhall and Clapham Junction. It half-empties and then re-fills.

I'm a busy boy. Being Cupid's not really my thing.

How much are you willing to pay?

Opportunistic fucker. I text back a reply:

Mmm. Well if he's not interested it's worth nothing . . . You spoken to him?

And then nothing. Fifteen minutes of radio silence from Jam. The train pulls into Barnes station, and I jump down onto the platform. I dawdle along the dark path, which leads away from the station. Trees line it, their bare branches scraping against my jacket whenever I stray too far into the shadows. I pause under a streetlight. Find a picture of Seb and zoom in on his six-pack. Moving to London was supposed to mean growing up, a new start, and instead I'm perving over a boy like a teenager. I call Jam.

He answers on the second ring. He's laughing, great peals of belly laughter.

"Jenson?" He finally stops laughing for long enough to say my name, or a variant of it, anyway. "How much?"

"Nothing! Well, four pounds, maybe. Max."

"Interesting. I reckon in a couple of days you'll pay more. The smart man would hold out."

I grumble into the phone, "This is so annoying. Have you spoken to him?"

"Nah, nah, nah – it's confidential. Seb and I have a professional relationship."

I moan and hear Jam laugh again, a hyena laugh – completely unrestrained.

"I'm loving this," he says. "My day was a bit dull until now. I'll be honest, Jenson, I do have a price in my head."

"Uh-huh. Do share?"

"Thirty quid."

I let out a horrified splutter. "Bet you don't even have his number!"

"Why would I try to sell a product I don't have? Twenty-five."

"Fifteen."

"Behave. Meet in the middle: twenty."

"That still seems rather high. For a phone number."

"Twenty. Final offer, Jenson."

"Seventeen?"

Jam laughs again. "Now you're just being silly. Why are you playing with coins? Twenty. I'll also accept it in alcohol."

"Ugh," I moan, snapping off a wayward branch. "Fine. Twenty. Deal."

"Good girl. What a lucky man Seb is! Just give me a couple of minutes."

"I can't believe I honestly thought you'd just give me it straight away, like a normal person."

Jam laughs again. He laughs so much I think he might lose his voice. It's pleasant and infuriating. And then he hangs up. A frustrated hiss escapes my lips. I continue down the path, until the flat I share with Bob comes into view. I can see into the kitchen, where he's chomping and chewing on something. A shiver runs down my spine, and I pull my coat tighter.

My phone buzzes as I'm unlocking the door. Jam has messaged me.

> Hi. It's been a pleasure doing business with you. You owe me £20.

Below is Seb's mobile number.

CHAPTER THREE

Thursday 3rd February

I head to the office bathroom ten minutes before work finishes. Despite my best efforts, Seb's messages have been somewhat lacking, so – with the encouragement of Saz, who seems determined not to let me wallow in the self-pity that accompanies unrequited lust – I've taken the matter of romance in London into my own hands by downloading some dating apps. Granted, there's clearly more to the city than its singletons, but swiping through profiles has proven a welcome distraction whenever I find myself at a loose end, or find my mind drifting dangerously close to memories of life back home. The life I've left.

I unzip my makeup bag and take out blusher. I have a date tonight and, as such, improving the appearance of my dull, dry face is imperative.

"Oh, someone looks nice!" Saz says as she barges into the bathroom.

"No one on reception?" I ask, examining my teeth for rogue pieces of food.

Saz has a wink which looks more like a pained spasm, and she uses it now, crumpling her snub nose, accidentally shutting both green eyes.

"OnIt Insurance will survive without receptionists for two minutes, I'm sure. Having a wee won't get us fired, it's a human right or something. Anyway, your date with what's-his-face still on for tonight?"

"Liam? Yep." My teeth are food-free, so I start brushing my hair, willing it to become bouffant and glossy, rather than limp.

"Oooh, show me show me show me him."

I've been avoiding letting Saz too near my dating profile; she got a little too excited upon learning I'd set my preferences to both men and women. But I relent now, taking out my phone and clicking onto Matchum, my current dating app of choice, and the place on which I virtually met Liam. Our messages have been entertaining but not bizarre, his pictures are all taken in a good light, and his social media checks out. Beyond having a mutual friend in common (if you can call Fiona Nunn, a low-level school bitch who never spoke to me, a "friend") there's nothing noteworthy. No Twitter rants, no cringey TikToks, and no exes lingering in any of his Instagram pictures. All in all, he's promising.

I attempt to scroll to his profile, but a prompt, seemingly from Matchum itself, blocks me.

Meet your perfect match before they disappear!

"Yeah fit, he's fit," Saz says, too busy pushing clips into her blonde curls to actually look at my phone. By the time I've closed the prompt and clicked onto Liam's profile, she's waltzed into a cubicle. She continues our conversation whilst pissing: "A fit guy will probably want action. *Naked* action."

"Naked action? What a grown-up way of putting it," I say, giving up on my hair and tying it into a ponytail. "It's a first date. I'm not having sex with him."

The toilet flushes and Saz emerges.

"Well, he'll be expecting it, so I hope you're all . . ." She pauses to mime shaving her pubes. "Tidy down below."

"It's winter – you could hide half a stationery cupboard down there at the moment."

"OMG! Jen, no! I've got a razor in my bag, I can put the cleaning sign up outside the bathroom!"

A snort of laughter escapes my lips. "I'm not stripping down and shaving my bikini line in the office, Saz."

"Shut up, you don't know what you're saying. Gotta smarten it up."

I pile makeup into my bag and head to the door. "Have a nice evening. Try and make it out of here without indecently exposing yourself – or anyone else."

I leave the shiny lime green of OnIt Insurance's office and head out into the night. I push my way through the hustle and bustle of central London – a city made sinister by the dark sky above, sharp buildings looming from the shadows.

The Waterloo and City line ruins any chance I had of not looking flustered, but still I drag a comb through my fringe as I exit Waterloo station and head for the river. I pull my skirt down, push my fringe back, try not to think too much. My first dating app date. He could be catfishing me. He might think *I'm* catfishing *him* – my photos are a couple of years out of date, after all. He could be boring, he might have a funny voice, there might be lots of awkward silence. I might get drunk and say something stupid. I might stay sober and still say something stupid. He might—

I feel someone grab at my waist as I reach the shadows under Waterloo Bridge.

"Aaah!" I jump, looking down at the hand gripping me, and then up at the face of the man it belongs to.

"Hey! Sorry, Jen, right?" asks Liam.

"Ah. God. Yes, sorry. Christ, you did well to spot me. I mean, how did you know it was me? The awkward walk or, oh God, I don't actually look like my photos, do I?"

"The big 'Jen' tattoo on your forehead, actually," he replies. He's American and I knew this, but still the accent surprises me. He squeezes me tight against his long black coat, an awkward hug.

Then we stand opposite each other, neither of us knowing what to say. I'm painfully aware that I'm assessing him and he's assessing me right back. What an odd thing to do, to effectively interview someone for the position of your partner.

"There's a bar or café or something, it's got booze, just over there?" Liam leaves the question to hang in the air.

"Sure," I say.

We leave the shadows and walk into the crowded bar. As we queue, I sneak glances at Liam, trying to figure out how he matches up to his photos. He's hot, with slim limbs and neat, dark hair. But there's something about his face I can't put my finger on. A harshness to his bone structure I didn't anticipate, perhaps.

"Wine, Jen?" he asks me. We're at the front of the queue.

"Sure," I say.

"White?"

"Sure." *Jesus Christ, Jen, change the record.*

He orders a bottle of Pinot Grigio and sounds cool doing it; I'd definitely have pronounced it, 'Pee-not Gree-gee-oh' and incurred scathing looks for my troubles. It's busy inside so we take a glass each and the bottle outside. The weather's mild for this time of year, and sitting outside is made bearable by heaters.

"So, you're a receptionist, right?" he asks once we've settled into our seats. He's got long, thin fingers, which he uses to open the wine and pour us both a glass.

"Uh-yuh-yep."

"Well, I'm literally raging you're not in the sexy skirt and heels they make you wear."

"We don't have a uniform, what with it being the twenty-first century," I say, then instantly feel awkward and take a large gulp of my wine.

"No, course not. Equal rights and all that." He waves an arm in the air, as if holding a placard. "What a shame. Being a receptionist the dream?"

"Not exactly," I say, thinking briefly of all the time I devoted to drawing, painting and researching. The afternoons spent in whichever galleries didn't charge an entry fee, conjuring up foolish daydreams about doing something creative one day. I shake these thoughts away and re-focus on Liam. "But it's something. It's paying for me to be in London – just about, anyway."

"Yeah, London prices suck. How long you been here?"

"A month. Ish."

"Holy shit. A London newbie. What are you running away from?"

I flinch. A drop of wine splashes out, onto my hand.

"Jeez," Liam continues, "that was a joke, but you totally reacted. You on the run? Do something bad?"

I glance to my right. I close my eyes briefly – only briefly – but it's enough time for a familiar image to fill my brain. A body, facing down, floating and lifeless. I look back at Liam. "No. Nothing bad."

Liam leans closer to me, clasping his long, bony fingers together. He raises one bushy eyebrow.

"C'mon, Jen, tell me the truth. What did you do? You can ruuuun but you can't hide . . . Besides, everyone loves a bad girl." A mischievous, eager light dances across his eyes. "Were you violent? Tie someone up? Keep them in a secret lair?"

My turn to raise my eyebrows. "You've thought through a few scenarios?"

He shrugs. "Pain can be sexy. I'd let you tie me up and take me away. Maybe I'd do the same to you in return."

My eyes widen. I take another drink. Shift my gaze between Liam's eyes and his fingers as a tingling sensation ripples through my body. I'm halfway between turned on and terrified.

"How's the living sitch?" Liam asks, before I can accept his bondage-cum-kidnap offer.

"Ahh, mmm. I moved down pretty suddenly, so just took a place I'd only viewed online. And it *seemed* really nice – one bedroom and a bathroom on the second floor, a kitchen and living room on the first floor, a little hallway on the ground floor. Couldn't believe it, whole place to myself for eight hundred a month. I moved in and it turns out the landlord, Bob, lives there. He lives, full-time, in the living room."

"No! No!" Liam smacks the table in shock. "No! And he didn't say before you moved in? Jen, that's like, hella illegal. Holy shit! What's he like?"

"Creepy. Very creepy. Bald but with a massive black 'tache and a huge nose. I swear all he wears are grubby pyjamas. And he always comes into the kitchen whenever he hears me and stands as close as possible."

Liam shakes his head. "Can't believe you thought you could live alone in London for eight hundred a month. What a noob."

"Could rent a bloody mansion in Middlesbrough for that price," I fire back.

"Alright, alright. Why you still there, though?"

"Year-long contract."

"Holy shit. I'd be raging." He shakes his head but he's grinning in amusement. He picks up his half-empty wine glass. "Well. Cheers to that."

We clink glasses and the ice is broken. We make our way through the bottle and Liam gets looser and more expressive. He doesn't touch me, but his hands are all over the place, rising and falling with his eyebrows and illustrating every story he tells. He fidgets and, as we near the end of the bottle, it's increasingly hard for me to keep track of where his hands go – playing with the bottle top or tapping at the table.

"Another bottle?"

"Please," I say, regretting the word as soon as it escapes my lips. Saz plus a hangover is going to be an ordeal.

Liam stands up, taps me on the shoulder and then heads inside. I lean forward and look around. We're the only hardy souls left in the outdoor area, with just the Thames for company. I straighten up, trying to see over the wall and down to the river, but the dark water is scarcely distinguishable from its inky surroundings. I rub my eyes, remember I'm wearing mascara and eyeliner and pull my hands away, cursing.

I'm fishing in my pocket for a mirror when my phone vibrates. I take it out, expecting the caller to be Liam, asking what kind of wine I want. It's not.

I answer, and she doesn't even give me time to speak.

"Jen . . . sss . . . you need to come, come help me." My mum, on the other end of the phone and 250 miles away, lets out a mighty sob.

"What?"

"Mmm need you back, Jen. Mmm."

"What's happened?" I attempt to keep my voice level. Strange, speaking to my pissed mum when I'm well on my way to being in a similar state, maybe only a bottle behind. Even stranger, given the strained nature of our communication ever since I left for London. Ever since the argument that forced that decision.

She sobs down the phone and I can't make out any of the words she says.

"Mum, are you okay?"

She cries harder, emits a great, pained moan. I pull my coat closer; it's the first time I've felt cold all evening.

"Sss, it's your . . . your dad, Jen."

Cold. Cold treacle seems to dribble down my spine. I shudder.

"What do you mean?"

"Isss has a bottle. Just one bottle and – and what your dad did . . . what you did . . ."

She cries harder, muttering things I wish I couldn't hear. The rush of the Thames is suddenly all-consuming, despite the fact I'm metres from it.

"Mum. Drink some water, go to bed. Or go see Priti next door. Please. Promise me?"

Liam comes back outside, wine in hand. Shit.

"Mum," I hiss into the phone. "Promise."

"Oh . . . okay. Comes back to me, Jen."

"I will soon. Maybe. I love you," I say, and hang up.

"Sorry," I say to Liam.

"No, it's fine, as long as that wasn't one of those calls where you text your mate saying it's a shocker of a date and she rings you with some made-up emergency and you bail on me," he replies, pouring us each a generous glass.

"No."

"Good, cos when I was walking over, literally that's what I thought."

"No, just my mum."

He shifts back in his seat, pops his collar up for some reason. "You close to her?"

"Ish. It's complicated."

"What does she do?"

"Used to work in a care home." I take a big gulp of wine and feel it slip down my throat, warming my body, blurring my peripheral vision, the inconvenient edge bits of my life.

"My mom doesn't work. Doesn't need to – my dad's a pretty big dog at Intel," Liam says, and begins telling me about his family: Dad from the Philippines, American mum, nice house in California, one younger sister at boarding school in England somewhere. Something about a cat. Or two. A man has taken a seat at a table a dozen metres from ours. I squint, trying to bring him into focus. He lights a fag and turns to stare at me.

"What's your dad do?"

"Huh?"

"What's your dad do?"

"Oh." I take another sizeable gulp. "He's dead."

There are two ways of replying to this proclamation: you can either ignore it or ask about it.

Liam goes with the former.

"No brothers or sisters?"

"Nope."

"Cool. Hey, you hear they're opening a bar in the Thames? Like actually *in* the Thames?"

Wine fills my body and the evening gets easier. I stare at Liam's lips, think about running my hands through his hair. Think about kissing him. People leave the bar, pulling on scarves and hats. Some of them stumble, stutter, slur like I do when I answer Liam, still talking at a million miles an hour. He laughs, shifts his chair closer to mine. The man with the fag leaves, I think. I squint, try to watch him disappear into the distance, into the dark. Bar staff come outside and begin turning off heaters. They ask us to leave.

"Let's bounce," Liam says.

We wind our way down backstreets and subways, skirting under and around the IMAX. Homeless people line the subway, some singing, some curled in a sleeping bag, hungry eyes watching us. The lights down here are purple-ish, flickering, dizzy. Words on the walls too, can't read them. It's louder when we're out of the subway, opposite Waterloo station. I nearly get hit by a bus. Then I nearly get hit by a bike. Liam laughs, grabs the sleeve of my coat, manoeuvres me up the steps, so many steps, into the station.

We're on the same train out of central. It must be the last train because it's full. We stand by the doors, falling all over the place, movements exaggerated.

"Holy shit, I smell chicken nuggets. Nugs, nugs, nugs!" Liam shouts, sniffing the air. I should be embarrassed, I think. If I was less full of wine, I'd be embarrassed.

The man with the chicken nuggets is drunk too, and starts yelling back at him.

"Mate, I'm literally just complimenting your chicken nuggets," replies Liam, falling about the carriage. I giggle, put my hand over his mouth. Breathe in the smells: sick and sweat and yes, chicken nuggets.

I get off the train at Barnes, determined not to go home with Liam, and he grabs me before I go, plants a clumsy kiss on my lips. His mouth is warm, wet. I exit the station grinning, and stagger down the dark, tree-lined path between the station and Bob's flat. To my disappointment, the kitchen light is still on. My heart sinks; Bob is still up, and I desperately need water, so I've no choice but to join him in the kitchen. He's at the small plastic table, reading a newspaper and eating smoked salmon and toast. He's wearing pyjamas – a grey top and tartan shorts – his stomach pushed up against the table.

I pause in the doorway, swaying slightly. I can't decide which animal he most resembles; I'm currently torn between an owl and a walrus. His glasses and little round mouth, constantly puckered into an 'o' shape, make me think owl. But his great horrid moustache, currently dusted in toast crumbs, his huge, bent nose and his enormous mass push me more in the walrus direction.

"Hi, Jen."

"Hi."

"Been out with a boy?" he mumbles through his moustache.

"Uh, yeah."

"Lucky boy," he says, picking up his fork and skewering a flake of salmon.

"Mmm."

I look down. I'm permanently seething at him for lying to me about the living situation, and yet I haven't confronted him, I've just let rage bubble up inside me. Still, I'm trying desperately not to sour the atmosphere, and to give him the benefit of the doubt.

"Done much this evening?" I ask, as pleasantly as possible.

"Crosswords."

Christ, it's like drawing blood from a stone.

"Oh yeah. Any, any good ones?"

"Any good crosswords?" He raises an eyebrow, as if *I'm* the weird one.

"Any good clues, then?"

"Depression of jet setter. Five, three."

The words mean sweet f-all to me, but still I turn them over in my mind, as if expecting my sluggish, tipsy brain to come up with an answer.

"You won't get it," says Bob, after a minute or so. "And that's a good thing."

I roll my eyes, somewhat offended, and stumble over to the kitchen cabinet. For reasons unbeknownst to me, he keeps his toolkit alongside his cups, so I have to push aside spanners and screwdrivers in order to reach anything that could be used as a drinking vessel. I reach for the glasses, inspect all of them, decide they're too filthy to be used and settle on a semi-clean periodic table mug, which I fill with water. Bob shuffles over to stand next to me and starts washing his plate. Our feet are almost touching. The side of his stomach brushes against mine.

I down my water and exit the kitchen with another full glass as swiftly as possible. But I pause at the foot of the second flight of stairs: the door to Bob's room is half open. It's always locked or inhabited by him, so I've not actually seen inside since I moved in. I'm overwhelmed by a funny, mouldy smell.

I've barely had time to clock the colour of the duvet (off-white) when he comes storming past me and into his room. He shuts the door in a hurry, and it almost hits my nose.

"Fucking weird," I mouth at the door.

The flat is silent, bar the sound of Bob locking me out, and the kitchen tap, still running next door. I walk back into the kitchen and over to the sink. The breadknife and his fish-covered plate have been abandoned in the sink, along with the sponge. I turn the tap off.

I would laugh, if I wasn't trapped here with him.

CHAPTER FOUR

Friday 11th February

I catch the six o'clock train from King's Cross to Edinburgh with a knot of worry in my stomach. I'm going home – all the way home – after five weeks away. Not a long time by any standards, but it's the most time I've ever spent apart from Mum. Her call has been playing on my mind since the date with Liam, and eventually guilt spurs me into buying a ticket. Seeing her is what I need to do, yet I can't shake the feeling that returning – even for a visit – is wrong. A literal step in the wrong direction. The possibility of being sucked back into the life I left feels all too real, as though my feet might get trapped in the sand on Redcar Beach, as though guilt might clamp my shoes down, rendering escape impossible.

The train north is noisy, packed and delayed. I spend my time procrastinating – scrolling through my phone rather than making a start on any of the books I felt certain I'd be able to wolf down over what's likely to be an uncomfortable weekend. Seb is yet to reply to my last three messages, but I've managed to convince myself that clicking onto his profile picture a dozen times might prompt a response. Madness. I will myself to focus on Liam, whose messages are always laced with sarcasm, but are at least consistent.

It's a relief to pack away both my phone and unopened book and alight at Darlington. I catch the little two-carriage train to Redcar Central. By the time it trundles into the station, the temperature has dropped below freezing, and a sea breeze has pushed its way into town.

I don't go straight home. Instead I detour, wanting to keep the reality – she'll be drunk and he won't be there – at bay for just a few moments longer. I pass the back end of the High Street (betting shops, nail salons and barbers, all of them closed). Side roads branch from this street, leading to little white, grey and yellow terrace houses. I don't turn off. I keep going straight, towards the sea. The town clock strikes ten as I reach the beach and I stand still, pausing to let Redcar sink back into my bones. It's not London. It's too quiet for London, too dark for London. And it smells too good: salty, cold, crisp, if any of those can be classified as smells. They're what the wind wraps round me.

I continue along the deserted beachfront, with the sea to my right, crumbling terrace houses to my left and the old steelworks, stretching up into the sky like metal skeletons, in front. I veer from the path and walk over the dunes, a fresh challenge for my legs: having to hold my body steady on the shifting sand. Thoughts of being trapped in the sand linger, so I shake my head and pretend I'm back on my bike, with Mum on hers ahead. I pretend it's a rare sunny day, a rare sober day. I try to force myself back to a time when that was enough for me, and when I could kid myself it was enough for her, too.

I head back inland after ten minutes, aware I can't delay any longer. I head back towards houses, lights and people. The roads are wide, and the small houses seem antisocial, as far back as possible. There's glass on the paths and kids in tracksuits round the bus stop and there's a chip shop, which I can smell from fifty metres away. I love it, a little bit. Despite everything.

Mum's house is one of the last on Broadway West. It's the middle of ten terrace houses: a neat redbrick, white-window affair, with the world's tiniest concrete garden. I pause and then knock. She opens the door and smells embrace me – the warm red wine of my mum, and the musky old-book smell of the house. I love the smell of both, though one is killing her.

She's so happy to see me, it's almost painful. I hug her, allowing her to plant kisses on my cheeks. All the while I'm cringing, not sure how to mirror her enthusiasm. I shrug her off once her grip on me loosens, and then head upstairs and dump my bag in my old bedroom. It hasn't been changed since I left. Unsurprising, really; I booked train tickets straight after our argument and left a few hours later. Mum was probably expecting me to return almost immediately, despite tens of phone calls to the contrary. My stuffed owl is still on the single bed. My Stray Café T-shirt hangs over a chair, unwashed after my final shift, smelling of coffee beans and bacon sandwiches. An eclectic mix of posters cover the walls: Queen, Harry Potter, Joy Division, Submarine. I should take it all down really. But this house and Mum's life are empty enough, and doing so would probably make my move seem too final for her. Besides, Dad's things are still in the house, over a year later.

I go back downstairs and join her in the living room, a small space at the back of the house, with a killer view of Trunk Road Industrial Estate and the steelworks beyond that. They're burning things tonight. Bright flames flash against the black sky, flickering off the living room furniture and casting Mum's face in an orange glow.

She pours me a glass of wine and tops up her own, hand shaking slightly. My beach detour has cost us precious sober time together.

"So, how's the Big Smoke? No regrets, I hope?" she asks, her tone almost aggressively jovial.

"It's keeping me distracted. And it's warmer than up here." I settle into an armchair. Everything in the house is heavy. Heavy colours and heavy materials – maroon, brown, teal, velvet, leather, wood.

"Oh Jen! It's not that grim up north!"

"I know. Just a bit colder."

I take a sip of my wine and let my eyes linger on her. The grey mane of hair which tickles her lower back. Her well-lined face. Her eyes, carbon copies of mine: hazel with flecks of green. Hers are bloodshot. Mine might be bloodshot, I've not looked at myself for a while. The main difference is her mouth, the last remaining pretty part of her body, clinging on as the rest crumbles around it.

I draw breath, knowing we need to talk about why I left. She can't take back the cruel things she said, but enough time has passed that I just about feel brave enough to have a proper conversation. All the unspoken words are making the house feel even heavier than usual. But Mum speaks before I get the chance.

"I – hic – I killed Richard," she says quickly, each word hard to distinguish from the one before.

"What?"

"I . . . Richard. He's dead," Mum says, bringing her glass high to cover her face. I can still see tears, though, as they slip down her cheeks. She brings the rim of the glass to her lips and takes a glug. I imagine tears mixing with Merlot, making it salty, making it taste even more like despair.

"How'd he die?" I ask.

Her eyes dart downwards. I follow her gaze to a small patch which is slightly darker than the rest of the burgundy carpet.

"Stood on him," she says. "It was early morning, I'd just woken up, was still half asleep, I didn't see him."

This is a lie. She will have stood on her pet rat at night, whilst pissed. My eyes shift to the rat cage and the piano beside it. Mum's two prized possessions. To my horror, the kids at school would refer to her as the Drunk Rat Woman. They didn't know she was more than that, didn't know she could play any song you wanted on the piano, didn't know she cooked the world's best lasagne or knew every Agatha Christie novel by heart. You couldn't blame them, she smelled of Lambrini, not lasagne, and walked around with a rat in one hand, not a copy of *Murder on the Orient Express.*

My phone vibrates. I put down my drink, pull my eyes away from Ross and Rosie, the two surviving rats, and pick it up. My bottom lip drops. Seb. Seb has messaged me. He's sent a picture of an espresso martini and a sentence:

> The night doesn't feel right without you grilling me on my age or mocking my taste in art. Do you want to come join?!

Fucking typical. *Of course* he'd pick the one weekend I'm stuck up here with Mum. Still, the fact he's thinking of me is brilliant, regardless of whether I'm currently capable of exploiting those thoughts.

"Something tickled you?" asks Mum, spotting the grin on my face.

"No, just a text from a friend."

I stand up and move round to the drawer in which Mum keeps some of Dad's old doodles. Tucked away. Safe, but out of sight. There are hundreds, but I know them by heart and flick through to one of my favourites, a stick man surrounded by other stick men, all leaping about to get his attention, overwhelming him. I take a picture and send it to Seb, along with a message:

> I'm in demand tonight, a bit like this guy. Sorry. Maybe another time?

I laugh and place my phone down. Trail my fingers along the tatty bit of notepaper. Dad's drawings were rough and ready, like him. I smooth it out, flattening all four corners. And I notice, for the first time ever, that there are two small, round watermarks in the right-hand corner. I trail a finger over the two crusted splodges. My eyelids feel heavy. But I can't close my eyes. If I close my eyes, I'll see him floating, I'll see—

"It's a boy, isn't it?"

"Huh?" I glance back at Mum. Her own tears have dried.

"It's a boy, isn't it? Who's texting you?" she asks again.

I turn the corner back over, folding it down hard. I place Dad's cartoons back in the drawer and return to Mum.

"Yes, it's a boy," I say as I sit down.

"I always hoped you'd meet a boy up here."

"Well, it didn't happen," I say, taking a gulp of wine.

"You should look for a boy up here, Jen," says Mum. "I'll kidnap every boy in London so you have no choice, if I have to."

"Stop being daft."

"I would. Honest." She fiddles with the silver pendant she wears around her neck.

"I'm not moving back up here," I say, taking a drink of wine. Of the three velour armchairs in the middle of the room, I occupy one and Mum occupies another. The third armchair is forever destined to be empty. I've run away from it, from what happened to the person who is supposed to be sitting in it. I ran all the way to London. Mum normally has two empty armchairs to look at, and nowhere to run but the drinks cabinet. She takes a swig of her wine, as if it were water.

I sink further into the armchair, with an image of my future in the armchair to my left and the ghost of my past in the empty armchair to my right. I take another drink.

"It's dangerous in London. They'll have you back in the café, they loved you in that café. Remember Doris? Doris and Bert? They miss you. Every time I bump into them, they say their cups of tea just don't taste right anymore. And what we argued about . . . I can barely remember. But I've said sorry. Didn't mean it. I've changed. Come back and live with me."

I lower my eyes, lose myself in the wine, the delicious, blood-red poison.

"I can't," I say.

"Why?"

"I just can't."

If I move back up here, I'll turn into her.

CHAPTER FIVE

Thursday 24th February

"Basically, I think Liam's a quite attractive dickhead who said a few weird things, but just enough nice things that I'm still interested," I say to Saz through a mouthful of tuna baguette. We're finishing lunch at reception, one eye on our respective sandwiches, one eye on the *Daily Mail* sidebar of shame.

"And you last saw him?"

"Our first date. So a few weeks ago. But seeing him tonight. He's going skiing and wants to see me before."

"Wow – long time between first date and second. That's cos you didn't sleep with him," she says, shaking her head like a wise old village elder.

"Nah, it's cos it's been Valentine's Day. He didn't want to go on a date a week either side of the fourteenth."

"Wow. He sounds like a *real* catch."

"When he gets drunk, he messages me some kind of cute things. Like apparently, I'm the sixth most attractive girl he's seen in London. And that's pretty high, when you think about the millions of people in the city. And sometimes if we run out of things to message each other about, we just send a 'fact of the day'. Did you know slugs have 27,000 teeth?"

Saz raises an eyebrow and fixes her green eyes on my face. "Are you dating a man or a Wikipedia page?"

"You've got to admit, that's a great fact."

"Oh, a fantastic fact. So romantic. I can't wait for the slug-themed wedding."

I roll my eyes and pick up my baguette. I hold the bread in one hand and a pen in the other. Between work, commuting, attempting to stay fit, ignoring Mum's calls and avoiding Bob, you'd have thought I would barely have time to think about Seb. But I have been. Continuously. Even Liam's daily facts can't force him from my head.

So I've been doodling in an old notepad, attempting to exorcise him via the medium of low-quality art. Caricatures of Bob and Liam have also made it onto the pages. They're terrible, but it's relaxing. I go over Bob's nose at the same time as taking another bite of bread.

"You need to draw me one day," says Saz, peering over. "As long as you're flattering."

"You'd want me to ignore your witch nose and buck teeth? Couldn't do it, I'd lose all my artistic integrity. They'd kick me out the club."

"Oh ha-ha. I've got a lovely nose," says Saz, patting it as if to double check. "You are good though. Talented."

"Thanks. My dad was the real drawing talent. I was more into paints and fabric and stuff. Not as easy to keep in a handbag, though."

"He's an artist?"

"Oh. No. He . . . he died just over a year ago."

Saz nods, and it's as if I'm seeing her – the real her – for the first time. Her smile slips and she meets my gaze. Her brashness seems to retreat, and there's a hint of vulnerability about her expression. It's so intimate, I almost look away.

"Sorry to hear that," she says. "My mum died when I was younger. Not that that . . . Not that that's any consolation."

"Woo, dead parent club," I say, voice flat.

"Yeah . . ." She trails off and then seems to force herself to perk up. I'm about to tell her that she doesn't need to, she doesn't have to act in front of me, but she speaks before I get the chance. "But made me who I am today! She was always saying to follow my dreams. Get out of Margate! Not that there's anything wrong with Margate – lovely place. But she was like, 'Go to New York! Do Broadway! Expand your horizons!' Course, London receptionist isn't quite that, but we move."

I nod. "I'm sure she'd be really proud."

Saz opens her mouth to reply, but her phone starts ringing. She looks down, and a mixture of annoyance and giddiness crosses her face. It's an expression I've only ever seen used when someone you fancy does something to piss you off.

"Oh, secret lover?" I ask, but she doesn't reply, preferring instead to answer her phone grinning, and give me the finger as she struts off towards the kitchen.

I return to my notepad and to my baguette, taking a bite and shading in Bob's moustache.

"Oh, Jen. Hi," says a voice I wasn't expecting to hear. I look up and see Seb of all people, wearing a suit and a sheepish smile. He watches me as I watch him. I realise I'm still eating a baguette. A blob of mayo falls onto my keyboard.

"Shit." I flap around for a napkin, can't find one. I end up ripping out the sheet of paper I was drawing on and using that to wipe my keyboard clean. I look back up to see that Seb's mouth has pulled itself into an ear-to-ear smile, and the remainder of his face has followed suit: nose upturned, eyes sparkling, tiny lines crinkled around the edges of them.

"Nice drawings," he says.

"Oh, uh-huh. Just randomers I found on the internet. Any resemblance to a real-life person is purely coincidental," I say, crumpling up the drawing of Seb's face, whilst real-life Seb stifles a laugh.

"I forgot Jam said you work here. I do quite a bit of business with OnIt's property insurance team, so you might see me now and again." He flashes another quick, wide smile. "How you finding things, anyway?"

"Good. Pretty good. And I'm not usually so unprofessional," I say, resisting the less-than-professional urge to ask why he never replies to my texts. "Can I help you?"

"As a matter of fact, I think you might be able to. I've a meeting with Freya Black, I've got a hotel in Chicago I'm hoping she can insure."

I call Freya, but she doesn't answer.

"Two seconds," I say, dialling again with one hand and using the other to type out an email to her. Seb lingers by reception, smiling. When my hands can do no more, I start plaiting my hair – the only way of guaranteeing I can't spill or break anything in his presence. He watches as I tie a bobble in the end of it, and then his gaze shifts to the bowl of hard-boiled sweets on the right corner of the desk. He picks one up.

"May I?"

"Of course, they're literally for people like you," I say.

"Ah, miscreants like me, easily wooed by sugary treats." Seb unwraps it and briefly stops smiling to pop the sweet into his mouth. "Oh. Lemon. Ahh."

I laugh, stand up and peer into the sweet bowl.

"I think yellow is snot-flavoured, actually," I tell him.

"Oh, I see. Red's flavour is blood and green's flavour is spinach?"

"No, actually I think green is algae."

Seb fishes out a green sweet, unwraps it and crunches down. "Nope, definitely spinach. Disgusting."

"Top tip: red is the nicest."

"Oh yeah?" He raises an eyebrow.

Christ, he has the most expressive face – pulled in one direction, towards one emotion, by a small change of a single feature. He picks out a red sweet and tries to hand it to me.

"We're not really supposed to," I tell him. His face is half-a-metre from mine. He's simultaneously sexy and shy – a steady gaze contrasts against the way he fiddles with his folders. I want his voice closer, that deep purr right in my ear.

There's a ping as an email lands in my inbox. Reluctantly, I shift away.

"Ahh. It's Freya. Something about one of her children projectile-vomiting all over his maths teacher. She's had to go pick him up."

Seb makes a popping sound with his mouth. "Naaaht what I was expecting. That's scuppered my plans." He taps his folders against the desk, and then looks at me. "You free? It's still your lunch break, right? Want to have our own 'meeting'?"

A . . . sex 'meeting' or a date 'meeting'? Irrelevant; I'll take either. I try to force a more nonchalant reply from my lips. "I still have a little time left. Guess I could fit you in."

"Perfect. You've already eaten, in which case . . . yeah, I know where we can go."

He turns on his heel before I have a chance to respond. I grab my coat and join him in the lift, just before the doors close.

We head along Fenchurch Street, coming to a stop at the base of the Fenchurch Building, a skyscraper in the shape of a walkie-talkie. A queue of people brandishing paper tickets and shaking in the wintry air snakes around it.

"Been up to the Sky Garden yet?" Seb asks.

"Err, no. And by the looks of that queue, I'm not going to any time soon."

Seb laughs. "Oh, we won't use *that* entrance."

He heads in via the front of the building instead, flashing a pass and leaning in close to a receptionist, saying something I can't hear. She giggles, blushes and then hands me a pass of my own. It's as easy as that: we pass through barriers, whizz up in one of the lifts and emerge into the Sky Garden.

"Well, that was . . . something," I say, blinking around at the enormous rooftop, sheltered on all sides by glass, dotted with lush green plants and featuring a breath-taking view of South London.

"Drink?" Seb asks.

"Uh, yes please. A juice or a lemonade would be great."

Seb heads to the bar whilst I meander around the plants, coming to a stop at a table under a lemon tree. He joins me a couple of minutes later, handing over my drink.

"Thanks. This is very special," I say, meaning it. This kind of scenario would have been impossible for me to envisage mere months ago.

Seb smiles and shrugs off his coat, revealing a white shirt pulled taut over his shoulder muscles. It's chilly up here, but I don't trust my cheeks not to turn an alarming shade of red, so I avert my gaze and take a sip.

"Oh. Alcoholic?" I ask.

"A little. I'm sure you'll still be able to answer the phones." There's a hint of derision to his voice I'm probably imagining. Regardless, I feel obliged to defend myself.

"Oh. Yeah. You know, I didn't always want to be a receptionist. And the job can be challenging at times, actually."

"Yeah, I'm sure it can," Seb replies, taking a sip from his own drink. "What did you want to be?"

What do you want to be? Something people seem to ask as soon as you can speak, despite the fact it's one of the hardest, most existential questions out there. But the only thing worse than being asked "what do you want to be?" is being asked "what *did* you want to be?"

I shift in my seat. "I like art. Think I mentioned as much last time I saw you."

Seb grins. "You did. You said your dad used to draw."

I blush, thrilled that he remembers. "Yeah, but . . . a career in art or in media just seemed so . . . indulgent. Even a degree seemed wildly indulgent, sort of a bit risky and selfish and inappropriate, considering . . ."

"Considering what?"

"Where I come from, I guess. Not just the lack of money in my family, but the lack of money in the town I grew up in, the whole area really. It just always felt so wrong to me to spend thousands and thousands of pounds on a creative degree, when I wasn't even sure there'd be a job at the end of it. Just seemed like a thing that wasn't meant for me."

He nods and shifts his chair closer to mine. The hairs on my forearms rise.

"I mean, I didn't give up completely. Took Saturday classes at a local college. Meant I could still work through the week, help my family out that way."

I shift my gaze from Seb (no easy feat) and stare out at the view, at the skyscrapers of Canary Wharf to the east. The edges of the buildings grow hazy, blurring with the sky. Sometimes Dad and I would work the same jobs – him a cook at the Stray Café, me a waitress. Or both of us on the tills at the local Aldi. The silly gestures we'd make when none of the shoppers were looking. The secret signals. The caricatures of co-workers he'd slip me. The way his face would light up whenever we caught one another's eye. His face then. His face later – bloated and swollen and sloughed.

Seb's hand has found its way onto my thigh. He squeezes my leg, and then pulls me in for a hug. I'm caught off guard, but I relent quickly, melting into his body. It's been so long since I hugged someone, and he feels strong and safe and warm. His thumb draws circles over my thigh, edging its way up.

We part eventually of course, moving onto more light-hearted topics and finishing up our drinks. We pass by the bathrooms as we're leaving, and Seb cocks his head in their direction.

"Fancy a quickie?"

I laugh. "No."

"There's a disabled toilet one floor down, not many people know about it."

I pause, trying to ascertain whether he's joking or not. His face naturally sits in a smile, making him near impossible to read.

His smile stretches that bit wider, the lines by his eyes deepening. "Joke. Joking. Let me walk you back to your office."

I laugh, relieved.

"This was fun," he says, when we're outside the building that houses OnIt Insurance. "Not my usual business meeting."

"It was fun. Good to connect . . . emotionally, I guess." Oh God, what absolute cringe.

Seb's lips twitch, but he doesn't reply. Instead, he takes my hand and presses something into it. Then he kisses my cheek and walks off up Gracechurch Street.

I uncurl my right hand. One of the red sweets from reception is in my palm. I unwrap it and press it against my tongue.

Not blood. Obviously not blood.

Strawberry.

CHAPTER SIX

Thursday 24th February

Mine and Liam's second date is at the Tate Modern, a location I had to pester him to agree to. I want to see *London*, not just London's bars. There are no tube stations near the Tate, so I brave the freezing temperatures and walk from the City to Southwark. I pause on the Millennium Bridge, standing side by side with photographers, dawdlers and some of the hardier tourists. London. It's beautiful. Ninety-five per cent of the time, it's a bitch: busy, polluted, indifferent. But five per cent of the time it floors me. The Thames cuts through the heart of the city, through incredible buildings and beneath almighty bridges. I'm mesmerised by the power of the water, simultaneously repelled and attracted to it. All too aware of what the shifting velvet is capable of, as it flows out to sea, carrying with it all of London's sins, all of London's secrets.

I look until snow starts falling, and then I move onwards, towards the Tate, tourists, prams, screaming babies and loud traders flogging hot chestnuts. Reality seeps back in. London becomes London again.

I meet Liam in the Turbine Hall, a vast space which has been transformed into a cosmic playground: planets hanging from the ceiling, constellations beneath our feet. It's bold, breath-taking, busy.

"It's like a shit version of Disneyland," says Liam.

I shake my head but don't say anything.

"Literally, that's what art galleries are: shit versions of theme parks," he says. My expectations for the night slowly readjust themselves. I'd imagined us people-watching, making up stories about the stranger pieces of art, giggling at the nudes, our bodies pressed into each other, hands wandering as we drank in the soft curves of other people's flesh, brought to life in paint and oil. In my mind, our night would end back in the Turbine Hall; we'd be lying against the starry carpet, gazing up at the planets, swapping tales, sharing secrets. In my mind, Liam magically transformed into Seb.

I'm a fucking idiot.

Liam hates it. All of it. Paula Rego is "fucking creepy", David Hockney is "lame", Marcel Duchamp is "hella weird" and the Guerrilla Girls are "boring feminist shit". Initially I disagree, but eventually I surrender, nodding along to his scathing reviews, his moaning, his all-consuming boredom. We complete the free exhibits in half an hour; that must be a record.

"Let's go get drunk," he says when we're back in the Turbine Hall.

"Sure," I say, hoping the glimpses of nice Liam I saw on our first date might reappear once he has a drink in hand.

We step back out into the night, wander along the river to the closest pub and order a glass of wine each. We're served by a waitress with a magnetism about her, which Liam doesn't seem to notice but I'm drawn to. Her hand brushes against mine as she passes us our glasses, and I shiver. With an effort, I force my gaze from her alabaster skin and back to Liam. He takes a big gulp and a smile spreads across his face for the first time tonight.

"Better. Sorry, I was so over that art, Jen."

"This all you do with girls, then? Take them drinking?" I push my body into the leather of the couch, taking a second to inhale the pub: the smell of warm, rich comfort food, the low chatter of two-dozen people enjoying a pint or a leg of lamb, the crisp taste of wine against my tongue.

"Basically. I just get bored, you know? Tried getting dinner with a girl once: hella boring, would not recommend."

I grip the neck of my glass tighter. Part of me wants to tell him he's a prick, the other part wants to know how many girls he's taken out. Whether he's still taking other girls out.

"So this is my life now: getting pissed at every bar in London with you?"

"Holy shit, slow down, Jen, this is literally the second time I've met you."

I nod through gritted teeth. We drink simultaneously, neither looking at the other. My gaze shifts back to the waitress, at the other end of the bar now.

"So you're never with anyone long enough to eat food with them?" I ask.

"Told you – I got food with that one chick. And never again."

"That's ridiculous."

He shrugs. "I seem to have a five- or six-date max threshold. Then just over it. Overrr it. Gotta make them disappear." He snaps his fingers. He says the most awful things with the biggest grin on his face.

I must look startled because he quickly amends his statement.

"Joking, jeez, Jen. I mean, I have *had* a girlfriend. I'm not a complete animal."

"Oh yeah? How long did that last, before you decided to dispose of her?"

"Like three or four months. And technically, she ended things with me. But I *seriously* got my own back, so who's the real winner?" Again, an awful statement, but spoken with a Cheshire-cat grin. I haven't a clue whether he's joking or not. I choose to ignore what I don't like.

"Three or four months? Is that even classified as a relationship?"

"Sure it is!" he replies, indignant. "Alright, Miss Sophisticated, how long was yours? You were married, right? You've got five kids? Or at least two? Where they hiding? Come on, come out mini-Jens."

He starts looking under the table, around other people's legs, in search of my imaginary children. I can't help but laugh.

"I went out with a boy for a year in school. And I dated people on and off up until a year or so ago." Up until I couldn't face people, had to remove them from my life. Or they removed themselves, did the work for me.

"So, my short, grown-up relationship doesn't count, but the one you had as a *child* does?" Liam asks, mocking. He places a finger over my lips before I can argue. "What's your type then, Miss Sophisticated?"

I take another drink before answering, "I like a nice smile. Smiley people."

I also like brown eyes, muscles, tits, chiselled cheekbones. I won't tell him the tits part. I take another quick glance at the waitress.

"I can do smiley," he says, sticking a finger into each corner of his mouth and pulling it wide.

"You're very smiley. Concerningly so," I agree. "What's your type?"

"I like plaited hair."

I laugh and roll my eyes, wave my plait at him. "Sure you do – how convenient."

"I do, honestly, not just saying that." He leans closer and takes hold of my hair, runs a long finger down the bumps of my plait. He's handsome. Straight eyelashes, glowing skin, a pointed chin. He's pretty in ways I didn't realise when I first looked at him, prettier now that I've noted the nuances in his expressions, the way his tongue pokes out between his teeth when he smiles, the way his fringe flops forward whenever he gets excited. He's too pretty for me, I think.

I swirl my wine, suddenly self-conscious.

Still, an hour later, his lips are on mine. We kiss in the cold, in the dark, in Southwark's dimly lit back alleys. His hands run over my body, and mine over his. I feel his flesh under his jumper, the tone and texture of the muscle, beat of heart beneath breastbone. He's neither hard nor soft to the touch – a sort of in-between, the body of someone who is active but not a gym-goer, fit but indulgent. I wonder, as my tongue pushes against his, what he thinks of my body. I realise I don't really care. Having his hands run over me is enough. This is the most attractive I ever feel. When a man is caressing my body. When a man is approving it. I am a bad feminist.

"Let's go back to yours," he eventually mumbles into my neck.

"Mine? Really?" I ask, pushing him off me.

"Yeah."

"Why not yours?"

"If you come back to mine, I have to introduce you to my flatmates. Awkward, literally over that and not even tried it yet."

"I have a flatmate too. A hella weird one, remember?" Ugh, I'm using his phrases. Someone shoot me.

"No, you have a fifty-something-year-old bald guy who owns the place and just moved you in so he could wank over your knickers. If I see him, I'll punch him. Deal?"

"We haven't discussed me bringing people back, I don't know if he'll be weird about it. He's kind of weird about a lot of things."

"Jen, you pay to live there. You're allowed guests."

I start pulling brown wool from my dad's coat. I dither. I paid far too much for a Hollywood before work. I'm bald down below, pre-pubescent. It would be a shame to waste that.

"Sure," I say.

None of the lights are on in the flat, and for this I am grateful. Bob's car is round the back, though. I tell Liam we need to be quiet as I unlock the front door.

"Hide your shoes, please."

Liam obeys, hiding his trainers behind the entrance curtain. I lock the door and we tiptoe up the first flight of stairs. Along the landing. I pause outside of Bob's room, but I can't hear anything. We pass the kitchen and turn left to head up the second flight of stairs, past the bathroom and into my bedroom. I turn my light on.

"I can breathe again now, right?" asks Liam.

"Sure, quietly."

"How pissed off would you be if I jumped up and down real loud?"

"Very."

"Well, I cum pretty hard, so don't be too pissed about that."

I roll my eyes and start faffing about my room, picking clothes off the floor and putting them in the laundry basket, standing fallen books back up on their shelf. My room is perfectly decent: reasonably large and filled with half a shop's worth of Ikea furniture. It's in the roof of the house, so the ceiling slopes down, and I'm prone to hitting my head on it. The walls are painted yellow, the carpet is beige, my duvet cover is cream. It's an impersonal room, decorated how you might an unborn baby's, gender unknown.

Liam grabs my hand. I have one hand in his and the other clutching a copy of *One of Us is Lying*. I release the book. We kiss. His tongue forces my mouth open, it darts back and forth between my teeth. His hands move under my top, warm against my cold torso. He moves backwards, pulling me towards the bed.

"Just . . ." I pull away. "Just to let you know it's not actually a double bed. It's two singles pushed together. And one of the legs of one of the single beds is broken, so the right single is wobbly."

"Shhh."

He pulls me onto the left single and removes my top. I climb onto him, kiss him, unbutton his shirt. I get up as he removes his shirt and turn the lights off. My room is dark now – not yellow but near black, the only light coming from the passing traffic. The ceiling flashes in sync with the traffic lights outside: green, amber, red. I take a breath and re-join Liam.

We finish taking one another's clothes off in silence. His body is thin, thinner than mine. His thighs look half the width of mine, breadsticks next to hunks of ham. I should really have a rule about dating men with slimmer legs than me.

He pushes me onto my back.

"No pubes, huh?" he says, examining me. "Shame – I kinda like a bush."

For fuck's sake.

"Be hot if I filmed it," he says, grinning. My body stiffens, so he quickly adds, "Joking, joking – jeez, I'm joking."

There's no discussion over whether we're taking it fast or slow, no debate to be had. Liam pulls a condom over his dick then pushes himself into me, as if I owe him this, as if two dates is enough, as if it's his right to fuck me. My consent is assumed, and even I'm not sure whether he's correct or incorrect in assuming this. I say nothing. I don't think too much, either. And Liam's clinical about it. Missionary, with his hands pressed against my mattress and his chest arched away from me. His head is bowed, his gaze doesn't shift from my torso and his legs don't touch mine. He doesn't speak to me, he doesn't look at me and, apart from his dick, moving steadily in and out, he doesn't touch me.

He hisses his way to a quiet climax then pulls out, rolling as far away from me as possible.

"You lied," I say. "You don't orgasm that loudly."

"I do if it's good."

"Oh."

My hands ball into fists, fingernails press themselves into my palms. I glance at his thin neck, the Adam's apple sticking out, taunting me, almost.

Liam kisses my forehead and I unclench my fists. I claim a corner of the duvet and lie down. I thought Liam might cuddle me, wrap me up in one of his arms, that we might fall asleep cocooned into one another. He doesn't. He lies on the right single bed, chooses a wobbly sleep over one next to me. I reach over and put my hand on his arm. He lets it stay there for a minute or two before rolling away.

It takes me a while to fall asleep. I stare up at the ceiling. Green. Amber. Red.

Strawberry.

Friday 25th February

Bob is awake come morning time; I hear the mumble of the kitchen television as soon as I open my eyes. My heart sinks and I bite my lip.

Liam is completely wrapped up in the duvet and he wakes slowly, opening sleep-crusted eyes to stare at me.

"Heyyy, Jen."

"Hey."

There's a zit under his lip. I think about picking it off. He starts picking at it himself instead, pulling sleep from the corners of his eyes and flicking it down the gap between my beds. I'm going to have to vacuum that later.

"Got any food?" he asks.

"I'll check," I say, getting up and pulling on pyjamas. I head to my door and push it open.

I can smell Bob as well as hear him. Haddock and eggs, the buzz of the television, the scrape of knife and fork against plate, his heavy breathing. The kitchen door is always propped open and has a clear view onto the landing. I'd rather Bob didn't meet Liam, but sneaking him out appears impossible.

I head back into my room to find Liam sitting up, still wrapped in the duvet, eating a packet of Doritos.

"Doritos?"

"Doritos Doritos Doritos! Remembered I had some in my bag."

"I hate Doritos," I say. Hate the smell, hate the texture. He eats them quickly, too quickly, and starts pulling on clothes.

"Hey, hey," I protest. "Where are you going?"

"Erm, out, as in work. I have shit to do, lots of it."

I take hold of his wrists and plant a kiss on his lips. He tastes of Doritos. Horrible.

"Yeah, you can't go yet," I say once we finish kissing. "Bob's in the kitchen."

"No!" Liam's fringe falls forward. He pushes it back. "Oh wow, can't wait to meet him!"

"You *cannot* meet him," I say, squeezing his wrists hard.

"Yeah, I was totally gonna punch him, remember?"

"No," I say, squeezing harder.

"I mean, yeah, no, that was a joke. But literally I do need to go. Work then packing for skiing."

"Please. Just give it five minutes. Ten tops. If he's not gone in ten, I'll let you go."

Liam laughs. "Jen, you can't hold me hostage in your room. You might want to kidnap me, but you can't. Besides, what's Bob going to do if he sees me? Kill me? Kill you?"

"Well, no, but—"

"Cool, so I'm outta here."

"Hey, no, wait." I put on as many of my own things as I can: bra and blue blouse and black skirt. I grab a comb and as much makeup as I can stuff into my bag. I'll get ready in the office bathroom. Probably with three purple eyeliners and no foundation, but needs must.

Liam pushes my door open and I follow. He clatters down the first flight of stairs, loud, obnoxious. We pass the kitchen and I sneak a glance at Bob: sitting at the plastic table, stomach protruding between his T-shirt and shorts, a forkful of haddock frozen halfway between his plate and mouth, which is resting in a little shocked 'o' shape. His grip on the knife seems to tighten, flesh pulled taut over his knuckles.

I race down the stairs and out of the front door before he can make a comment about my having a guy over. Liam and I walk away from the flat, towards the station. I glance back just before we round the corner. Bob is at the kitchen window. We lock eyes as I move out of sight.

CHAPTER SEVEN

Thursday 24th March

Liam has been absent from my phone, whilst Mum has taken over. I'm hardly surprised; Liam's social media is littered with boozy après-ski videos and – by the looks of it – multiple me-shaped replacements. Poor sods. Mum, meanwhile, has only two rats and a dozen wine bottles for company. Guilt (and love, I guess) is what keeps me answering her calls, though I always feel drained and depressed after our conversations end.

Work is drawing to a close, and my phone pings.

"Oh no," I groan, glancing down at the message.

"Your mum again?" Saz asks, from next to me.

"Worse – Bob. What a weird message: Cheese and wine night, tonight, 8pm. All flatmates."

Saz shakes her head. "That's hilarious."

"We don't even have flatmates. What does he mean by 'all flatmates'? The only flatmates are me and him, and we're definitely not mates."

"Maybe he's kidnapped a load of people and keeps them in his room? Maybe you're finally gonna meet them tonight?"

"Don't. Honestly, I wouldn't put it past him."

I lower my forehead onto the desk.

"Let's go out tonight, then," says Saz. "You and me, maybe Jam too? Then you can bail on any awkward fish and flat small talk."

I raise my forehead off the desk just as my phone receives a second message:

I've got brie.

"Yeah, okay. Let's go for drinks."

*

An hour later, and we're outside Wandsworth Town train station. Saz seems to fizz with nerves and excitement as we watch Jam approach with two of his mates – Pete and . . . Pete?

"Jenson!" Jam bellows as he steps through the ticket barriers. "I'm honoured. What a treat to see you again."

He grabs me in a tight hug and then turns to Saz, with decidedly less enthusiasm.

"Saz. Alright?"

Both Petes are as insipid as I remembered, and Saz looks a little crestfallen, so I bring the conversation round to her as we walk from the train station to the bar.

"So, what's the friendship origin story between you two?" I ask Jam. "You got her a job, right? Is that the only way you know how to make friends?"

Jam laughs. "Jenson, Jenson, Jenson. I'm too sober for you to be so rude. Saz and I met a long time ago."

"On a dark, dark day!" Saz interjects, suddenly perkier.

"Behave! Nah, nah, nah, nah. Saz reached out to me one day – granted, she was a bit like you, needed a job. She wanted to be an actress, but I gave her a reality check, promised to get her a glamorous city job instead. Course I took one look at her – peroxide poodle on her head and she had these big dreamcatcher earrings back then – and I thought, 'oh strike me down, this bird is not going to be easy to place'. But I'm a busy boy: worked my magic and eventually she landed the reception job. Hardest client ever."

"Shut up, I have not been your hardest client!"

They bicker until we arrive at The Waterfront, a fancy glass bar on the banks of the Thames. As soon as we step inside, Jam refocuses his attention on me.

"Jenson – a pint of Guinness if you will." He pats my shoulder and nods in the direction of the bar.

"I will not."

"Nah, nah, nah, behave. You do owe me."

I sigh, he's right. I still owe him twenty pounds, or roughly three London beers. I traipse over to the bar and order him a beer and myself a glass of wine. As I wait, I look around, out of the floor-to-ceiling windows and back outside, at the Thames as it flows past. Dark. Deadly. Inviting, in its own strange way.

"Worst twenty pounds I've ever spent, by the way," I tell Jam when I re-join him, Saz and the Petes at a circular table next to the windows.

He shrugs. "You asked for Seb's number, I sold you Seb's number. I'm not responsible for your subsequent romantic failure."

"I didn't *fail* fail," I say, picking at a loose button on my blouse. "He sometimes replies. Sometimes really quickly. With emojis and everything. I mean, he even took me out for a drink! At lunch! Saz couldn't believe it when I told her. But then he ignored my messages after. Which he does quite a lot."

"So, you keep messaging until he replies, right? One more message? Two more messages? One message a day for a week? One message an hour for the past three weeks?"

I scowl, and take a big drink of wine. "I sometimes message him. He's probably busy."

"You should *see* her messages," Saz interjects, smirking. "Bloody funny, defo a bit creepy."

I glare at Saz.

"Oh Jenson, Jenson, Jenson," says Jam, grinning over his beer. "You're much too young and far too common for Seb. Just see it as a bit of fun sex with a nice lad. And leave it at that."

"I do really like him, though. Feel like he really listens to me."

"Behave. You just like the thought of being with someone hot and successful with a super-rich family who can take you on fancy holidays."

With a shrug, I take another sip of my drink. "Shoot me."

Saz giggles. She looks better than usual tonight: black blouse exposing the top half of her bust, her peroxide hair straightened so it brushes her collarbones, mascara on her eyelashes, making her small green eyes look wider. She shuffles closer to Jam. I watch them for a second or two before taking out my phone and scrolling through my many unanswered messages to Seb. He was last active an hour ago. Sighing, I take another drink.

My phone starts ringing and, in my enthusiasm to check whether Seb is the caller, I almost lose half my wine. But it's not Seb, it's Liam. I hesitate, and then I answer.

"Yo, Jenny!"

"Err, hi? Haven't heard from you in a while."

"You not? My bad– time got away from me. You missing your daily facts? I owe you some, right? How about this one: you're hot and I'm horny. Where are you?"

"I'm with my friends at The Waterfront . . . are you drunk?"

"The Waterfront – sweet, I live close by. Cool, I'll text when I'm near."

For fuck's sake. Why do people only call me when they're pissed?

"I'm actually not really so sure I want to see—"

"Of course you want to see me! Holy shit, Jen, the connection we have . . . discombobulating. See you in a few."

He hangs up and I pull a face at my phone – the kind of expression I usually only reserve for when I've downed a tequila. I take a large drink of wine, hoping Liam gets lost on his way over.

Ten metres behind Jam, Saz and one of the Petes, the door swings open. I sit up – Liam said he lives close, but surely not *that* close? The smoke from Pete's vape clears just in time for me to see two men enter and head for the bar. One of them is wearing a knee-length navy coat over a suit. He has brown, tousled hair. My stomach drops.

"Shit," I say. I reach for Saz's hand. "That's Seb. That's *Seb*."

"What?" she says, too loud. "Seb? *The* Seb?"

"Yes. Shut up."

"OMG, where?"

"Literally just behind you."

Jam has spotted Seb too. He pushes his chair back, but I grab his arm.

"What the hell?" I say. "Did you know he'd be here?"

"Nah, nah, nah. Promise. No idea," he says, smirking. Jam shrugs me away and saunters over to Seb, putting an arm around him. Seb jumps and grins. He's quickly joined by both Petes, who he gives one-armed hugs. Saz and I stay seated and watch as Seb introduces the trio to his companion: a small, manic-looking guy in his early thirties.

"Long legs, broad shoulders, he is fit, Jen. He is *fit*," says Saz.

"Yep, I know."

Seb briefly turns his head, and his chocolate eyes meet mine. My body jolts, the same reaction I had to catching his eye the first night I met him. We both look away quickly.

"You should go see him," says Saz.

"And say what? 'Hey, it looks like I'm stalking you. Why haven't you replied to my messages?'"

Saz laughs, "Yeah, maybe not. We'll just sit here awkwardly all night then. He really is hot though."

Jam eventually returns to Saz and me, with a shot of sambuca for us both.

"Luckily for you, Jenson, Seb is with a client, not a date," he says.

"Can you imagine?" says Saz after downing her shot. "That would be so bloody awkward."

I shake my head. He's even attractive from behind, his crisp shirt once again pulled taut across his shoulders. When he turns, I can see the moles on his neck and cheek, the creases that form at the edges of his mouth and eyes each time he smiles.

After a couple of shots, and in part to shut Saz and Jam up, I bite the bullet and approach Seb. I tap his back and hear Saz and Jam giggle when nothing happens. It takes a few excruciating taps before he eventually spins round. There's no surprise on his face when he sees me (we have shared multiple awkward glances, after all) but he does the open-mouth smile I've looked at so often in pictures.

"Hello you."

"Heyyy." Panic, panic, internal panic as I flounder for a response. "Sorry, it looks like I'm stalking you. I'm not."

His laugh makes his cheek mole jump up and his eyes sparkle. "Well, I came in after you, so the police might conclude it was me doing the stalking."

"True, I'll watch my back in that case," I say, with a wink so clumsy even Saz would be embarrassed.

I order a drink. Lemonade: I need to be sober (ish). I can feel Jam and Saz's eyes on my back.

"So. Kind of made my week going to the Sky Garden the other

day," I say once the drink is in my hand and Seb's client is busy chatting to Vaping Pete.

"Made your week? Blimey."

"I mean, no. Yeah. No. Sorry," I halt my stupid mouth by taking a substantial gulp of lemonade. Once I've swallowed, I continue talking, taking the conversation in what I hope is a more sophisticated direction. "What kind of music do you like? I saw the guitar and piano in your room."

"Huh, you're observant," Seb says. I'm not sure if he means it as a compliment. "Old stuff – jazz, the blues. My parents wanted me to try everything, the guitar and piano stuck."

I take another sip to dampen the enthusiasm of my reply. "I love the blues. And jazz. It's all my dad really played when I was growing up."

My attempts to woo him with grown-up conversation go well until one of the Petes commandeers his attention with a question about cricket or rugby. Seb turns away so I sidle back to Saz, a smile stretching across my face.

"It's going well, isn't it?" I ask.

"Honestly, Jen, he is bloody fit, but I've been trying to listen in and he's so posh I can't understand him, so it might be going well, it might not, I honestly couldn't tell you."

"It's going well," I repeat, answering for her. If I say it enough, then surely it's the truth.

I watch Seb, and I'm not alone: he receives plenty of attention from other women, and I feel eyes burn into my back whenever I get close. He chats to his client, he chats to Jam, he chats to both Petes. He even chats to Saz at one point, and I watch, nervous about the grenade of embarrassing tales she might release. He smiles the whole time, making it impossible to ascertain how much he's enjoying himself, how genuine he is. He's right, I am observant. But I'm not telepathic.

My phone rings, and for once, I know who it is. I answer.

"Hey, Liam."

"I'm outside, you gonna come meet me? Then we can bounce."

"Why don't you just come in?"

"Why don't youuu come meet me?"

I sigh and hang up. Hopefully I can persuade him to leave. Or if not, I guess I might be able to use him to make Seb jealous. I pull my coat on and head back out into the night. Liam is leaning against a low metal wall which separates the path from the river. He grabs my hand and gives me a peck on the cheek. It's oddly formal. Like an interview.

"Think I'm tanned?" Liam asks me. First question.

"It's quite dark. And you're wearing a lot of clothes. So hard to tell," I reply snippily.

"Outrageous! My face and hands are *so* tanned!" he practically shouts.

"Are those the parts people want tanned these days?"

He doesn't laugh, and instead reaches into the pocket of his duffle coat.

"Got you a present," he says, sticking his hand out.

In spite of myself, I feel my mouth spread into a smile that must look idiotic, like I'm expecting him to give me a ring or a love letter.

He doesn't. He uncurls his fingers and in his palm is half a block of chocolate.

"Got to the airport, thought 'should I get Jen something?' – this was on offer in duty-free, and yeah, perfect for you. Ate a bit on the flight though."

I accept the nibbled chocolate. Maybe I could save it and add it to some kind of shrine to our relationship, alongside bar receipts and empty Doritos packets.

"Anyway, you ready to head back to mine?" he asks. My eyebrows raise in surprise, as I recall how set he was on me not coming over to his. But perhaps his flatmates are out? Or perhaps he's reached a whole new level of desperate for sex?

"No. I'm having drinks with my friends. You're welcome to come join us, but otherwise . . ."

Liam pops his coat collar up, rolls his eyes. "Come on, Jen, don't pretend you're not dying to get in my bed. It's a privilege, coming round mine."

A genuine peal of laughter escapes my lips; the audacity of men never fails to summon a sincere smile. After a few seconds, Liam must get the message. He stalks towards The Waterfront, almost stumbling into the glass door. I follow him, and we don't stop until we're at the bar.

"Two double vodka lemonades," he demands, resting a forearm across the bar.

"Is one of those for me?" I ask, half taking the piss.

"Will it get you back to my flat quicker?"

"Err . . ."

"Then no, they're both for me."

I glance around, wondering whether Seb has clocked us. Though I doubt the frosty display between Liam and I would do much to spur him into a fight for my affections. Regardless, I can't see him. His client is still talking to the Petes, whilst Jam and Saz are at our table – Jam with his back to me, but Saz facing me, mouth slightly open. I give her a smile and a little wave, but her expression remains confused. She stands up, pushes her chair aside and hurries over.

"This?" she says, grabbing my sleeve and dragging me a couple of metres from Liam, who's sloppily downing one of his drinks. "*This* is the guy you've been dating?"

"Err, yep. Liam," I reply. "I know he's not quite Seb's level of unattainably unreal, but he's not too bad. From the outside, at least."

Saz opens her mouth and then closes it as she watches Liam sway about with a look of disgust on her face. Her grip on my sleeve grows tighter.

"Yo, Jenny, you ignoring me?"

I turn around to see Liam, who's using his right hand to point a wobbly accusatory finger at me, and his left to hold the second glass of vodka and lemonade. He takes a hearty swig.

"I'm just speaking to my friend," I say, offering him a strained smile.

"Blonde chick? Stop stealing my girl, you want her or something?"

"No," says Saz. Her eyes, which are normally small, normally creased at the corners with laughter, are currently fixed in a glare.

"Then stop looking at me like that, jeez." He downs his drink and then turns to me. "Jen, let's go – your friends are giving me the creeps."

"I really don't—"

He grabs my free sleeve, rendering me scarecrow-esque: one arm in Saz's grasp, the other in Liam's.

"Stop pretending you're frigid – I know it doesn't take much to get you to open your legs," he says. His voice carries; fellow drinkers try not to react, but I know they'll have heard the insult. I'm suddenly far too hot in my dad's thick coat. Heat seems to rise through my neck and to my cheeks. A bead of sweat drips down my forehead.

I try to shake Liam's hand from my arm, but his grip is strong. I don't want to cause a scene but . . . but I feel trapped, bullied, forced down a path I don't want to travel.

Liam continues, "Come on, I know you're up for it, you little slu—"

"Don't call her that! Don't you dare!" Saz shouts, releasing me to square up to Liam, glowering. She shoves him, and he's finally thrown off balance, a victim of his own drunkenness. He steadies himself and waggles one long, bony finger in the general direction of my face.

"Believe me, you don't want to mess me around, Jen. You don't want to piss me off."

He moves his finger closer, so close it almost touches my nose. And the features that I found so attractive on our last date seem to twist: his cheekbones seem sharper, his eyebrows menacingly bushy, his lips twisted into a sinister smirk.

"Everything okay here?"

A voice that's neither mine, Saz's nor Liam's. I look to my right and see Seb, standing next to us.

"Piss off, white knight," says Liam, grabbing my arm again.

Seb ignores him. "Jen, everything okay?"

I shake my head. Seb is subtle but effective. He's four or five inches taller than Liam, and he's broader too; with minimal effort, he manoeuvres Liam away from me. Liam resists, of course – shouting and swearing – but eventually they're out the door. I hear Seb tell the bouncers that Liam has had too much to drink, and then I lose sight of the pair of them.

I breathe a little easier, feeling some of my earlier panic disintegrate. I can't help but swoon over Seb's interference. Bad. Feminist.

"What a dick. You okay?" asks Saz. I nod. She waits a couple more seconds before taking out her phone and stepping away. I should follow, but my feet seem glued to the spot.

"Jenson? What went on there?" I feel Jam's hand on my waist.

"Just some drunk guy being an idiot. It's no big deal," I tell him.

"Nah, nah, nah. If he was harassing you, it's a big deal. Seb took him away?"

"Uh, yeah."

Jam clicks his tongue. "I'd better go find them, then. Get yourself another shot, Jenson."

Jam squeezes my waist and then follows Seb and Liam, out of the glass door. I shake my head – relieved to finally be free of hands gripping my coat – and turn back to our table. Seb's client and the Petes are still chatting, seemingly completely oblivious to everything which just happened, whilst Saz is on her phone.

She shoots me a smile, hangs up and then walks over, coat and bag tucked under her arm.

"I'm so sorry to have to nip off after that palaver – God, what a wanker," she says. "I'll have to vet your next bloody online match!"

"Aha, yeah, maybe you will. Everything okay?"

"Oh, yeah. I'm fine. My sister just rang me though – she's broken a nail or something. Some minor problem, but my legendary sympathy is required."

"Didn't know you had a—"

"A sister, yeah. Stepsister, technically . . . but that's a long story and doesn't get me off the hook for these kinds of so-called emergencies." She rolls her eyes, and then leans in close to me. "Text me when you get home. *If* you get home."

She does her signature clumsy wink, and then dashes away with more urgency than I'd anticipated. Perhaps her sister's emergency is more serious than she's letting on.

I return to the bar, heeding Jam's advice and buying myself a shot. After downing it, I stick my index finger inside the sticky glass and twirl it as I look out across the tables. Vaping Pete leaves after ten minutes or so. And then Seb returns, giving me a small smile. Jam doesn't come back. I should leave, too. If I was sensible, if I had any dignity, I would leave. But I don't. I linger. I linger like a bad smell, on the outskirts of conversations, on the edge of the remaining group: Pete, the client, Seb. It's desperate. Is it desperate? I keep mouthing 'thanks' at Seb, and occasionally, his eyes catch mine. We both know without saying anything: I'm coming back to his tonight. That makes him as desperate as me, I think.

The client must take pity on me because he asks my name.

"Jen," I tell him.

"Sweet. I'm AJ. I'm here hoping Seb can get my property empire insured. And when we're not talking business, Seb's showing me the town."

"American?" I ask. The guy has grown more manic with every drink he's consumed: blond hair sticking up at angles from his head, polka dot bow tie twisted, wet patches – signs of a reckless wrist, a night enjoyed – down his shirt.

"New York. You a friend of Seb's?"

"Kind of."

"Oh. You're *that* kind of friend. Yeah, I hear he has a few of those. Some of them are pretty crazy, from what I've heard," says AJ, a remark I try to forget.

But I *am* one of *those* friends, my role made apparent by the awkward dance Seb and I do around each other: always a metre or two apart, never speaking, only ever casting quick glances at one another, checking our ride for the night is still around. And always being watched. Half a dozen eyes follow me whenever I get close to Seb.

I alternate between soft and alcoholic drinks, a tactic which keeps my mind clear but fills my bladder. I head to the toilet, and when I emerge, bright lights have been turned on, and the illusion of atmosphere that the bar had managed to create – sexy, intimate – has evaporated. Dazed drinkers are trickling out of the door, blinking. I look around but can't see anyone I recognise. Grabbing my coat and bag, I join the current of people. We head out into the dark, into the chilly March air.

"Looking for Seb?" asks a voice I hardly recognise. It's Pete, ten metres from me, leaning against the rail that separates the path from the river. Ordinarily, he's mute. Or I just don't listen to him, I guess.

"Err, kind of." I pull my coat tight and shuffle next to him, gaze drawn to the murky Thames.

"He had to go somewhere. He does that sometimes – he's a flaky guy. And AJ's still doing lines in the toilets, as far as I can tell."

"Oh." Hurt. Confusion. These emotions briefly overwhelm me. I stare harder into the water. It's velvet, trickling under and over itself. Hiding things. The sting of Seb's rejection seems to lessen with every second I spend staring at the shifting midnight.

"So, we could? You know? If you wanted to?"

"What?" I turn my head, away from the river and towards Pete's sizeable face.

"You could come back to mine."

I dither. A dithering ditherer. I'm a terrible people-pleaser, godawful at telling people what they don't want to hear. Politeness, I suppose. And probably a deep craving to be liked. I try to assess Pete as quickly as possible. He's strong of nose, weak of chin. Fine-looking. But not for me, no matter how tricky I might find that to tell him. But I've already dealt with one forceful man tonight, I'm not in the mood for another.

"You were going to fuck Seb, why not me?" he continues.

"I've got a cheese and wine night with my landlord. Yep. So, got to go."

"It's 1 a.m."

"That's when we do our cheese and wine nights."

And with that I leave. I return to the thing I've spent all night trying to avoid, riding the 337 along Upper Richmond Road. Whilst the bus trundles along, I check my phone. I've received messages from Bob, obviously.

Don't forget – 8 p.m. There are crackers

Jen, cheese and wine?

Remember, it is 11 weeks since you moved in with me. Looking forward to celebrating that anniversary

Jen are you okay?

Jen, are you with the man who was here a few weeks ago?

Jen, do you need help? In trouble?

In trouble with that man?

Jen, I'm coming to find you

Fucking hell. I've got a mum up north and a mum down here. I reply, apologising for my absence, and hop off the bus.

Bob isn't in when I reach the flat. His car isn't round the back, and none of the lights are on. I pause outside his room. I'd be able to hear him breathing or snoring, I'm sure of it. But all I can hear are the clocks which hang in every corner of the flat, ticking down to dawn.

CHAPTER EIGHT

Sunday 3rd April

Thankfully, Liam doesn't get in contact after that night at The Waterfront but, less thankfully, neither does Seb. March bleeds into April, the nights get lighter, and flowers dot the ground. The natural crevices of London erupt into colour: pink and green and yellow. So bright, such a contrast from the barren land before, it almost hurts my eyes.

Seb disposing of Liam and then leaving without explanation has made me want him more, and I think about increasingly elaborate ways of bumping into him: from joining his gym to eating lunch outside his office every day to spending my weekends traipsing up and down the King's Road, outside his flat. I construct elaborate fantasies of us bumping into each other and me sweeping him off his feet. Because surely if he sees me enough, if he talks to me enough, he'll fall for me. He'll ask me to be his girlfriend and then . . . then what? I join his family on fox hunts and pheasant shoots and ski trips? I attend dinner parties with his boarding-school friends? I stare and stare at his beautiful face until his flesh sags, the lines around his eyes and lips deepening, spreading like a river around his face. Until he's not a god anymore, but a human, and I see him as such, and the illusion is gone.

I'm a dog chasing its own tail; any victory will be hollow, a reality which doesn't match up to my fantasy. And yet still I want him.

Saz has been on a last-minute holiday for the past week, so I've had no one to digest Seb's behaviour with, no one to stop me pining. I should venture out but, truth be told, I'm still a touch intimidated by London, by the crowds and the tube system, and the dark river that divides the city. I still haven't made many friends, and there are only so many spinning classes I can be bothered to drag myself to, so I spend many a drawn-out weekend in the flat with Bob. He commandeers the kitchen from 7 a.m. until 10 p.m., chopping up fish and chicken and strange-smelling meat I struggle to identify. So I stay in my room, listening to knives on flesh and planning Seb-ensnaring traps: kidnapping and seducing him. My gaze drifts between my phone screen and the four yellow walls of my room. I spend my Sunday purposefully making a probability tree and accidentally memorising every crack of my bedroom walls. The probability tree reads as follows:

Probability of you replying to this:
No = 0.5
Yes = 0.5

Probability of me subsequently replying to your message:
No = 0.2
Yes = 0.8

Probability of you wanting to go for drinks:
No = 0.6
Yes = 0.4

Probability of me wanting to go for drinks:
No = 0.2
Yes = 0.8

Probability of being free on the same night:
No = 0.2
Yes = 0.8

Probability of us both turning up:
No = 0.5
Yes = 0.5

It's not an optimistic model. My predicted probability of both Seb and I going for a drink is a measly five per cent. I look at what I've created for a while, and then a small, mental part of my brain decides to send him a photo of it. Perhaps he'll think I'm quirky and endearing. Or mathematically minded, at least.

Thirty minutes pass without a response. I don't look quirky or endearing or mathematical. I look unhinged. I'm about to delete my message when he responds:

> Lol. Slow Sunday? You're over-optimistic about us being free on the same night.

Holy shit, he's replied. Did not expect that. I can't help it, a smile spreads across my face. I type back:

> Oh, I just really love maths. I make probability trees for every life decision – which shoes to wear, which skirt. Takes a solid 3 hours just to get dressed each day.
>
> Joking, please don't tell Jam, he'd ruin me.
>
> The odds just rose from 5.1% to 12.8% . . .

He replies quickly:

> Haha, that sounds stressful if you ask me. Being free on the same night still the stumbling block, though.

I force myself to do other things – pick my clothes up, read a chapter of *American Psycho* – before replying:

> Oh yeah, my room is a mess – 50% furniture, 50% old probability trees. In the interest of completing this probability tree and moving on to my next – do you want to go for a drink?
>
> Odds are on 'no' at 60%

He sees my message but goes offline. I wait for ten minutes, swiping absently through profiles on Matchum, and then I pocket my phone and make myself go downstairs to the kitchen. I've not had a drink for four hours and I've not eaten for at least six; I've got to put my own survival above my hatred of being in a confined space with Bob. He's sitting at the plastic table, watching television and eating tuna, with his laptop and a newspaper beneath his right elbow.

He's wearing a grey T-shirt and tartan pyjamas, which he's rolled up to his knees. An improvement on the shorts, I suppose. He turns his owl head and emits a grunt.

"Hi, Jen. How are you finding *American Psycho*?"

I'm briefly confused, before remembering I was reading it earlier. I must have left it lying around in the kitchen at some point. "I'm, uh . . . it's an interesting book."

"Too violent for me."

"Mmm. But, uh, how are you?" The guilt I feel for missing his cheese and wine night seems to have manifested itself in an insatiable desire to check on his wellbeing – not that I care much for the answer.

"Same old. Road outside is still busy. Way busier than when I bought the place."

"Oh, uh-huh. When did you get this place?"

"Uhhh . . . Higgins won the snooker . . . Icelandic banks collapsed . . . bought this place six years after the golden jubilee, or maybe seven?"

"You know what, I don't need to know."

"Been here fifteen years, give or take. Was cheaper back then. And quieter too!" Bob gestures in the direction of the window. The traffic is all too audible, and he starts muttering about it.

"Yep."

I can never quite figure out Bob's financial situation. I'm ninety-nine per cent certain he told me he was an accountant (there's a small margin of error, of course, for I don't think I've ever managed to give him my full attention). Is that enough to get you a place in London? Was it enough when whoever the hell Higgins is won the snooker? My guess would be yes, but then again, I also thought you could live alone here for £800 per month, so maybe I'm not the best person to ask.

A pan is bubbling away on the hob. I move past Bob and stand beside it. I see his moustache hairs everywhere: on the taps, the tiles, plates. And shorter hairs too – maybe eyebrow hairs or, worse, pubes. It's as if he goes around moulting on everything. I shudder and open the cupboard, pushing past his toolkit to grab myself a glass. I pour myself some water and then lean against the sink, watching the television over his shoulder. He's watching a quiz show, with an old man asking a younger man questions.

"Which element is the fourteenth to appear on the periodic table?" asks the quizmaster.

"Silicon," mumbles Bob, through a mouthful of tuna. The contestant gives the same answer a beat or two later.

"Impressive," I say.

Bob shrugs. "Ex was a chemist."

"Oh yeah, did you . . ." I pause, torn between asking whether they did literal experiments together or whether there was much figurative chemistry in their relationship, despite the fact neither question makes much sense, and I don't care for either answer. "Did you . . . err, did she have her own Bunsen burner?"

Bob shifts his gaze from the television to raise his eyebrows at me. He thinks I'm a weirdo. My weird landlord is genuinely weirded out by *me*. He turns back to the television just as the quizmaster asks how many hearts earthworms have.

"Five," Bob says, at the same time as the contestant.

"Correct," says the quizmaster. "And which type of slug frequently chews off its partner's penis after mating?"

"The banana slug," answers Bob, instants after the quizmaster has finished his question. The contestant gives the same answer a second or two later.

"Wow. You really know your molluscs?" I ask.

Bob doesn't turn around. "General knowledge."

It bloody isn't.

Boiling water from the pan hits my arm. I wipe it away and peer inside, at bubbles that half-conceal yet another strange-looking meat. Another glance at Bob, who's still absorbed by niche trivia. I take my water and packet of crisps, and I'm just about to exit the kitchen when Bob bangs his fist on the table.

"Robert Pickman! That was Robert Pickman who fed his victims to pigs!" He flails his palm at the television, in exasperation and disgust. "Bloody gameshow. Who doesn't know that?"

I pause just behind him, eyes narrowed, nervous laughter bubbling about my throat. He shoves his tuna away and pulls his laptop close. He flips open the lid and types in the password:

J – E – N—

My eyes widen, but my phone vibrates and, in a pathetic display of lust over logic, I miss the remainder of the creepy password as I fish it from my pocket. Seb has sent three messages. I leave Bob to his indignant muttering and head back to my room.

Lol you can't ruin all the fun and just skip to the end!

I'm already out every night this week apart from tomorrow.

And much as I would like to help you complete ever more complicated probability trees, it's probably not the best start to the week.

I sigh, unsure whether he's being genuine or just letting me down gently. I open Instagram and begin clicking through people's stories – a variety of insipid pictures. Avocado on toast. Manicured nails. Cherry blossom outside St Paul's. A missing post of a dark-haired boy. A French bulldog puppy. Holy shit – a *missing* post? I click back, and my stomach drops.

Fiona-bloody-school-bitch-Nunn has shared a picture of Liam, and above his head are seven letters, printed in red and in capitals.

MISSING

Missing? How can someone who was so, so . . . present and loud and irritating be *missing*? I . . . I . . . God, the word seems to sting, each letter slicing into my brain. I snap my head from side to side, searching for Dad's coat.

And then, hands shaking, I click on the link. It takes me to the Instagram page of Tala Garcia. Her profile is adorned with pictures of Liam, and pleas for information. I click on one of her posts – a dark CCTV still of Liam alone, leaning on the wall opposite The Waterfront. Under the picture, she's written:

PLEASE HELP. My brother Liam (27 y/o, 5ft9) hasn't been heard from since the 24th of March.

The 24th of March. Thursday the 24th of March. Eyes watering, I look harder at the CCTV picture. There's one thing I know for certain. And that's the fact that I'm just out of shot, probably exiting the bar, heading for Liam. I'm seconds – *metres* – from being the last person Liam was captured with. Fuck. Who saw us together that evening? Is more CCTV footage going to be unearthed?

Tears spill from my eyelids and I paw them away. I shiver, as though someone has blown against the back of my neck. This is horrible. And far too familiar. I drag myself off the bed and grab Dad's coat from the hook on my door. I squeeze the fur hard beneath my fingers, feeling each damaged, tatty bit of fluff. I pull out one clump, and then another, hands still shaking.

My phone, still on the bed, buzzes. Another message from Seb.

Jen? You're not ignoring me, are you?

I turn it off and throw it into a corner. Sit on the end of my bed, pull my legs in close, so that my knees are touching my chin. I'm shaking. Shaking and breathless.

I try to calm myself. Count numbers. Imagine the river. Imagine dropping my problems into the waves, letting them drown.

CHAPTER NINE

Monday 11th April

Liam's disappearance is simultaneously something I'm scared to face and can't look away from. I'm torn over whether I should play detective, but I'm also torn over whether I should take what I know to the actual detectives. But would they listen? Would they believe me? Or would they twist things, somehow find a way to blame me?

So I don't tell anyone about his disappearance. It's a form of denial, almost: by not talking about it, I can pretend the dark shadow looming over my new life isn't real. And yet his face dominates certain corners of social media – there's a *Find Liam Garcia* Facebook page, and his sister shares constant updates. The photos get a couple of hundred likes, a dozen sympathetic comments, but they're largely ignored. A fully grown man hasn't been heard from for two and a half weeks, it's hardly front-page news.

I'm drawn to the virtual updates on his disappearance, but I'm also drawn to the physical. Twice daily, my train stops at Wandsworth Town station, and I have to fight the urge to re-trace my steps back to The Waterfront. To walk in the footsteps of old Jen, who might well have been one of the last people to see him alive. I should go to the police. I really should. But I'm not sure I can face the embarrassment and frustration of once again not being believed, not being listened to. I know all too well what poor Tala is going through, and yet I'm conflicted. I want to help her. But I can't get myself more involved. I can't re-live another disappearance.

Saz is finally back from Ibiza, and I'm thankful for the distraction.

"So, how was the hol?" I ask, mere seconds after she's logged on.

"God, *so* expensive. Like, ten pounds for a water! Can you believe it! And actually not that warm. Still fun, though."

"I guess it is still the off-season. Any fit men?"

Lips still hovering over the rim of her coffee cup, Saz shoots me a smug side-eye. "The. Fittest. Men."

"Helping you get over that guy you were on and off with?"

"Ha yeah, you could say that."

"Well, I'm very jealous. Who'd you go with?"

Saz looks at me suspiciously. "It's nine o'clock on Monday morning! Too early for twenty questions."

"Oh, yeah. Sorry. Just been bored without you." And in desperate need of another voice to drown out my constant thoughts about Liam and his family. I take a drink of my tea. Lukewarm.

"Just went with my stepsister," Saz eventually says, whilst scrolling through her inbox. "Six hundred emails! Six hundred! I was only away two weeks!"

"You know the company falls apart without you," I say with a wry smile. "Anyway, tell me about your stepsister. I didn't know you had one until that night at The Waterfront." My ignorance in respect of Saz's life makes me feel guilty. I'm so caught up in my own problems that I seldom bother to scratch beneath the surface of anyone else.

Saz shrugs. "Oh yeah, when I had to go help find her favourite bikini, would you believe. But honestly, she's cool. I've always looked up to her a lot. You remember what I said about my mum?" she says, and I nod. Our conversation about a mutual loss of a parent is probably the only serious chat we've ever had. "Well, my dad started dating another woman a couple of years later. I was only ten at the time, and I remember being so nervous hearing that this new woman had a daughter seven years older than me. But I didn't have to worry – she was kind and funny and cool and honestly became like a mum to me. Did all the things mums are supposed to do – made me feel warm and safe and looked out for, you know?"

I don't respond straight away. Because I don't know. I nod my head once, and Saz keeps talking.

"Our parents didn't stay together, but we kept in touch. Together through the good times and the bad. And there have been some *bad* times. But I always do what's right by her."

I set my mug down. Do I always do the right thing for someone else? Should I? If anyone were to influence my decisions, it would be Dad. I would want to do the right thing in his memory. I dip a finger into my tea, plunge my nail beneath the surface. Cold. But what *is* the right thing? The police didn't help Dad; I'm not sure I can bring myself to trust them.

Come home time, I've had a change of heart. Hard though it might be to put my past experiences aside, if what I know about the evening of the 24th March can help return Liam to his family, it's worth contacting the police. I find a quiet bench amongst the trees of Barnes Common, and take out my phone.

Tala's posts included the telephone number of Hammersmith Police Station. I click onto her Instagram page, my eyes peeled for the MISSING picture she uploaded last week.

"Shit."

I don't get that far. There's a new post. Just a black square, with white writing across it:

> Update: Liam's body has been pulled from the Thames. He drowned. I'm heartbroken. Want to thank everyone for their help in trying to find him.

He's dead. Fuck, he's dead. My heart beats a little faster and I glance around, suddenly certain I'm being watched.

Liam's body has been pulled from the river. Liam drowned. He … I know exactly what he'll look like. His flesh will be scarred from rocks and branches. His clothes will be soaked, muddy, ripped. His skin will be wrinkled, saturated with water. And it will be sloughed, too. His nails will be soft and purple. He'll look bloated. Stuffed full of the thing that killed him.

I don't realise I'm throwing up until the liquid – milky and uninspiring – is out of my mouth and splattered onto the grass in front of me. I wipe my damp forehead with the back of my right hand, and my sick-stained lips with the back of my left hand.

I shudder, wondering whether this will escalate things, whether the police will look harder, see how connected I was to Liam. Whether I should be worried about being dragged into this, whether I should start planning for that possibility now.

CHAPTER TEN

Wednesday 27th April

The taste of sick seems to linger in my mouth for the next couple of weeks, making my teeth feel crusty, my tongue fuzzy and sour. And I'm paranoid – going over my final moments with Liam with a fine-tooth comb, trying to recall how many eyes were on us, how many people might have seen us argue. Whether they might put two and two together, decide his death is suspicious. Christ, I wish I could share my worries with Mum, but she's drunk whenever I call her, slurring her words and mumbling about rats. Ordinarily, she'd be my main concern, but for once her alcoholism has to take a back seat.

When Jam messages Saz and me asking if we're free for drinks, I leap at the invite – if only as a distraction. I try to swallow the taste of sick away for good as the two of us make our way from the office to his proposed destination.

The Ship turns out to be a sprawling riverside pub overlooked by fancy glass apartments and adorned with fairy lights. Saz and I make ourselves comfortable at a wooden picnic table looking out across the dusky river. My gaze drifts across it, following swirling eddies and floating debris. I can feel my mind drifting, too, wanting to add its own grizzly image to the scene. One floating body. No, not one floating body. Two.

"Lads!" Jam arrives, and I snap myself away from the river, making a concentrated effort to plaster a smile onto my face and push sinister thoughts from my brain. He places four drinks on the table and then sits himself down next to Saz.

"Feeling thirsty tonight, are we?" I ask, eyeing up his selection of beverages.

Jam flashes me a quick smile. "You're a funny one, Jenson, I'll give you that. But nah, nah, nah. This is a beer for me, a wine for you . . ." He pauses to hand me a glass. "A pink gin for Saz, and a sherry for Daniel."

"*Daniel?*" I ask.

"A *sherry*? Who is this guy, a seventy-three-year-old woman?" Saz adds.

"Crikey, who put two pence in the pair of you tonight? Daniel is one of my clients, I've just recruited him for OnIt Insurance. I thought it might be nice for him to meet the office gossips before he starts – you know, get the worst introductions out of the way first."

Saz gives him the finger, before scowling down at her drink. "You know I'm not a pink gin fan."

"Thought pink gin was your drink?" Jam shrugs.

"Shut up! How long have you known me? Prefer a rosé, or a tequila sunrise, or a Malibu and Coke."

"Behave." Jam gives her a playful shove. He smirks at me. "Saz'll drink anything that's put in front of her. It'll get her into trouble one day."

An uneasy laugh escapes my lips. I look down at the red wine in my hand. Give it a swirl.

"So, Jenson – heard from that sleaze at the bar again?" Jam asks.

My stomach drops.

"Liam?" It's obvious that Jam hasn't made the connection between my "sleaze" and the missing man, but I still feel I'm being inspected. "Nope! Nothing! I barely knew him!" I snap. I can't be implicated in this. By anyone. If Jam thinks I'm suspicious, it's plausible the police will too.

I look up, and both Saz and Jam are frowning. I look back down, at the crimson poison in my glass. I look to my right, at the river, so deep and dangerous. Sweat tickles my brow.

"Evening, all," says a deep voice from behind me.

"Daniel!" Jam says, standing up and wrapping the mystery man in a one-armed hug. "Let me introduce you to Saz and Jen, the best receptionists in London – recruited by yours truly, of course."

Daniel greets me in a flurry of aftershave and adjectives. He pulls me into a hug and my skirt almost splits.

"Jen, amazing, you look divine, beautiful, truly."

He releases me and I get my first proper look. A well-preserved man a couple of decades older than I am. He's wearing a white shirt with three buttons undone, exposing both black and grey chest hair. His tan skin is turning leathery, his bright white teeth are clearly veneers. He's got dark, shoulder-length hair which has been gelled back from his face, exposing a receding hairline. He's attractive, but – upon clocking his skin-tight black jeans – the term "mutton dressed as lamb" springs to mind.

"Ahh, London at dusk with a host of new pals and a stiff sherry," says Daniel, settling next to me on the bench. "A toast, if I may?"

"Uh, yeah, sure. To . . . err . . . dusk and new friends," says Saz, sarcasm dripping from her every word. The four of us clink glasses, and then Jam leans across the table, resting his chin in his hands and allowing a wide grin to stretch across his face.

"So, Daniel here is the new head of Marine Underwriting at OnIt Insurance. He doesn't start for a couple of weeks – you two cheeky chaps are getting a sneak peek."

"Lucky ladies indeed," adds Daniel, scooching himself a couple of inches closer to me. "But you make me sound far more important than I am. Really, I'm just one of the guys. Down with the kids. I party until dawn. And my pint-drinking skills are legendary."

Saz snorts into her pink gin. She tries to disguise her laughter with a coughing fit and a tactically placed napkin which covers half of her face. Jam scowls at her – the look of a husband who's been married for a dozen years too long – but Daniel doesn't seem to have noticed.

"I'm far more fascinating than the corporate shackles that restrict me," he says, shaking his wrists. "But, Jen, any questions for me? For your new head of Marine Underwriting?"

"Uhh . . ." I look at Saz, hoping she can help me out with a question, or that we can, at the very least, share a smirk of disbelief. But Saz's gaze is fixed on her phone.

"I'm going for a smoke," she says, suddenly.

"Oh, you have ciga—" I say, but she's up and across the decking before I can finish my question. I watch as she disappears into the dusk.

"My one weakness – the old cigarinios," says Daniel, also getting to his feet. "Any mention of a puff and I'm gasping. Back in a tick."

He waves a cigarette packet in front of Jam and me and then waltzes away under the fairy lights.

I turn to Jam. "Well he's a bit bizarre. And I didn't think Saz smoked."

Jam shrugs. "She does when she's drunk. Or in one of her dumb, giggly moods."

He rolls his eyes, more annoyance in his expression than I've seen before. He downs his pint and runs a finger around the rim.

"All the time, then," I say, trying to make a joke.

"And she wonders why I don't take her seriously," continues Jam, still humourless. "I mean, would you?"

I can't tell whether the question is rhetorical or not, but I've no desire to sit and bitch about Saz. I tell Jam I'm going to get everyone another drink, and then I head inside. I prop myself against the wooden bar, between a group of selfie-snapping girls and a couple of flat-cap-wearing men. The smell of garlic bread and chicken wings drifts up my nose, and I have to fight the urge to buy everyone a round of starters rather than booze.

The pub television – hanging to the left of a cabinet of whiskies – soon forces food from my mind. Because Liam is displayed across the screen. His dark hair, pearly teeth, bushy brows. All pixelated and aggressively bright. Not an image I want to see. In fact, the very thing I've come to the pub to forget. The upper half of my body turns, but my feet remain glued to the spot. As ever, I can't look away.

His face is replaced with the image of a reporter, wearing a smart tartan coat, clutching a microphone and standing at the edge of the Thames. The television has been muted, but subtitles flash across the bottom of the screen:

This is the place where Liam Garcia's body was found a

> couple of weeks ago. It was initially assumed that his death was the result of misadventure. However, autopsy results found no—

The barman moves to grab a cocktail umbrella, obscuring my view of the television. I shove my way through the selfie girls and dash to the base of the television. The image has changed – a close-up of the murky Thames now dominates the screen – but, as far as I can tell, I don't appear to have missed any of the story.

> —water in his lungs. Police are now investigating the possibility that he died before entering the Thames.

Murder.

The police think he was murdered.

The hairs on the back of my neck rise. I sneak a glance around the pub. It suddenly seems all too shadowy, and all too close to the place Liam was last seen alive.

Fuck the garlic bread. I need a drink. A strong one.

Daniel, Jam and Saz are all back at our table by the time I re-emerge, balancing four shots and four double vodka lemonades on a tray.

"Jenson!" shouts Jam, all smiles again in front of his client. "What a lad!"

"Oooh, yes please," says Saz, grabbing a shot and a vodka lemonade before I've even set the tray down. She necks both of them, and immediately offers to buy the next round.

"Err, sure."

The remainder of the evening continues in a similar vein and I'm grateful, as it offers some distraction. I know that the update on Liam will contaminate my mind for the foreseeable future, but – for now – I attempt to shove him into a different part of my brain.

Saz seems determined to get herself absolutely steaming. Jam and I go along with it for a little while, before I start pouring my drinks away (good God, what a waste of money) and Jam heads for home, muttering about Saz being a child under his breath. We never get to see Daniel's supposedly legendary pint-downing but, to be fair to him, he does his best to keep up with Saz – turning his face puce in the process.

He wipes sweat from his brow and leans in close to me. "Man oh man, your friend can drink."

"Yep. I didn't think she was going to go this hard. On a work night."

"Be nice to hang together without her, don't you think, bubba?"

It takes a second or two for me to realise that *I* am "bubba".

"Uh, I guess I'll see you in the office, sure," I say.

Daniel laughs – deep and disingenuous. "You're funny. Really, you're funny. Here, take my card." He hands me a business card so simultaneously vague and showy it can only have been made by him. "And give me a bell when you're up for an adventure."

He leaves before I have time to decline or accept, reversing off the decking and saluting me as he goes. When I turn back to Saz, she's flopped across the table, smirking.

"You gonna call him, b-hic-ubba?"

"I don't think so. He was very . . . full on. Plus, he's basically going to be our boss," I say, crumpling his card and stuffing it in my pocket.

"Booo. Office romance is a . . . rite of passage. A London bucket list thing – like eating a jellied eel or going up Big Ben."

Ha – I knew you could go up Big Ben.

"Giz his number and I'll-hic-call him," Saz continues, waving her hand in my face.

"Absolutely not. You're coming home. With me."

"Ooooh, lucky me."

She's too pissed to make her own way back to her Haggerston flat-share, but Saz's safety isn't my only motivation for bringing her home with me. No. It's late, it's dark and (even though I've done a semi-decent job of compartmentalising it) the news about Liam has terrified me. Granted, the police might be wrong – Liam might not have been murdered. And even if he was murdered, there's absolutely nothing to suggest said murderer would be coming for me. Still, I feel safer as a pair. On the off-chance we bump into Liam's killer, I'd rather face him with Saz, even if she would do little more to help than act as a semi-comatose shield.

We catch the train from Wandsworth to Barnes, and she grips my arm as we stagger up Rocks Lane.

"How's ya love life then, little Jen Beeny?" Saz asks.

I grip her arm tighter and try to steer her away from a tree she seems set on stumbling into. Talking about my so-called love life would involve thinking about Liam, so I flip the question around. "How's *your* love life?"

"Oh, bad! So bad!" she says, with more enthusiasm than I had anticipated. "Dating, oh kind of dating the same guy I've always been . . . but on and off but . . ."

"Oh no, the Ibiza men didn't work then?"

Saz hiccups and shakes her head.

"Got a picture of this guy?" I ask. "He must be unreal to hold your interest for so long."

"Oh no, I can't . . . could but I won't. Have my stepsister telling me how bad he is for me twenty-four-eleven, twenty-four . . . aaaaaall the time. Can't have it from you, too."

"Okay. Well, here if you need a chat."

"Men, Jen! Jen, men men!"

"Ingenious rhyme. You'll be pleased to know you're about to meet a new man," I say, as we round the corner and the flat comes into view. The kitchen light is still on. Bob's omnipresent body is evidently slumped against the plastic table. Saz perks up.

"Don't say anything to him," I say, sensing her anticipation.

"I'm defo-hic-saying something to him. Never been so bloody excited to meet someone in my life."

Groaning, I unlock the door and we step inside.

"Wow. Wow. Jen, it bloody stinks of fish," giggles Saz as she removes her boots.

"Yep. I reckon he bleeds omega three."

"Almost like he's deliberately making it smell extra fishy to hide some other smell," she continues. "Now *that's* fishy. Get it?"

I roll my eyes and begin climbing the first flight of stairs. I'm proven right; his body is pressed between plastic chair and plastic table. The plate in front of him is empty, but no prizes for guessing what recently occupied it.

"Hello," slurs Saz, barely stifling a giggle. She does a funny little shimmy and a wave. Bob's eyebrows raise, his eyes, behind his glasses, widen, and his small mouth opens. I've never seen him look more like an owl.

"She's too drunk to be able to make it home safely, so I'm keeping an eye on her here." Before Bob can respond, I pull Saz up the second flight of stairs and into my room.

"OMG, Jen, it's honestly hilarious that you live with him. He's even weirder than I imagined. Whenever I feel . . . I feels, sad, I just thinks about the fact you live with a random fifty-year-old and it always . . . always cheers me up."

"I'm glad my misery brings you so much joy," I say. I change into pyjamas and chuck Saz a spare pair. I start folding my clothes away whilst Saz examines my room. She wobbles the unstable bed and pulls back my curtain to look out at the road below.

"There are weird clocks in this flat," she says.

"Oh yeah?"

"Yeah. Flashing dots in them, even though theys just ordinary clocks. One in the hall was doing the same."

"You're drunk."

Saz shrugs and throws herself onto the wobbly bed. I wince as the block of wood keeping it level almost escapes.

Her upbeat façade disappears as soon as I turn the light off. I hear her crying softly on the wobbly bed. I lay a hand over her shoulder and give her a squeeze. I endeavour to remember to talk to her about it when she's sober.

"Sorry, Jen. Just got so drunk."

"It's okay. Only eight hours of work to get through tomorrow," I say.

For the second time this evening, my attempt at humour falls flat. Saz groans.

"Shut up – forgots all about that."

"Mmm. Get some sleep."

She doesn't sleep straight away. About ten minutes later, she mumbles, "You gonna message Daniel?"

His business card is already in the bin. I shake my head.

"No. No, I'm not."

CHAPTER ELEVEN

Monday 16th May

It turns out that Liam's death isn't as easy to compartmentalise as I hoped it might be. As much as I might want to bury my head in the sand and pretend that I never met him, it's now his body that I see whenever I close my eyes. So I message Daniel. Obviously. I message Daniel because I need distracting, because Seb never replies to me and because nights alone with Bob are, if possible, getting more unbearable. And I can't face going onto Matchum again. Not after Liam.

And ultimately because I'm an idiot. Again, obvious.

I learn four things about Daniel during our WhatsApp chats:

1. We have no virtual chemistry. Nada, none, *niente*, *gar nichts*. Try as I might, each message remains simple and formal.
2. He ignores any vaguely serious questions I send his way. He doesn't tell me much about himself, other than that he's "Devonshire's answer to James Bond" and his friends describe him as an "international man of mystery". I laugh, cringe and send screenshots to Saz.
3. His profile picture is of him on a mountain. It's too distant for me to make any kind of judgement.
4. His joining date is the 23rd of May, and yet he's absolutely insistent we meet beforehand. He says he's going to turn up at the office, and no arguments from me can dissuade him. He tells me that I am a lucky lady, and that he'll tell my boss how welcoming I've been to him.

Despite myself, I dress that bit nicer for the day he claims he's going to collect me for lunch: heels, the white blouse and a knee-length skirt so tight I can barely walk.

"How's my lucky lady?" Saz asks when I arrive at reception. After a hangover that seemed to last two weeks, subdued Saz is finally gone, and she seems – just about – back to her normal self, which makes it easier for me to pretend everything is fine. I don't even mind that much that she's using her newfound energy to take the piss out of me.

"Ha. Ha."

"You look . . ." She scans my outfit, eyes widening. "You look ready to pull yourself a sugar daddy."

"Please don't say that." I sit at the desk and unzip my skirt a little. "I can't even remember if I fancied him. Really, this is just a professional lunch – he's going to tell our boss and everything."

"Uh-huh, sure. That's why you're wearing heels. I never see you in heels."

"For good reason. They're stupid. And painful. And impractical. If a zombie invasion happened now, I'd be fucked."

"I dunno – you could take them off and you'd have a decent weapon. For stabbing."

"Stabbing who now?" asks a voice that isn't mine and isn't Saz's. I look up: Seb is at reception. His chocolate eyes are wide, and his mouth spreads itself into a mischievous grin.

"Sorry," I say, "bit of a weird conversation to catch us in the middle of."

"Most of your conversations are weird, so the chance of me catching you in the middle of one is high." He leans against the desk, edging closer to me. "Perhaps you could create a probability tree for that?"

I blush, and his grin stretches wider. He has a meeting, but he doesn't go straight to it. Instead, he lingers at the reception desk.

"How are you then, Jen?" he asks. Out of the corner of my eye, I see Saz lean closer, clearly desperate to hear every word.

I almost tell Seb that I'm pissed off about the fact that any messages I send him go largely unanswered. He's too goddamn pretty, though, so I just mumble something about being okay.

"Well, you look . . . far better than okay," he says, scanning me.

"Oh, thanks," I say, taken aback. I look round at Saz with wide eyes, only to find her mirroring my expression.

"Not going on a date, are you?" Seb leans back, taps his files into order and raises one thick eyebrow. "Cos I'll get jealous if you are."

He flashes a quick smile and strolls off before I can reply.

"I thought you said he didn't like you?" Saz says once he's out of earshot. Her green eyes are still wide, and she's pulled one of her curls taut.

"I didn't think he did," I say, my gaze shifting to the space Seb occupied seconds ago. "I've no idea what he's up to."

Daniel arrives at midday, wearing a waistcoat, a tie, and seven or eight gold rings on his fingers. I don't think I've ever seen so much jewellery on any man, woman or child, and I try not to gawp too much.

"I'm an edgy guy," he tells me, flashing a quick smile. I can't tell if he's being serious or sarcastic, so I nod once and shuffle out from behind the reception desk. He asks if he can freshen up in the office bathrooms, and comments on my appearance half a dozen times as I show him the way. I should find this sweet, but it's too much: I'm "prepossessing", "winsome", "handsome", "beguiling", "pulchritudinous". It's like wandering around with a thesaurus in tow.

I nip into the women's bathroom whilst he's in the men's. Before today, there was an outside chance I could fancy Daniel, but he's just too odd – even for me. Besides, having Seb at reception has reminded me who I'm *actually* into. I stare at my reflection in the mirror, steeling myself for a lunch that looks set to be bizarre, but hopefully – at the very least – filling.

When I re-emerge, Daniel is nowhere to be seen, so I topple back along the corridor.

"Hey," I say, upon seeing his body draped across the reception desk. His face is close to Saz's, and I can just about see her expression: shock. No, not shock – her eyes are too watery, her face is too pale. Fear. Daniel turns away from her, but she keeps her eyes fixed on him. Suddenly embarrassed at what criminally embarrassing thing he might be saying to her, I cut their conversation short.

"Okay, Daniel, shall we make a move?" I ask.

"Indeed!" he says. "Pip, pip – One Lombard waits for no man!"

He storms towards the lifts and I follow, a dutiful dog. I offer Saz a reassuring smile and mouth, "It's just lunch, I'll be fine", as the lift doors close.

One Lombard is lovely, that much can't be denied. It's got high ceilings and white tablecloths, and a circular bar in the centre, with an extravagant flower display balanced in the middle. Our fellow diners wear almost exclusively suits. Suits eating lamb, suits talking about exchange rates, suits eyeing up the waitresses.

I sit down at our table in the centre of the restaurant, and can feel eyes on us, judging. I tell myself we look like father and daughter, or employer and employee to outsiders, but of course we don't. We look like a sugar daddy and a gold digger. I shiver at the knowledge, picking up the large, gold embossed menu, if only to hide my face.

"Decided what you're eating?" I ask.

"Oh, I eat anything. I'm a man of the world, I've had it all on my travels."

I nod, desperately trying not to scoff at his sentence, and scan the menu. All ludicrously expensive. I decide on the Thai beef salad, a safe bet in case I end up paying. A waiter comes over to the table, and I can tell from the angle of his eyebrows he's passing silent judgement. I squirm a little.

"Ready to order?"

"The house white for me and the same for my ravishing lucky lady," says Daniel, before I have chance to open my mouth. "And I'll have the Thai beef salad. Same for you, bubba?"

"Err, yep, same please." Maybe the guy isn't as flush as he makes out.

"Perfect, wonderful," says Daniel, handing our menus back to the waiter and then refocusing his attention on me. I get the full force of his wide eyes. The man never blinks.

"Now, tell me about the most adventurous scenario in which you've ever found yourself."

Oh, good lord.

"Wow." Is that a normal lunchtime question? Our wine arrives and I take a long drink, wishing it was something stronger. "Umm, I don't know. I've been rock-climbing. I went to Spain a couple of years ago."

"Spain? Beautiful country. Rock-climbing? Fantastic sport. I've done both. Multiple times. I've rock-climbed *in* Spain, believe it or not – my nickname isn't Double-O-Devonshire for nothing."

I almost choke at this. But Daniel carries on in full flow, taking no notice that I'm fighting for breath or that what he's said is anything other than totally normal.

"But *my* most adventurous moment? Tough. I've sailed in the Atlantic. I've been on safari – two actually! I single-handedly rescued a drowning dog on Oddicombe beach. Hey – *Death Ship*, the film – you know it?"

I'm learning fast that Daniel likes to answer his own questions. I'm fairly sure he's just asked me to lunch so people don't think he's talking to himself. Which he effectively is. I have neither accurate nor interesting answers to "What's your greatest achievement?", "For how long can you hold your breath?" or "What are your six favourite cuisines?", so have to spend an inordinate amount of time nodding along as he expands on each.

It's a relief when the Thai beef salad arrives. I can't decide how fast to eat it: too fast and I'm left idle, no excuse not to talk; too slow and lunch stretches on longer. I start shovelling rocket into my mouth. Daniel is able to eat without looking at his plate, maintaining steady eye contact throughout.

"I mean, this is lovely: the richness of the beef, the crisp tang of the radish. Just needs a little . . . a little something. Chilli, perhaps? Mozzarella?"

I mumble that it's fine, but there's no stopping Daniel; he summons over an unfortunate waiter, who nods in a confused manner as Daniel breaks down the ingredients in the salad, and then uhms and ahhs about what's missing.

"Sriracha? Mayo? Just something to give it a kick? Oh no, I know," he says, whilst rifling through rocket. "Beef. Not enough beef. If you could take it back and add some more beef in, that would be just the solution."

"Err . . . I'll see what I can do." The waiter picks up Daniel's salad and heads back towards the kitchen.

"Honestly." Daniel turns to me. "I counted eleven bits of beef. In a *beef* salad. Scandalous."

"Uh-huh," I mumble, cringing into my chair.

I'm not a salad fan, so it takes a while to force myself through the cold meat and wilted greens. As soon as Daniel finishes his beefed-up salad, I make a big show of checking the time, exclaiming that I've got a to-do list as long as my arm and insisting on getting back to work. Eventually, I manage to convince him that he can't charm my boss into letting me stay out all afternoon, and we leave the restaurant through a velvet curtain, back to the real world.

We pause at the crossroads opposite the Bank of England as people, cars and bikes zip noisily past. I have a horrible feeling Daniel is about to launch into a mushy monologue, so I get in there first.

"Well, thanks for the lunch. And see you in the office. It'll be great to *work* with you." I put so much emphasis on the word "work", my voice breaks.

"Anytime. Work hard, play harder though, right?" He smiles and undoes two shirt buttons. "See you soon, bubba."

He leans in for a kiss, but I back away, almost falling off the kerb.

"Err no . . . I mean. Goodbye. See you in the office," I say, before turning and hobbling along Cornhill, at a frustratingly slow pace. This really would be an awful zombie invasion outfit.

I feel Daniel's eyes on my back the whole way.

CHAPTER TWELVE

Friday 27th May

I had been expecting Daniel to arrive at the office the following Monday, regaling his new employees with tales of his ongoing excellence, but he doesn't show all week. When I mention this to Saz, the patron saint of office gossip, she's texting Jam in an instant.

"If anyone knows, Jam'll know," she says.

I nod, but I'm more interested in our location than Daniel's. Saz has taken it upon herself to become my "unofficial London tour guide". This arrangement came about when she started quizzing me on places I'd visited and grew more and more comically shocked as I told her that, no, I hadn't visited Notting Hill, or Hampstead Pergola or Kew Gardens and that no, I hadn't even heard of Kynance Mews. So this evening we're in Camden, meandering along the canal and around market stalls.

"Bloody hell, Jam is the slowest replier," Saz moans, and I force my attention from a fabulously dressed group of goths and back to her.

"Ha, well, thank God you're not dating him, I reckon he'd be a right pain. Probably take three to five business days to reply to anything serious, keep his tie on in bed and charge you for orgasms."

It's a joke, but Saz gives me a funny look. "You've actually thought about dating him?"

"No. God, no. He was my recruiter, and now he's morphed into a random sort of friend. I have no plans to take his transformation further, trust me."

"Good. Definitely don't date him, Jen."

"Oh, literally zero chance of that."

"Good, cos—" Saz is suddenly distracted by a food stall at the edge of the canal. "Bubble waffles! Always wanted one of these!"

I'm sceptical about the cones filled with sauce and sweets, but Saz pulls out her "I'm your unofficial London tour guide" card and insists I get one. Bananas, marshmallows, cream and batter probably isn't the dinner of champions, but I tell myself it's acceptable on a Friday, when I'm out and about without parental supervision. I'm a fully grown woman, of course, but I choose to overlook that fact as I stuff more sugar into my gob.

We meander further into the market, under a ceiling of colourful umbrellas, and between stalls selling indie posters. I'm just swallowing the last bit of waffle when Saz grabs my arm.

"OMG, totally forgot about this shop. Right up your street. You'll love it, Jen."

She drags me between two giant metal figurines, and into a shop called Cyberdog.

"Are you sure this is a shop?" I ask, blinking around in awe. Between the loud music, obscene amount of neon and darkened atmosphere, it feels decidedly more like a nightclub. Saz doesn't answer, instead choosing to canter down a set of escalators and round a corner, rushing past items I could have spent all evening staring at: luminous, paint-splattered jackets, six-inch-high trainers, and dresses that would only really look appropriate on aliens. We head downstairs, beneath a neon sign which reads *Future Lovers*. And into what can only be described as a sex shop for extra-terrestrials.

I pick up a pair of feathery, yellow boxers.

"*This* is right up my street?"

Saz grins, mischievous as ever. "You can take your dates here. It's probably an amnesiac."

"I'm going to assume you mean aphrodisiac."

We brush past PVC thongs and light-up whips, struggling to keep a straight face.

"Honestly, I think this would just intimidate my dates," I say, eyeing up a leather, intergalactic police outfit.

"Fine. You can take your friends here when they come visit."

Friends. There's even less chance of that happening. I used to have them, of course. A group I'd go around with at school. A handful I hung out with after school ended. The couple who attempted to comfort me after what happened to Dad. But I was beyond consolation, didn't want to know. Needed to close down, close off . . .

"Oh, he's finally bloody replied!" Saz shouts, before I have to say something, thank the lord.

"Jam?"

"Yep. He's seriously pissed off. Apparently, Daniel got offered another job in Dubai and just bailed."

"Good for us though. He was so strange."

"Ha, bet you're secretly gutted not to be getting your sugar daddy, aren't you, bubba?"

"Please don't call me that."

"Sorry, lucky lady." Saz can't hide her giggles as she continues to mock me, waving a lime dildo far too close to my face.

I roll my eyes and lead Saz out of the shop, back out into Camden, which is basking in the low, midsummer sun. My mood aligns with the weather; I'm grateful my life can continue free from any awkward Daniel encounters.

Tuesday 7th June

But apparently working in different companies in different countries isn't enough to keep him off my back, something which becomes apparent with the arrival of an enormous bouquet of flowers one Tuesday afternoon.

"For Miss Jennifer Beeny," says a delivery man as he sets them down in front of me.

Saz and I turn towards each other at the same time, eyes wide.

"Seb?" I say to her, indulging myself in a brief daydream, wondering if this is his way of finally asking me out properly.

"Oh my God, can you imagine? How romantic."

I accept the enormous bouquet and rummage through the leaves. I'm no good with flowers but there's surely every variety in this bundle: roses and lilies and the ones which look a bit like cabbage. There's a note beneath an aggressive orange bud. I pull it out. It's not from Seb, that much is clear immediately. The note says:

Hey bubba, sorry things didn't work out – I know you had big plans for us. But don't be too sad, I'll look you up when I'm back from Dubai.

12.04am, 30th May, 25°N, 55°E
Shifting sand dunes, a starry blanket
00Devonshire

"It's from Daniel," I say.

"*Daniel*?" Saz shuffles over to me and takes the note. "How surprising."

"Quite surprising, yeah. He's utterly deluded," I tell her.

The flowers – which were tacky but in a sort of romantic way when I had thought they were from Seb – become uglier the more I stare at them. I glance up just in time to see a gaggle of workers step out of the lift. The group clock my flowers (how could they not; they're huge and horrific) and start chuckling before turning into the office.

"Right, they've got to go," I say, moving the bouquet behind the desk. I snatch the note from Saz's fingers. "And no, before you ask, I'm not going to reply to him. Please don't get me stamps and parchment. Or a bloody owl. It's all going in the bin."

Alas, the office bins are all too small to accommodate half a flower shop, so I end up leaving with the bouquet once work finishes. I meander about the city, growing hot and impatient in the search for a decent-sized bin. I catch my breath outside of O'Neil's, a cute little bookstore which has just opened on Lime Street. The window display is delightful: silver and gold ribbons twisting through hardbacks, or dangling down from the ceiling, creating book baubles. I shift the bouquet this way and that, ensuring I'm able to take in each book without a rogue leaf obscuring my view.

"Are you like me? Someone who prefers physical bookstores to the online version?" asks a lilting voice from next to me. I peer around the cabbage flower to find a stunning girl looking at me. She has a small, upturned nose, porcelain skin, dark blue eyes and the loveliest hair: thick auburn curls which my fingers want to run through, my fingers want to pull. There's something otherworldly about her, as though she's just stepped out of a pre-Raphaelite painting. She's vaguely familiar-looking, too; I have an inkling I passed her as I was leaving the office.

"Sorry, were you talking to me?" I ask.

She smiles. "Only if you want me to be."

There's an . . . atmosphere. Ordinarily, I'm rubbish at clocking when girls are interested in me. But the edges of this girl's lips are upturned, her eyes are warm, kind and staring at me so intently my stomach flips.

"Yes. Yes, I am like you. There's something so much more personal and exciting about a physical bookstore. I . . . you know . . . the smell of the books. The rustle of pages as other customers flick through them, finding something new to treasure. The window displays – adding an extra layer of wonder to the whole experience."

Christ, I'm speaking like a Shakespearean character. Daniel has clearly rubbed off on me. Still, the girl doesn't seem put off. Her smile widens, revealing pointy incisors.

"You're so right. *So* right. Gosh, it's so refreshing to meet someone who just gets it." She pauses and seems to look at me with even more intensity. She shifts her gaze down to my bouquet, and I'm almost relieved – my heartrate slows just a little. "I mean . . . I would ask for your number, but looks as though you've got a boyfriend. Or a girlfriend."

"Oh! No! Oh God no! These flowers are from no one! Absolutely no one! No boyfriend for me. And no girlfriend, either. Not that I'd be against a girlfriend. Not I, I just don't . . ." All of my earlier eloquence is lost as my mouth motors on, spewing out more and more shit.

"Well, I'd love your number. And maybe your name, too, if that's not pushing my luck."

I nod, flattered by the attention of such a stunning woman. I'm finally glad of the bouquet because it gives my cheeks – surely crimson – some coverage.

I tell her my number and she nods, typing it into her phone.

"Fab. I'll drop you a text . . ." She pauses and looks at me with her eyebrows ever so slightly raised, as if she's waiting for me to continue.

"Jen! Jen! Sorry, my name's Jen!"

"Cool. Nice to meet you, Jen. I'm Scarlet."

For the first time in ages, the noise of what happened to Liam is turned down a bit in my head. Pathetic, maybe. But I'll take anything I can get at this point. I'm in such a daze, I don't even realise I'm still carrying the huge bunch of flowers when I arrive back home. I don't want them in my room, so I leave them in the kitchen, hoping they'll cover up the smell of fish. My mood is so buoyed, I don't even feel irritated when Bob texts me asking who 00Devonshire is and for a flat meeting about his pollen allergy.

CHAPTER THIRTEEN

Friday 17th June

The investigation into Liam's murder rumbles on. To my knowledge, he never makes it onto the television again, but a couple of articles deep within the *Metro* are devoted to him, and whenever I click onto Tala's profile there are fresh posts. She's on a one-woman mission to discover who is responsible for her brother's death. I would be doing the same thing if I was her. My heart aches for her, but I can't get myself more involved.

It's been a few weeks since I last saw an article about Liam, so I'm caught off-guard whilst flipping through the newspaper on the train home.

My stomach drops when I see him. His wide, malicious smile is squished in between a story about a donkey who has been nursed back to health, and a precocious little maths prodigy. I do what I always do when I see information about Liam. Look away. Slow my breathing. Tell myself I'm going to flip to the next page, or scroll onwards. And then – slowly, oh so slowly – my eyes drift over. It's like passing a car crash. The more I look and the more I learn, the worse I feel. And yet I can't stop myself.

> Fresh hope for the investigation into the death of 27-year-old Liam Garcia, as an anonymous witness brings key information. Liam's body was found on the 11th of April, just over two weeks after he disappeared on the 24th of March. Dragged from the Thames, it was initially assumed that Liam had drowned – an act of misadventure. But his autopsy suggested his death may have occurred under suspicious circumstances. Police are said to be keen to

> identify a woman Liam was seen with on the night of his disappearance. The woman is believed to be in her early twenties.

I slam the newspaper shut and scrunch the paper between my fists.

I can't be blamed for anyone else's death.

I unclench my fists and look at my palms – now stained with Liam's inky image. I'm being silly, and paranoid. Liam was a serial dater of women in their early twenties, and he wasn't exactly picky; I wouldn't be surprised if he met someone else when he left the bar. And besides, *I* stayed in the bar. It was Seb that escorted him outside. And then I went home alone. I'm completely innocent. I rub my palms against my trousers, attempting to rid myself of ink and the feeling that fingers are starting to point in my direction.

Bob keeps his eyes fixed on me as I heat up noodles in the kitchen on my return. Ordinarily, I can block him out, but today it proves too much; I book train tickets to visit Mum. If there's one positive to her drinking, it's the fact she's seldom sober enough to properly focus on me. A miniscule positive, which is overshadowed by the guilt I feel about her addiction. The guilt I feel about leaving her to fester alone, drinking and drinking. How horribly that seems certain to end. And the guilt I feel every time she looks at me, too. She must hate me.

I hate me.

But I still owe her my company. I catch a train north, glad to leave London and thoughts of Liam behind. Friday night is pleasant, albeit brief. We get a late dinner: fish, chips and scraps from the takeaway down the road. I drink water and so does Mum. I make the mistake of commenting on her lack of alcohol.

"I don't need it, I don't. I've stopped," she says.

I'm sceptical, oh Lord I am deeply sceptical, but I nod and tell her I'm pleased to hear it.

"We should go cycling tomorrow, like the old days?" I suggest through a mouthful of batter.

"Yeah. Yes, we should. Bikes are out back. Haven't touched mine since you left me."

I flinch but bite my tongue.

"Well, it's a date," I say. I lay my hand on top of hers, and I'm almost embarrassed by the difference between them. Mum's hand is bony, the skin on it paper-thin, the webs between each finger dry and irritated. My hands, by comparison, are plump and nourished. I feel like the cat who got all the cream, leaving its companion to starve.

Mum pulls her hand out from underneath mine.

"Looking forward to it," she says. She brings her glass of water up to meet her lips. The bony hand holding it shakes.

Saturday 18th June

She lied to me. I know it as soon as I wake up. The house reeks: a sickly heavy raisin smell and something worse – cod that has been digested and then puked back up. I enter the living room and I'm confronted by a scene I've seen dozens of times before: sick on the shag carpet, a rat running loose, three empty wine bottles on one armchair and my mum hanging from another, her skirt lopsided and orange vomit masking her mouth, like a vile lipstick.

I check she's still breathing before I allow myself to think about how much I want to kill her. I want to pull her silver pendant tighter and tighter around her neck, until she can't breathe. I want to stuff her scraggly grey hair into her mouth, more and more until she chokes on it. I want to smash one of the wine bottles she loves so much over her head, watch as blood streams from her temples.

My mum is drinking herself to death and there's fuck all I can do about it.

I put the rat (Rosie or Rumpelstiltskin or Rodelina or whatever the fuck its name is) back in its cage. I move the empty bottles from the armchair into the recycling bin. I scrape the bigger bits of sick into a dustpan and attack the remainder with bleach and a cloth. I can't find house spray, so I fill the room with deodorant (*Meadow Days* – who the fuck spends the day in a meadow?) and then, finally, I face Mum.

"Thought you'd stopped drinking?" I ask.

She stirs, half opens one eye, moves her head to the left.

"Not drink. Ill. Flu."

"Oh yeah? Really bad flu, huh?"

"Mmm."

"I don't believe that shit anymore," I mumble. With some difficulty, I scoop her up and take her body out of the lounge. She resists as I carry her up the stairs, but I squeeze her limbs tighter.

The last person I stripped naked was Liam, months ago. Stripping Mum feels more invasive, more degrading. The single similarity between the two situations is that they're both alcohol-induced, but where Liam smelt of Scotch whisky, Mum smells of half-digested Pinot Noir. I put her sick-stained clothes into a plastic bag and coax her into the bathtub.

"Tell me if it's too cold. Or too hot," I say as I point the water coming from the shower head at her naked body. As I hose her down, I think that age is turning her into a bird. There are crow's lines at the side of her eyes, and the plumpness of her face is disintegrating, leaving behind a beak of a nose. Her feet, crossed at the ankles, are bony, angular, bird claws. Breakable. And she's increasingly scatty, too, bird-brained. I'm not sure if that's age or alcohol.

I shampoo, condition and scrub Mum. I towel her body dry and touch crevices and corners that should be private, should be off limits. She no longer smells so bad. But for the heaviness of her body, the clumsiness of her actions, it's possible to pretend she hasn't spent the night drinking herself into a stupor. I tuck her into bed, and almost instantly she wriggles, trying to get out.

"Stay in bed."

She wriggles more so I push her bony shoulders hard into the mattress.

"Stay in bed. Sleep."

I hold her longer, harder, until all resistance ceases. Her eyes meet mine and she nods, slightly. I turn to leave.

"Love you, Jen."

I turn back. Her head and shoulders are pressed into the pillow, as if she's too scared to move, but her hazel eyes are on me. I sigh. I look at the mouth which read books to me, the hands which taught me to play piano, the ears which listened to my problems and my dreams.

"I love you too. But you're hard to love." It's terrifying and exhilarating to finally admit this to her. Shame she won't remember anything I say. "Every time my phone rings, I think this is it, that my luck and your luck has finally run out. That you've been found dead in a pile of your own vomit."

"And I . . . I worry. About you in London. And about you being attacked or falling into the river. And I . . . worry."

I sigh again, not sure how to reply.

"I miss you," mumbles Mum.

"I miss you too."

"So come back."

"I can't."

There's a pause. She pushes her shoulders up off the pillow.

"You left me."

I shake my head and take a step backwards. "I had to. After what you said . . . I can't be here with you. I can't be here knowing what you think of me."

I'm being suffocated by the house: its dark colours, the heavy fabrics, the smell of musky books and sick and red wine, the overwhelming feeling of despair. I leave. I drag my bike out of the shed (it's rusty and cobweb-covered and smaller than I remember, but it's workable) and I go. I cycle hard, harder and harder until the only thing I can think about is the burning sensation in my quads.

I cycle up Coatham Lane and onto Trunk Road, which is a dual carriageway, not a road that's meant to be cycled on. Cars fly past at seventy miles an hour, their wing mirrors just centimetres from my hips. I don't care. I need to feel something other than sadness.

I'm surrounded by abandoned industry: warehouses and chimneys and containers on either side of the road. I pedal harder. My lips are dry, my legs are burning and my stomach drops every time a lorry passes me, but I've stopped thinking about *her*. Industry bleeds into civilisation as I breach Middlesbrough. I pass a giant Asda, a car garage, a McDonald's.

A small red car passes close enough to wobble my bike. I pause to catch my breath and will my heart to slow. And then I turn right, onto a quieter road. It takes me over the railway and past the Riverside Stadium. It's quiet, the car park is empty – no football today, not a soul about.

I abandon my bike and run towards the river, stopping only when the barriers force me to. I grip the cold metal hard. The river Tees – wide and a murky brown – is in front of me. Beyond that, there are a couple of giant grey warehouses. And to the left there's the Transporter Bridge; an old blue giant which, for a pound or two, takes cars and pedestrians over the river. The river. I look down at it. The Tees is not so different from the Thames. I squeeze the metal barrier harder. I pull the smells and sounds into my body, trying to absorb the scene: seagull cries and the stench of rust. I close my eyes.

This is where my dad died.

The river took him, in the same way a different river took Liam. The muddy water dragged him away from me, and from Mum. It froze him and choked him. The police didn't help, they hindered. And I hindered, too. But he's well and truly gone now, and nothing I do can get him back. Nothing I do will get Liam back, either. He's as lost to his family as Dad is to us. The thought of both of them is killing me.

Thinking doesn't help though. You can't outthink nature, the deadly pull of the water. I open my eyes and duck under the barrier, my toes hanging over the edge.

Mesmerising. I raise one foot, as if ready to step forwards and face the same fate as the others. My phone vibrates. I take it from my pocket hoping, as always, that the texter is Seb.

It's not Seb (it's never Seb) – it's a number I don't recognise. I take half a step back to lean against the barriers and unlock my phone.

Hey Jen, it's Scarlet, your fellow IRL bookstore lover! I can't stop thinking about your pretty smile. And the fact you're a fellow book enthusiast, of course. Got any favourite quotes? Xx

I drag myself from the river and duck back under the metal bar. Scarlet's profile picture is goofy: her clutching a baby cactus, auburn locks spilling over her shoulders. Men never open conversations like this. Not to say that their openings aren't interesting, but they're generally brief: a question, a compliment, a greeting. Never a kiss. Never more than one sentence. Scarlet seems . . . different. I have a plethora of quotes and scenes and observations to offload – about films, art, books, real life. Perhaps I've finally found someone who would be interested.

I take a last look out across the river. And then I reply.

CHAPTER FOURTEEN

Monday 4th July

Talking to women is different to talking to men. I've always thought as much, but interacting with Scarlet solidifies it. There's an intensity and depth from the get-go, something I've not had with any of the men I've dated. Scarlet and I only message a couple of times a day, but each message is a paragraph or two long, and the subject matter is always reasonably intense: death row or where the universe ends or the emotional states of characters in films. She peppers her messages with exclamation marks, emojis and kisses. There's a thoughtfulness to them that I find refreshing. I feel like I could tell her anything. I mean, apart from the Liam-shaped elephant in the room, of course. But it's something.

I'm replying to her most recent messages on a Monday afternoon, when Saz sighs and swivels in her chair.

"God I'm bored. Two hours 'til freedom," she says.

"Working hard as well, aren't you?" I ask, peering over at her computer screen. She's got three windows open: the Nando's menu, Drama Studios London and a Bali travel blog.

"Says you, you've been staring at your phone all afternoon."

She's correct, of course.

"I won't tell if you won't," I say, doing an over-exaggerated wink, the kind Saz always does. She grins and winks back. "Anyway, I've been messaging someone new, want to see?"

Saz's reaction to Scarlet's profile picture is not what I had anticipated. Her bottom lip drops, and her eyes widen.

"You alright?" I ask, suddenly self-conscious. "You know I fancy girls, right?"

Saz nods her head and forces her lips into a strained smile.

"Yeah, yes, I do. You've never really acted on it, though."

"I mean, I've been on dates with women back home," I say. None of those dates ever went particularly well. I've never slept with a woman, and this always made me feel like I was an intruder, despite the fact I know it's something I want to try. But I always felt like whoever I was on a date with would sniff out that I didn't belong in the club, or be put off by my lack of experience. I'd clam up something chronic, and the poor girls would have to talk for the two of us. Needless to say, I've never had a second date with a woman.

"I definitely, definitely fancy girls, though," I continue. "And I just can't seem to emotionally connect with men. It's sex and banter and that's it. Maybe I'll find what I want with a woman."

"With that woman, though? With Scarlet?"

"Yeah," I say. I look at Saz again. She opens her mouth as though she's going to tell me something, but I speak before she can. "She's stunning. And interesting. And *interested*. She might be what I'm looking for."

Saz sighs and turns to look at me, resting her chin in her left palm.

"Do you even know what you're looking for, though? Or who you're looking for?"

"I do a bit. Someone like Adèle from *Blue is the Warmest Colour*, or Tom from *500 Days of Summer*, or Dean from *Blue Valentine*."

"Those are really sad films," says Saz.

"Yeah. But also really deep and soulmate-y."

"You want something that's fictional. You want something that doesn't even work out in the fictional world."

I pause, confused as to why Saz has saved this reaction for Scarlet. I can only pin it on the fact she's a girl, and Saz is . . . not as open-minded as she makes out? Repressing some homophobia? Or is Saz jealous? I almost laugh; surely not. There's zero sexual chemistry between the two of us. Regardless, I say, "You're being serious, aren't you? This is a serious chat? We never have serious chats."

"Well, you've just seemed sort of on a mission to get a boyfriend or girlfriend ever since you arrived in London. And you're twenty-three, it's okay to be single at twenty-three. It's okay to be single at any age. You can just enjoy London. You don't need a relationship to do that."

I turn away from my new agony aunt and face my computer. I start clicking through my emails, feeling awkward. And lonely, too, truth be told. I don't think it's London that's made me feel this way, though. There's been a sense of alone-ness for the past couple of years.

"You're still going to meet her, aren't you?" Saz asks.

"Yeah. I'm meeting her Friday."

"I really think you should reconsider."

I laugh, out of discomfort, more than anything. The only person she's warned me away from before is Jam, but that was different; she *knows* Jam. She knows he likely wouldn't be a good match for me. I feel the corners of my mouth droop. I'm still not entirely confident with my sexuality; the last thing I need is Saz being off with me about it.

Friday 8th July

The weather on Friday is apocalyptically bad. Rain falls heavy all day: fat grey drops that dribble down the windows and soak the pavements. The sky is a menacing dark grey, only disrupted by lightning that flashes every fifteen minutes or so. It seems an ominous omen for my date.

I'd planned to meet Scarlet at Southbank, to have drinks outside overlooking the Thames. However, a plan B is blatantly required. Not helpful, as I'm infinitely more nervous about meeting a girl than a guy, even without troublesome weather thrown into the mix. Whilst I find connecting virtually with women fine, whenever I meet them romantically in the flesh, all my courage deserts me. Men seem easier, somehow, more straightforward. As long as you're vaguely fit and somewhat flirty, they seem to be satisfied, on the first date at least. Women have always struck me as more complicated creatures, harder to impress. Hence my record of getting tongue-tied, of letting the pressure get to me.

I arrive in Waterloo just as the station clock hits 6 p.m. Rain is still pounding, drumming on the plastic roof overhead. I push through the crowd and wait next to the station M&S. I message Scarlet:

> I'm opposite platform 9. Riverside drinks might not be workable . . . x

She replies quickly:

> Fab, nearly there. Ya, maybe no, but I have a better idea xx

She's in the station and I'm nervous. I faff, putting my bag down then picking it up. Comb my fringe. Apply lipstick. Glance ahead at the thronging mass of bodies and then avert my gaze, worried I'm going to make eye contact with her two minutes too early and set an awkward tone for the entirety of our date. I rummage in my bag, just so I have something to do with my hands.

"Jen?" A voice from in front of me.

I stuff my phone into my bag and look ahead: Scarlet. Tall. Taller than I remember, probably two or three inches taller than me.

"You okay?" she asks. "You look kinda worried."

"Sorry. I'm not. Well, I am a bit, but in an excited way." Jesus, Jen, play it cool.

Scarlet smiles. She's wearing a low-cut jumper dress which exposes her toned shoulders, and multiple simple line tattoos. She's decorated with an abundance of accessories: a big dreamcatcher necklace, an armful of bangles and friendship bracelets, half a dozen pretty clips twisting her auburn hair into place. I suddenly feel too formal, in my blouse and pencil skirt. I move to hug her, undoing a button at the same time. A familiar feeling creeps up on me; I look far too straight.

We hug. Our embrace lasts two or three seconds longer than the average hug might, and in this time, I note things about her body: the similarity in size to mine, how easily my arms are able to wrap around her waist. I push my nose against her neck and breathe her in – lime and lemons.

"This weather is horrific," I say when we part.

"Tell me about it. I'm like, 'where's summer?' This is *not* summer," she replies. "Anyway, I was thinking – have you ever been to Leake Street?"

"Err, nope."

A grin spreads across her face. "You'll *love* it."

She turns and dashes through the crowd, a vision in emerald. I follow, her fiery hair a beacon. We head out of Waterloo and into the rain, both holding our bags over our heads, weaving between commuters and splashing through puddles. She stops abruptly two minutes later, and I almost crash into her.

"Ta-da," she says, stretching out her arm, revealing what we've just stopped outside of. A tunnel. But a tunnel unlike any other. It's so long I can hardly see the exit, and it's wide enough to accommodate bars and eateries. But – more notably – it's absolutely covered in graffiti.

"Cool, isn't it?" says Scarlet.

"Very."

I step inside, transfixed. Nearly every inch of wall and ceiling is covered in spray paint. A lot of it is standard – slogans and names in bubble writing, scribbles and messages done in a single black line – but there's a lot of art, too. Faces, painted in jaw-dropping detail. Lego characters with multi-coloured bricks framing them. Green aliens with goofy grins. Doodles scaled up and coloured in and running riot in this little corner of London.

Some of the artists are creating as we pass by, paint hissing from their spray bottle. There are kids on bikes and skateboards, a dance group body-popping under fluorescent lights and a fair few sodden dawdlers, who evidently entered the tunnel to escape the rain and have been met with more than they anticipated.

Scarlet and I meander up and down, taking it all in. My eyes dart about, following the neon tags and the ghoulish faces which decorate the arched ceiling, and the more intricate pieces; a painting of apples holds my gaze for a minute or two. Scarlet takes photos on her phone, but I feel more of an urge to sketch the art, so I ask if she minds and retrieve my notepad.

"You're pretty good," says Scarlet, peering over my shoulder.

"Oh, thanks," I reply, blushing. "It's not, like a serious thing, it's just . . . something someone I used to know used to do and it helps me feel close to them, I guess."

Christ, what a garble. I shut my notepad and continue walking.

When we've been up and down the length of the tunnel twice, we order a glass of wine from Draughts, and drink it on a bench in the tunnel, our backs resting on an electric pink drawing which says ENOUGH.

I sip my wine and sneak glances at Scarlet, focusing on her rather than my surroundings for the first time. She's pretty – she is *so* pretty – but I know all her tricks. I can see she's got spots hiding under a layer of foundation a shade or two too light for her skin. I can see that her eyeliner has smudged ever so slightly in the rain. I can tell that her hair is merely dyed red, and my eyes zone in on her dark roots. Tiny details that a man might overlook, but I focus on. These are the details that I analyse daily, on my own body. I wonder if she is inspecting me so thoroughly.

"So, you're a receptionist, right?" Scarlet asks, turning to fix her gaze on me.

"Yep." I don't know what else to say about that fact.

"Awesome. You enjoy it?"

I shrug. "It's alright – the pay is decent, the hours are fine, it's quite sociable."

"Fab. Is that what you wanted to be when you were fourteen?"

"No," I reply sharply. A little too sharply. "But I was an idiot at fourteen – I wanted to be an Olympic cyclist, or have an exhibition in the Tate – despite the prospect of either being stupidly slim. It was just going to happen. One of those magic things like falling in love or becoming rich."

What a depressing little spiel. I drink my wine and ask Scarlet what she does for a living.

"Ugh, long story," she says, taking a drink. She rolls her eyes, but she's smiling coyly. "I *used* to work for HADV – Humans Against Domestic Violence. I'd been there ever since I finished uni, so eight or nine years or something. It was a pretty incredible charity, giving support to people who had been sexually abused, or raped, or emotionally abused. I mainly worked with children with difficult family lives. It was – and I probably sound morbid for saying that helping abused children made me feel fulfilled – but it was an incredibly fulfilling job."

"No, no. I get it. I've only ever really worked because I needed money." Or, more accurately, my family needed money. "It sounds pretty amazing to make a difference doing something you're really passionate about."

Scarlet smiles. She has a dimple on her right cheek but not her left, and I find it adorable.

"It *was* pretty amazing. But I had to leave. Last year. For a really bullshit reason but, you know . . ."

I don't reply, waiting instead to see if she'll continue. She doesn't, she just takes another drink. I go to copy her, before realising that there's a hair at the bottom of my wine glass. It's short and dark, reminiscent of the hairs lying around Bob's kitchen. I set my glass down.

"Do you have any hobbies?" I ask, hoping to move the conversation on from a topic that Scarlet genuinely seems quite cut up about.

"I do. I like plants. I'm quite green-fingered, always looking after a dozen cacti and a wonky sunflower or two." She pauses to fiddle with her clips, twisting a curl back and off her forehead. "And I like rowing. Love rowing. Used to row more, but my club got shut down last year. Super sad."

"Oh. How come?"

"Little things – the boathouse was a bit run down, not fit for purpose. We kept losing members, wasn't financially viable. I keep meaning to look for another club but, you know." She shrugs her shoulders. "I've been busy with the whole losing my job thing. Fighting for justice. Trying to right a few wrongs, etcetera, etcetera."

There's something about her that I find utterly beguiling. She's older than me by six or seven years, and she seems to wear her extra life experience in a variety of different ways: both emotionally (her voice is even, inviting and she knows just when to offer up a reassuring smile) and physically (her story seems embedded into her appearance; I'm desperate to know the origin of each tattoo, details of the day on which she got each of her freckles, where each ring is from and what they all mean to her). I watch her lips as she kisses her glass. It's easy enough to imagine her kissing me, me kissing her. I inch my gaze lower. She's not worn a bra; I can see both nipples under the green dress. I imagine rolling the dress down, exposing her ribs, her belly button, her pelvis. I think about working my lips down her body, along the inside of each thigh.

"Indulge me, if you don't mind?" she says, and I return my gaze to her face, blushing slightly and grateful she can't read minds.

"Sure."

"I just find that first date questions can be a little stale, so I like to ask some slightly more random things."

Oh God, she's been to the same school of dating as Daniel. Scarlet must clock my expression because she laughs and continues, "Nothing too weird. Fun stuff. Like, what were you like as a kid?"

"Oh," I laugh. "That's a pretty normal question. I was just . . . I don't know. Quiet and curious and reasonably happy, I suppose. And obsessed with doing the newspaper Sudokus, not that I was great at them."

"Cute," says Scarlet. "Super cute. So you were a bit of a goody-two-shoes, then?"

I shrug. "I liked to try to keep people happy."

"Sweet." Scarlet places her hand on my wrist and runs a nail along my forearm. I shiver. "I was slightly less sweet. Used to be quite naughty. Nothing too bad, of course."

She squeezes my wrist and my body tingles.

"Uh . . . uh-huh."

"I used to steal things. Mainly just sweets from the corner shop – gobstoppers and toffees and Parma Violets. Never got caught. Not even once."

I laugh, nervous. "I tried that, and I got caught immediately. I crumbled as soon as the shopkeeper started interrogating me."

"Oh, you poor thing," Scarlet says, fixing her eyes on me. Once again, there's a spine-tingling intensity to her gaze. "Not a very good liar, then?"

"Really bad. I'm not even a very good truth-teller – kids at school would always blame whatever naughty thing they'd done on me. They knew I'd accidentally mumble and stutter my way into a detention."

"Oh Jen! What are we going to do with you?"

"I . . . don't know."

I dare myself to touch her. Slowly, I move my fingers so that they're resting against her wrist. She's got a number of tattoos: an open bird cage, a crescent moon, a leaf. I squeeze her wrist – squeeze the goose bumps, the delicate lines of ink, the light hair which covers them. I look into her eyes. Blue. Mischievous. Domineering. She leans her head towards mine. I close my eyes and kiss her, nudging her lips open with my tongue. We part after a few seconds, and I take a giddy swig of my wine.

I look down, and then behind her right ear.

And I freeze.

Bob.

Bob is in the tunnel, not fifty metres from us. He's making a phone call, and his clothes are dripping wet. He's yet to spot me, but I duck regardless.

"You okay?" asks Scarlet. "You're not embarrassed, are you?"

"No! God no! I just . . . err . . . have this twitching neck condition."

What a fucking weird thing to say. I glance back at Bob, who runs a hand through his sodden moustache. What on earth is he doing here? My mind jumps to the sinister: he's followed me. But how? *Why?*

"D'you want to go?" asks Scarlet.

"Oh, no. Nope."

I want to reassure her, to let her know that I am genuinely interested in her and in women, that I'm not just here as an experiment, but all I can think about is Bob. I would tell her about him, but my living with him is a lengthy, strange story which is unlikely to win me any attraction points. I allow myself one more glance in his direction. He still doesn't seem to have spotted me. I'm being silly, probably. This is just a coincidence. He's passing and he's ducked in here to take a phone call and escape the rain.

"Yeah, we should go," says Scarlet, finishing her wine.

We settle the bill (fifty-fifty; there's no awkward dance around whether someone should pay for it all), gather our bags and walk out of Leake Street Tunnel. I keep my head bowed as we walk, and my right hand glued to my face. Scarlet raises an eyebrow but doesn't comment. I daren't look back at Bob.

It's still raining outside, so we hurry up York Road and back into Waterloo station. Scarlet is catching the tube whilst I'm taking the train, so we pause under the station clock. She grabs my waist and squeezes it tight.

"We should hang out again, when you get over your . . . issues. I'll teach you the tricks of the trade when it comes to penny-sweet shoplifting," she says, attempting a wink. She laughs and releases me, disappearing into the depths of the Underground before I have a chance to respond.

I'm stuck to the spot for a dozen heartbeats, the image of her red hair burnt into my skull, the touch of her soft skin a ghost against my fingers.

I move backwards. One step back, then another, and then—

"Hi, Jen."

I know who I've bumped into before I spin around; the stench of eggs and fish overwhelms me, I seem to know the curves of his flesh intimately, despite my best efforts to avoid it. I turn and retreat from Bob, putting a solid two metres between us.

"Hi."

"Good evening? Getting the train back now?" he asks, blinking at me from behind his glasses.

Ugh, please no. The last thing I want is half an hour of small talk with Bob.

"Yeah, a pretty nice evening. I might be heading back now or – actually – just remembered, I desperately need milk and chocolate."

"I can come to the shop with you, I need some scampi."

Good God, he's a hard man to shake. I stutter, attempting to come up with a sure-fire way of ditching him.

"Were you on a date?" he asks before the cogs in my brain have had a sufficient amount of turning time.

"Uh, yeah. Yep."

"And it went badly? You look upset?"

Sound escapes my lips, halfway between a huff and an exasperated laugh.

"It went really well, actually. Right up until the end, when you . . . When I started feeling sick. Really sick, actually," I say, suddenly inspired. "So sick, I need to dash . . . to the bathrooms – the *women's* bathrooms."

I hurry away before he can offer to hold my hair back or provide sick bags. A delayed journey is preferrable to one spent uncomfortably close to Bob.

CHAPTER FIFTEEN

Sunday 31st July

I don't hear from Scarlet again, and thus my track record for getting a second date with a girl stands. I'm disappointed but I can't blame her, given how oddly I acted at the end of our evening together. So now, as ever, I'm stuck with Bob and thoughts of Liam and my dad.

Bob commandeers the kitchen for almost the entirety of the weekends, so I get up crazy early one Sunday in an attempt to have breakfast before he's awake. I've just poured milk onto my Weetabix when he emerges from his room (six-oh-motherfucking-nine) and comes into the kitchen. He hasn't put his glasses on yet (he hasn't put much on, just a stained white T-shirt and tartan shorts), so he looks less like an owl and more like a walrus today.

"Morning, Jen," he says as he makes his way over to the fridge and takes a whole trout out of it. Surely not. The man cannot be eating trout this early. He's not – he moves it to the freezer and then shuffles past me to the kettle. And thus, I've finally established how weird he really is: fucking weird, but not weird enough to cook himself a fish as the sun rises.

He makes himself a coffee but doesn't leave, just lingers in the doorway between the landing and the kitchen, with one eye on the road outside and one eye on me. I halve the number of Weetabix I was planning on eating and attempt to return to my room as quickly as possible. I get one foot on the first step when he turns to me.

"What are your plans today, Jen?"

"Errr . . ."

Bob takes a step closer to me. Our faces are level and only inches apart. I can see every nostril hair, the crusty pieces of sleep in the corner of his eyes, the puckered indents in his cheeks, scars from long ago acne.

"I won champagne at the pub quiz. We could share it today," he says. His gaze shifts from my face to something behind me, and then back to my face. He raises his hand and then lowers it, as if he was going to touch my waist. My body stiffens.

"I'm, uh, I'm busy. So, so busy. Hence why I'm up so early."

"Oh, no. Of course. I was just thinking, we missed the six-month anniversary. You moved in on the 4th of January. A good day. We should have celebrated. Should have celebrated our six months."

My eyebrows shoot up towards my hairline, and I'm sure my face will be resting in a comical expression, but I can't help it.

"4th of January." I cough. "Uh-huh, a good day. I mean, I would but, don't you have anyone else to have the champagne with? A girlfriend? Or a boyfriend?"

Bob's expression changes so briefly, I can't be certain I haven't imagined the anguish that danced across his eyes. He coughs. "Used to have a girlfriend. A fiancée. The chemist. She used to live here. Has always felt very quiet, ever since she left."

God, do I really want to have a deep chat with my landlord at this time in the morning? I can certainly relate to the emptiness that seems to sit in a house once someone you love is no longer present. I hesitate, before saying, "Oh ahh, I can imagine. But yep I, uh, I do really need to go. I'm really busy. Sorry, enjoy the champagne though."

I turn and rush up the stairs and away from him as fast as possible. Bob doesn't protest, and I only pause once, when I reach the top. I look back down in an attempt to see what he had been staring at. There's nothing on the wall apart from the clock. He surely didn't need to check it. I could have told him the time: too goddamn early for either of us to be awake. I huff into my room, pissed that he's effectively left me with two options: make myself scarce for the day or spend my Sunday downing champagne and having my landlord stare at my tits. I turn my mobile on, think about messaging Saz or Jam, asking if they want to hang out.

I've just typed out a message reminding Saz about being my unofficial tour guide, when I change my mind. I'm in London, for

God's sake, one of the most exciting cities in the world. I can enjoy it by myself, I don't need someone to steer me round. I'm still baffled by ninety per cent of the tube network, but I've got legs. And a map on my phone. And a smidge of independence.

I pack a bag and leave as soon as I fear Bob might think it's a reasonable time to pop open the champagne (circa 11 a.m.). London is in the throes of summer, with the temperature sitting pretty in the high twenties. I drift around Barnes Common, taking pictures of the sun-dappled trees and restraining myself from uploading them to Instagram. I get a sandwich from Alma Café and eat it on a bench overlooking the Thames. Then I amble further along, following the river as it travels back on itself, in a horseshoe shape. The river path, which encircles Barnes, is peaceful, with just a few joggers and dog walkers for company. It slopes down to a narrow pebble foreshore, which the Thames laps against.

Strange, how my perception of rivers changes near daily. Sometimes repelled, sometimes attracted. Sometimes sickened and sometimes soothed. My feelings ebb and flow, often in sync with the water itself.

I collapse onto the pebbles and wriggle off my trainers, allowing the water to nibble at my toes. I lie back. Raise a hand to protect my eyes from the sun.

I doze off, I think. I shut my eyes, and when I next open them, a trail of dribble has slipped from my lips, my right arm has cramp, and the sun is lower in the sky. I shake my arms and wriggle upwards, away from the river, which has completely submerged my feet.

"Ugh." I wipe my soaking feet on the weeds which stick up through the pebbles. I open my bag, take out a water bottle and start drinking from it. A message on my phone catches my attention as I'm putting my water bottle away:

When will you be back, Jen? Champagne tonight?

"Ughhhh."

He's evidently lonely and he's just trying to be friendly, probably, but he's a friend I neither expected nor asked for. I toss my phone back in my bag and pull out my notepad and a handful of pencils.

I draw the pebbles first. And then I draw the sky. The flats on the opposite shore. And then, finally I draw the river.

It's silk. Trickling over and under and around itself. Beautiful. Mysterious. And purple, today, reflecting the sunset. I take out a pink pencil and start shading. And then I take out a blue pencil. I add a hand, reaching up towards the surface. An arm. A face, with its mouth stretched open, eyes full of regret.

I slam the notepad shut, sending my pencils flying. Take a second to regain composure. And then – slowly, neatly – I re-pack all but one of my pencils. I take myself away from the river, to a bench ten metres back. I sit still, waiting a couple of minutes for my heartrate to slow. And then I check the time: 8.30 p.m. He should be here soon.

Alas, there's an ulterior motive behind today's innocent little dawdle and doodle. And, alas, I haven't heeded Saz's advice to give up on a London romance. I still spend an inordinate amount of time thinking about Seb. And quite frankly – between Liam's death, Daniel's departure and Scarlet's dumping – I think the gods are telling me that he's the one.

A casual stalk of his Strava profile lets me know exactly when and where he runs. Tuesday morning is a five-kilometre trot around Battersea Park. Thursday evening is interval training along the Serpentine. And Sunday evening is his long run. Always the same route: from Chelsea to Mortlake Crematorium, along the river one way, back on the opposite side of the river on his return. His heartrate always hovers at around 172 beats per minute, his pace stays consistent at four minutes per kilometre. Granted, these kinds of details are probably the line at which stalking crosses from casual to creepy, but I'm just working with the stats offered up by Strava. I can't help the fact they're incredibly intimate.

I cross and uncross my legs. Run a finger through my fringe. Apply a dash of tinted Vaseline. Look left and right along the river path. Open my notepad to its final page and start drawing spirals.

Footsteps and panting, from my left. I snap my head round and, sure enough, a sweaty Adonis is cantering through the shadows, heading in my direction. I stand up, step out onto the path and, and . . .

He runs straight past me. He doesn't even look. Shit.

"Hey!" I yell at Seb's retreating back. "Hey! You dropped this!"

He keeps running.

"HEY!" I shout. Fortune favours the brave.

Finally, he stops. He turns around slowly, squinting through the dusk.

"Jen . . . ?" he says, jogging towards me.

"Err, yep. Hi."

"Did you say I'd dropped something?"

"Yeah, err, your keys."

He reaches me and comes to a standstill. Fishes in his shorts pocket and pulls something out. "These keys?"

"Oh. Oh. Silly me. I must have mistaken . . . my keys . . . for your keys . . ."

"Right. Everything okay, Jen?"

The application of tinted Vaseline was pointless. Glossy lips can't stop me from looking crazy.

"Sorry. It's just . . . it was dark!" I do jazz hands, for some reason. Perfect. "And I didn't expect to see you."

"Naaaht true. I can tell when you're lying." He laughs, and I thank biology for the runner's high. He peers behind me, at my notepad, still lying out on the bench. "Still got that drawing of me?"

"That wasn't you."

Seb laughs. "Jen, again, a terrible liar. Plus, you're a decent enough artist that I recognise a picture of my face when I see one."

I'm glad it's dark because my cheeks – which are likely crimson – are hidden. We start ambling along the river, back in the direction of civilisation. It's eerily quiet here, and, despite my close proximity to Seb, I still find myself eager for the comfort of a crowd. There are no bikes, no walkers and no streetlights. The only light comes from the crescent moon and the distant buildings on the other side of the river.

We eventually reach the road. Seb turns to face me. Sweat is still glistening on his forehead. His curls are still damp.

"I would abandon my run and see you home, but I've got to be somewhere," he says.

"Where do you need to be?" I ask, my curiosity trumping good old-fashioned English restraint for once.

Seb flashes me a quick smile, his eyes glinting in the moonlight. "I forgot how many questions you ask."

"Sorry."

"It's alright. My brother's on holiday. Colombia. I promised I'd feed his cat."

"Oh. Right."

He chuckles at the confusion in my expression. Then he reaches for my waist and pulls me that bit closer. He kisses my jaw, but lingers long enough that it changes from a polite goodbye to . . . something *more*. His fingers stroke my ribcage. He's so attractive, even all sweaty. Perhaps stalking his runs really is the way to go. Or perhaps I should be a little more ambitious.

"Hey," I say. "Maybe we should actually go on a date one of these—"

He's gone before I can finish my question. He jogs back along the river path. I watch for as long as possible, until he's out of sight, eaten by the night.

Monday 1st August

Saz phones early the next morning to tell me she's too ill to come to work. She sounds stressed, rather than unwell, but I don't press, settling instead for generic concerned noises. It's a shame she isn't in the office; I wanted to discuss the Seb encounter in great detail. I arrange a lunch with Jam instead, hoping he can lend a sympathetic ear.

Jam, of course, does not.

"Sorry, let me get this straight. After you tracked Seb down like a deranged stalker, he left you, within minutes, to go and feed his brother's cat? Fucking what? What a fucking flannel. Jenson, lad, your chat must have been terrible," says Jam. We're eating chicken and chips at a table in Leadenhall Market. Jam starts laughing so hard I think the chips he's just eaten might come back up through his nostrils.

I roll my eyes and look around. It's lively at this time of day: underwriters getting their shoes polished, brokers in big groups drinking beer, tourists wandering around, gazing at the old-fashioned shops and cobbled streets in awe.

"I guess cats do need to be fed," I say, refocusing my attention on Jam.

"Nah, nah, nah, nah, don't skirt around this. He quite literally *ran* away from you . . . to go and feed a cat." Jam pauses to laugh again. "You've got to stop. My stomach actually hurts."

"Literally not even the worst bit," I say, taking a bite of chicken. "He ran away *as* I was asking him out on a date."

"Oh behave – Jenson, this is fucking tragic, it's made my week." Jam chokes down another bite of chicken between guffaws.

"I don't get him at all. Every time I see him, he's quite flirty, but he just won't commit to anything."

Jam shrugs. "Seb's a man. And he's busy."

"Not too busy for a cat."

Jam starts licking grease from his fingers whilst I glance at the crowds around us. Women in heels, men wearing suits. I turn back to Jam.

"I'm going to send him another message."

"Nah, I wouldn't bother."

"Sometimes he replies to my messages. Not always, but some of the time. And he did really *linger* when he kissed me goodbye yesterday."

"Ahh, the three-second jaw peck which means 'Marry me, Jen,'" says Jam, running his tongue over his pinkie. "But honestly, not a good idea."

"Why? I know he's too rich and too posh and too mature, but he also loves art, loves reading, loves the piano. He remembered what I told him about my dad. And he's so fit."

Jam starts speaking and then stops. He takes his glasses off and wipes them. He's impeccably smart: shoes polished, shirt pressed, a colourful tie every time I see him. He puts his glasses back on and rests his chin in his hands.

"Jenson, I've not been completely honest with you about Seb. There's a reason I've been quite against you getting involved with him."

"Why?" My eyes narrow in interest.

"He's charming on the outside, but he's cold. Really cold. Doesn't give a fuck about screwing people over to win an account or make money. And definitely doesn't give a fuck about any of the girls he nails and bails. Half the population of London can't stand him."

"What?"

"You've noticed it, surely? You hang around him enough. You must have noticed people watching him?"

"Err." I squeeze a chip between my greasy fingers. I think of the eyes that always seem to be on me whenever I get close to him.

Fluffy potato falls between my fingers.

"Look, Jenson." Jam pauses and leans across the table, so his lips are mere inches from my own. "He's got no moral compass. Stay away from him."

Jam's words irk me for the remainder of the afternoon. His warning doesn't match up with my experience of Seb – the dashing white knight who frogmarched Liam away from me. I chew on the end of a pen and send out emails requesting office supplies.

My usual ratio of work to procrastination is approximately 1:2 – for every five minutes I spend filling in spreadsheets or answering calls, I spend ten scrolling through my phone. I take my phone from my bag, ready for the first unofficial "break" of many, only to find that I have five missed calls from Mum. Nothing to worry about, I'm sure. She'll have lost a rat, or forgotten where her purse is, or . . . something. But my stomach still drops as I click onto her voicemail.

"Jen, have you? You've seen the news?" Mum's voice – hungover and horrified. It's thick with emotion, and, when it comes to her, that's rarely a good thing. There's a pause, and then her voice message continues. "So awful, that man, just like Dad? He's just like your dad, missing and then found washed up and . . . oh. The pictures. Disgusting pictures. Can't . . ."

No more words are distinguishable, just sobs and mumbles, splutters of distress. With every watery gurgle, my own panic increases, so I hang up and attempt to call her back. My left hand holds my phone tight against my ear, whilst my right searches Google: Man found drowned.

News articles from today are top of the search. I click onto the first one, an article written by a red-top news site.

River Thames death: Body of man found by cyclist.

My stomach flips. I'm transported back in time, to one year, eight months and twelve days ago. Switch 'Thames' for 'Tees' and the headline is identical. Mum is yet to answer; the phone continues to beep into my ear. Louder and louder. Faster and faster. My hands are shaking, but I scroll down and keep reading.

The body of a man in his forties was found by a cyclist late last night, on the banks of the Thames, near Hammersmith Bridge.

"Oh God," I whisper. Finally, my phone stops beeping, and I'm met with Mum's voicemail. I hang up and place my phone down, eyes still glued to the computer.

Because there are pictures, too. Disgusting, graphic pictures, which should never have been published. I have no idea how the website has gotten hold of the images, but they burn into my retina: the body of a man, lying face down in the river, caught between branches and rubbish. Another of the body on land, swollen beyond recognition. A close-up of a saturated, lifeless body part. It's so mangled, it takes me ten seconds to realise that I'm staring at a hand.

It's too similar to what happened, back then . . . I can't think straight. Can't breathe. I flap papers around the desk, just to be doing something with my hands, just to take my mind off the headline, the pictures, the fact that my heart is squeezing itself into a tight little fist.

I duck under the desk and call Mum again. This is what she does. Spends her nights drinking herself into a stupor, and spends her days trawling through news sites, looking for articles on London, or on drowning, on death. Desperate to destroy any progress she might have made, desperate to traumatise herself over again.

There's no answer. I try again. And again. And again. She doesn't pick up. Everything inside me seems to contract: windpipe and arteries, so that it feels like nothing works – not my lungs, not my heart.

"Pick up, pick up, pick up."

She doesn't. So I try Priti, her next-door neighbour. Priti, God bless her, answers on the second ring.

"Hello?"

"Hi, Priti, it's Jen Beeny, Leah's daughter. I'm so sorry to be ringing you out of the blue like this."

"That's quite alright, pet, this about your mam?"

"Yeah, she's not answering her phone."

"Let me go check on her."

Three minutes of silence from the other end of the phone. I count the lack of gasping as a good thing – evidence that Priti hasn't found Mum lifeless. But the complete silence is worrying, too, because it suggests that Mum isn't there. Sure enough, Priti confirms my suspicions.

"Sorry, pet, your mam isn't in."

"Yeah . . . I thought so. Thanks for checking, anyway."

I hang up before she can reply. Let my head loll back against the underside of the desk. Shit. I've no choice. I need to go find her.

Practical, emotionless Jen takes over, steering my body through tasks which need completing: begging my boss for last minute time off, booking train tickets north, packing everything into my bag. I do each without thinking much, pushed on by the knowledge that they're necessary steps, that doing each gets me to Mum quicker.

I go to shut down my computer and, for some reason, I finish reading the article:

> Hammersmith Police have confirmed that the victim is Daniel Brown, an insurance underwriter who lived in London. His death is being treated as suspicious, the force added.

Daniel Brown.

Daniel.

His death is being treated as suspicious.

What. The. Fuck.

She's where I thought she would be. St John's cemetery on Haverton Hill. A three-hour train journey and twenty-minute taxi ride away. The cemetery is right in the middle of the industrial estate, surrounded on all sides by where Dad used to work.

She's not even by his grave, for fuck's sake. She's spreadeagled on the grass, next to Abraham Harris's faded headstone, an empty bottle of vodka not far from her outstretched fingertips. I drag her up and stick two fingers down her throat, make her gag up as much alcohol as I can. And then we sit on the grass, between stone crosses and wonky slabs. Cemeteries are never a barrel of laughs, but there's something particularly uninviting about this one. Piles of scrap and debris. Rusty warehouses. Two giant concrete cooling towers, looming ominously. Smoke. Fire. The distant trundle of machinery. Teesside's dying industry, taking its last breaths.

I stay with her for two weeks. Not a glamorous summer holiday by any account. But it feels good to get out of London, good to put some distance between myself and Daniel's death. Between me and the police.

I throw away Mum's alcohol and keep a glass of water by her side at all times. I clean her house and cook basic, healthy meals. I make her sit at the table until every scrap on her plate has disappeared, even if it takes hours. We go for daily walks on the beach, heads bowed against the chilly sea air, despite the fact it's the height of summer. We don't talk about Dad and we don't talk about the article. I think about it plenty, though, trying to piece the logistics together in my head.

Daniel quit his new job to go to Dubai. And then what? Two months later he's dead on the banks of the Thames. My experience tells me it's a suicide. But the police are treating the death as suspicious. Perhaps it's time I stopped comparing Daniel's death with Dad's and focused instead on the glaring similarities of another recent, watery death.

The only problem with this, of course, is that I don't want to focus on Liam's death. I don't want to focus on any of the deaths. It would be like staring directly at the sun. So I turn away. I stop myself from going blind, but I can still feel myself getting burnt.

And each day spent with Mum is like wading further into quicksand. With each passing hour, I feel more and more trapped. I start wondering whether I invented my new London life, whether it's even possible to return. Fourteen days in and I manage to haul myself out, catch a train back.

I'm drained, but my mum is still breathing.

And so am I, just about.

CHAPTER SIXTEEN

Friday 2nd September

Saz throws a flat party at exactly the right time. It means an evening of beer pong, shots and drinking games, rather than the smell of fish, the sound of Bob muttering away to himself and my own morbid thoughts.

It's dark by the time I exit Haggerston station, but still relatively warm. I amble down the busy road, past takeaways, pubs, nail salons and chattering groups who block the pavement. A gaggle of pissed men are gathered around a phone box, giggling like schoolgirls and pointing at something.

"Oooh, dangerous woman – Gaz likes a feisty one, don't you, Gaz?"

"She might be a bit much if she's pushing men in rivers and that, mind you."

"You got your twenty-five-metre badge though, Gaz!"

"Aye. More booze?"

The group stumble into Sainsbury's, chattering about cigarettes and lager, and I approach the telephone box, eager to see what they were gawking at.

Two images. One is of Daniel's face. His big white veneers. His leathery skin. Intense, hazel eyes. Dark hair slicked back from his sizeable forehead. And the other image is of a girl in a brown coat, her face mostly concealed by an enormous bouquet of hideous flowers.

"What the fuck?"

I glance around, worried that somebody is watching me watching this poster. My heart is pounding, and I laugh once, out of nervousness or disbelief or something . . . something. This can't be real.

"Woman wanted in connection with the death of Daniel Brown.

We believe that this woman was his girlfriend in the months leading up to his death," I whisper out the details that run alongside the pictures. "We believe she was involved. Please help."

She was involved. We believe she was involved. Woman wanted in connection with the death of Daniel Brown. Please help.

My eyes start watering. *How* have I been linked to his death? It's nonsensical, baffling, *terrifying*. Guilt creeps up inside me, which is ridiculous. I can't be blamed for Daniel's death. Surely, I can't be getting blamed for Daniel's death. I had very little to do with Daniel, full stop. And yet, the poster . . . the accusations on the poster . . .

I tear it down and struggle over to the closest bench, head spinning. The words on the poster all seem to blur into one. Daniel's face merges with my body. I shake my head, trying to correct my vision, trying to make sense of what's in front of me. But I'm baffled. And, worst of all, I can't tell anyone. I can't risk losing my new friends over false, horrifying accusations. Telling Mum would be completely pointless. And the police? They'd either ignore me or, worse, believe the poster.

I crumple it up and force myself to stand. My knees are shaking, and my head is whirling and, and . . .

There are more posters. I'm stapled to a tree trunk, I'm wrapped around a lamppost. I pull them all down, squeezing the paper in my fists. I stumble, veer into the road, am almost hit by a bike. The cyclist screams something at me, but I can't hear what. There's a ringing in my ears. I've no idea if it's real or not.

The posters are real, I think. Another one is flapping around a bus stand and I grab at it, add it to the collection clutched between my fingers.

Anger bubbles up inside me, like water boiling above a hob. I fear I'm about to hiss scalding spit at the next person to walk past. But there's something else too . . . *Who the fuck took the photo?* This realisation is almost worse than anything else. It's not a bad CCTV photo, someone *took* this of me. I'm clearly being watched. But who by? This has to be a joke. But I'm not laughing. I don't know when I've been more scared.

I take a deep breath. There's water, glistening fifty metres from me. I hurry towards it and stand on the edge of Regent's Canal, my toes dangling from the path. I hold my arms out in front of me and release the missing posters. They hit the water and leave me: carried towards the Thames, or pushed down beneath the inky liquid. Gone.

I want to disappear too, but being alone – or, worse, being with Bob – fills me with dread. So I lock the posters in the part of my brain where I try and keep Daniel and Liam contained, plaster a strained smile across my face and head back towards Saz's flat, rubbing ink from my palms as I walk. I feel like I'm on autopilot, concentrating on putting one foot in front of the other. My heartrate has just about returned to normal when I knock. Saz's flatmate opens the door to me. She's pretty – tall and freckly.

"Hi, Ellie," I say, with only the smallest wobble in my voice. I stare hard at her face. Daniel seems to be imprinted on my brain. I try to replace the image of his hazel eyes with Ellie's blue ones, of his taut, tan skin with Ellie's freckles. She raises her eyebrows, so I shake myself out of my daze, embarrassed.

"I'll show you where to dump your bag," she says. I nod and follow her up to Saz's bedroom.

"Lots of bags," I say, eyeing the cluttered floor. "And more than the standard number of beds, too."

"Oh yeah, Saz not say? There's you, Saz and Jam in her bed tonight, and Pete and Zoe are on the blow-up mattress. Or maybe Zoe will be in the bed and Jam will be on the floor." She shrugs. "I'm sure you'll figure it out, I've got six people sleeping in my room!"

"Wow. Cosy flat."

"We'll all be too pissed to care."

I hope so; the flat Saz shares isn't particularly spacious. It's at the bottom of a block, with two bedrooms and a bathroom on the first floor, and a dining/kitchen/living room on the ground floor. One bathroom. Between thirty or so people. It'll be blocked within the hour.

I push toilet worries to the back of my mind and head downstairs, towards the music. Towards distraction. It's packed, with figures shrouded in shadows, illuminated only when light from the disco ball hits them. Their hands are on one another's waists, and their lips are glued to other lips, or wrapped around a bottle. If the back door leading out onto the yard wasn't open, I'm certain sweat would be dripping from the ceiling.

Jam and Saz are by the sink, pouring drinks into red plastic cups. They grin when they see me.

"I need a drink," I tell them. "A strong one."

"Oh, young Jenson – it'd be my honour," says Jam, his voice hardly audible over "Mr Brightside".

Saz gives me a wink and a wicked grin. "Three quarters vodka, one quarter lemonade it is."

Jam picks up an extra cup and pours the specified amounts of poison and mixer into it, before passing it over.

"Good lad, get it down you," he says.

I don't need telling twice. I chug it down, hoping to drown out all memories of Daniel's face, and the picture of me that was beside it. I don't know whether to be thankful for the godawful bouquet or aggravated by it; on one hand, the flowers render me near unrecognisable, but on the other they might serve as proof that I was his "girlfriend". Absolute bullshit.

As I drink, I push my way through the throng of people and outside into the yard. Partygoers are playing beer pong, snogging and falling about. Drunk or giddy, it's hard to tell. I take another gulp, watching. If I watch everyone, no one can watch me – right? There must be some logic in that. Somewhere.

There's no one too interesting here. No one who looks capable of following me around, snapping incriminating pictures. But then, what on earth *would* that look like? Not like any of the lads next to the speakers. Not the girl with fake eyelashes and pufferfish lips and hair extensions and heels. And not the girl standing next to her, wearing exclusively black and an expression of such disdain it makes my skin crawl.

The girl in black takes her phone out, and I swear she edges it in my direction. A hot flush overcomes me. There's a dribble of sweat on my forehead. I squeeze my cup and vodka slips down my forearm. Sticky. All so sticky.

A hand closes around my shoulder and I jump, yelling.

"Calm down, Jenson, I'm rescuing you!" says Jam, moving to face me. "You look like a massive loner."

His laugh – a great guffaw – conceals the fact that I stay quiet, too paranoid for humour.

"Err thanks, I guess," I say. "But I'm sure there were ways of doing that and not making me squeal. Keeping some of my dignity intact."

"Nah, nah, nah," Jam says. He starts walking across the yard and I follow. We come to a stop by a plastic table, and he continues speaking. "You've still got a little dignity. And I'm gonna take it away by thrashing you at beer pong."

He places red plastic cups on the table, nine on each side. Instead of filling them with beer though, he pours a couple of inches of vodka in each.

"Are you actually trying to murder me?"

Jam pauses his pouring to look up and grin. "Nah. I'm upping the stakes to get the best out of you."

I roll my eyes but place my hands on one end of the table regardless. It's sticky.

"Oooh, we playing beer pong?" Saz comes bounding over, with Ellie only a few paces behind.

"Vodka pong," I say.

"Shut up!" she says, increasingly excited. "Jam, I'll be on your team."

"No thanks, mate, you're shit," is his reply. Saz scowls and takes a step back to stand next to Ellie. Jam finishes pouring vodka into the cups and the game commences.

I'm fine and then I'm fucked. I drink one cup and then two then four and dribble vodka down my chin. Saz keeps butting in, interrupting, throwing balls towards Jam's cups and missing. He tells her to fuck off again and again and . . . and I've got two cups left and my dress is damp, one bit darker blue than the rest. Ahh fucker. I lean against the table, making the stain worse. It's wetter than before.

"You can't speak to people like that!" I hear a girl screech. I try to pull my head up but it's stuck, heavy, gaze fixed on spilt vodka. A spider is stuck on the table. It has six legs.

The screeching from the girl continues. I snap my neck up. Look to the right. To the straight ahead. To the left. Ellie is yelling and waving her drink around. Liquid jumps out and splatters onto the concrete below. She's so tall and her limbs are waving, stretched out like a stick insect. I look back to the table, to the spider struggling against pools of alcohol.

"I don't care! I don't care! Stop fucking her if you don't want to be with her! Stop fucking fucking her!" shouts Ellie.

I look back up. Ellie is still yelling and flailing, and Jam keeps shouting back. He's so short in comparison. Saz is watching, the quietest person for once. My head drops again, heavy, as if the sticky table is sucking me down. I force myself to look to the right. And I spot a familiar face.

"Pete! Vaping Pete!" I stumble over and place a hand on his shoulder, keeping myself steady. "Vaping Pete!"

"What did you call me?" He looks down at me, wearing a funny expression, upside down smiling one.

"Vaping Pete, I really, really love, and I never told you. You're a good guy and I've never telled you."

"Cool, thanks."

"Good guy, good guy." I pause. Sway. Think of something. "Hey, you know Seb? I know you knows you know Seb?"

"Yeah."

"So where's he at? Where's? He gots a girlfriend?"

"I don't know, I don't know him that well. He's out of the country a lot," says Pete. He moves to shrug me off and the ground beneath me shivers.

"D'you think. But. Does he ever speaks about me?" I ask, finding my balance.

"No, he never speaks about you."

"Ahhh. Sad. I likes him. So fit."

Vaping Pete's not so good with the info and the ground continues not to be still, so I cross the yard. Jam is shouting. Ellie is shouting. I go inside and through the sweat and up one stair and one stair and two. Left, into the wrong room and so out and right and into the bathroom. And I was correct, earlier, when I had my thoughts about the bathroom, it's all sick and bad smells. I sort of stumble and so grab the toilet seat and look down: orange sick with bits of brown blobs and it's swirling, like the ground. I grip the sticky seat harder. It smells of tuna or the sea and I'm reminded of Bob. Push myself away.

I head out of the bathroom and along, into and out of the wrong room, and finally into Saz's bedroom. It's a pretty room, big mirrors and so, so many photos. I pause by the photos and touch. A picture of her with elephants in Thailand. A picture of her as a child, being hugged by her mum. And there's this one photo frame which is soft and fluffy, and it houses a picture of a girl. A girl I think I've . . . Think I've seen before.

"Oh. Jenson." A voice from behind me. I turn. Jam.

"Hey, whatta you up to, friend?" I ask.

"Leaving."

"Nah, nah, nah, nah, nah." I'm starting to sound like Jam at this stage of my vodka journey, but I can't stop.

"Yeah, yeah, yeah. Saz is a state and Ellie's a psychopath. I'm out."

I move towards him. A bag gets in my way so I stumble but I'm fine, I'm fine, and I hold his shoulder and pull my mouth close to his ear and say, "You know . . . we's sharing a bed."

"What, are you staying? In this room?"

"So the sparrow crows, so it crows."

"Right. You're sharing a bed with me?"

"That's what I said I says."

Jam pulls away a little, rocks his head from side to side.

"Nah, I should still go," he says. He heads back downstairs and after a bit I follow.

He doesn't go. He gets me a glass of water, which I sip from and then lose. And he dances and he drinks and I copy him but my world is less stable. Sweat streams down my forehead and deep into my hair. There's banging – neighbours or police shouting about how it's too loud and complaints that it's too late for this, this racket. People dribble out or away and in not so many minutes I'm back in Saz's room, finding my way to her bed.

There's a big lump of big human in the bed. I feel its face: Saz. She's asleep. Asleep, I think. Climb in next to her. She doesn't move. The bed rocks, like being on a boat. And later there's another body which climbs in next to me. I touch just to be sure: Jam. He touches me back. And his fingertips trail my arms, shy. Fingertips get less shy, along my collarbones and up my thigh and under my pyjamas. Move my lips closer and we kiss. Kiss and kiss. I don't remember falling asleep.

CHAPTER SEVENTEEN

Monday 5th September

I snuck out of Saz's flat as soon as dawn broke, before anyone else was awake, hoping to run from my actions and never speak of them again. Kissing Jam was an embarrassing, drunken fever dream. It can't have been real, can it? And the posters of me and Daniel? In fact, Daniel's death, Liam's death, *Dad's* death – how can any of that have happened? They're not . . . They're not things which are supposed to happen. I squeeze each muscle in my body, hoping to shrink myself, perhaps, shrink my life and the things which have happened in it out of existence.

I come in on Monday expecting Saz to tease me relentlessly for getting so wasted at her party and for kissing Jam. But she doesn't mention the party at all. I guess she was pretty drunk herself, and clearly completely out of it whilst my lips were glued to Jam's. I would tell her (I've told her everything about my other London "romances", after all) but I recall her warning me not to date Jam. Not to be with him sexually in any capacity. So, not wanting to disappoint her, I hold my tongue, and am left to dwell in silence about who put the posters up, instead.

I spend every spare second checking to see if it counts as stalking or slander or something chargeable so I can get it to stop. Or at least I could, if I knew who was behind the posters. Throwing them away seemed like a good idea at the time, but now I don't have any evidence. Would I have shown the posters to the police, though? They'd likely just have believed I'd done exactly what I've been accused of.

In what seems to be a sickening twist of fate, police visit the office, and my paranoia increases. There's a pretty woman and a gangly man with a protruding Adam's apple. They step out of the lift opposite reception, and I tense up, assuming they're here to find out what they can about Daniel. I hope to high heaven all I'll need to do is show them around the office. I can't handle a morning of interrogation, a morning of attempting to convince them I was never his girlfriend, that I didn't kill him.

I slam my notepad (full of doodles of Daniel, Liam and rivers) shut and stand to attention, ready to be as efficient and unsuspicious as possible.

I'm rendered unnecessary; a couple of senior managers intercept the police officers before they reach reception. They're discreet, but I still hear mumbles of, "For Daniel Brown? Yes, this way."

I peer over the desk and watch as the group stride along the corridor and into one of the meeting rooms. I tap my fingers against the plastic surface. Like anyone else would be, I'm curious about what's going to be discussed. Does OnIt Insurance really have any information of use for the police? Daniel didn't even spend a day here. This was, however, his link to me.

But I'm innocent. I was never Daniel's girlfriend. Not even close. But a little voice in my head keeps telling me that miscarriages of justice happen all the time.

I shove my chair back and rush down the corridor, nearly tripping over my shoes. The meeting room door is shut, of course. I start thinking up ways of listening in: barging in with teas and coffees and leaving the door propped open on my way out, or offering to take minutes. That's a thing a receptionist could do, right?

Indecision immobilises me; instead, I stand next to the door, grateful for any snippets of conversation which make it through.

"... eccentric, but sound of mind when we interviewed him ..."

"... no, no he didn't aggravate anyone here. He didn't have time to aggravate anyone here ..."

"... no, he told us he'd gotten a better offer via letter. We asked to meet him to discuss his decision, but he never replied ..."

There's a scraping of a chair, as someone in the meeting room stands up. I take a step back, terrified of getting caught. And my bottle (not that I ever had much of it) completely deserts me. I turn back towards reception, only stopping to nip into the bathrooms. I'm just about to pull the bathroom door open, when I hear a sob from inside. I pause, palm wrapped around the lime green plastic handle.

"Yes, think you might be right . . ." I hear the voice from inside say. Another almighty sob is emitted. "Hate to say it but . . . think you might be right."

The sobber is Saz. I think about turning around, heading back to reception and acting as though nothing has happened, but I can't do it. I pull open the door and step into the bathroom. Only one of the cubicles is occupied.

"Saz," I say, rapping my knuckles lightly against the door.

I hear her hang up and blow her nose. She unlocks the cubicle door and emerges. She shoots me a watery smile, but her eyes don't meet mine.

"Are you okay?" I ask the dumbest question available.

"Yeah, I'm fine. Honestly." She pulls her lips into another smile and heads to a sink, where she starts washing her hands with an unprecedented level of concentration.

"I can always listen. You can always talk to me," I say. I reach out to touch her shoulder, and then pull my arm away, awkward.

"Yeah, I know," Saz says, applying soap to her palms for the third time.

"Is it work? Cos I can do more, if you want to give me some of your workload. You know I don't really try that hard."

For the first time, a genuine smile crosses Saz's face. "Yeah, trust me, I know that. But no, course it's not that. Just . . . that guy."

"Oh. The one who isn't good for you?"

"That's him."

"You feel like telling me a bit more about him?"

"It would . . . make things weird. Stuff you're better off not knowing."

Stuff I want to know, though. I want her to let me help, to trust me completely. I know all the trivial bits of Saz and none of the deep stuff, not who this man is, not how her stepsister is doing, not why she was funny about me mentioning dating Jam, not what her aspirations are beyond OnIt Insurance. I'm briefly frustrated by this, but all I do is nod. I stare straight ahead, into the mirror. Saz looks up too, and our eyes meet. I touch her elbow, try to manoeuvre her out of the bathroom with a promise of snacks in my bag.

She resists.

"Sorry, I just . . . need to ring someone back," she says, holding her phone up.

"Oh, sure."

"Try and leave me some chocolate, though, ey?" She smiles. I turn to leave, only glancing back once more, as I'm about to exit.

Saz's eyes are fixed on her phone, and her smile has disappeared.

Thursday 29th September

For the next couple of weeks, every time I walk past a poster, I'm certain it'll show me. Doesn't matter if the poster is for a concert, or a new phone, or a missing cat, my reaction is always the same: furious squinting, followed by rushing over and standing with my nose two inches from the paper. When I've established that, no, my sweaty fringe and an accusation of murder don't decorate the picture in front of me, I take a step back and glance around. And, more often than not, when I look about, I clock someone whose phone is pointing in my direction. My panic escalates once again and I pull my coat collar higher, brush my hair in front of my face and scurry away, head bowed.

There's a knot in my stomach, constantly. And the faint, acidic taste of sick. This is not a healthy way to exist. Not at all.

Jam celebrates his birthday one Thursday evening, and I attempt to spend a full two hours not worrying about anything. The setting helps: a big, comforting group of us are eating finger food at a pub squeezed between the ornate roof and cobbled ground of Leadenhall Market. I had hoped Seb would be here, but I'm yet to see him. Damn those Thursday night interval runs.

Jam sidles up to me, sausage roll in hand. "You remember Saz's party?"

"Course I do," I say. "D'you think I've got amnesia? It was only a few weeks ago."

Jam smirks at my response. My stomach drops because it's the smirk of a man who is chomping at the bit to bring up our kisses. Kisses that I've just about managed to convince myself most definitely *did not* happen.

Jam places his palm between my shoulder blades and leans in close. "And do you remember what *we* did at Saz's party?"

My face grows hot and my eyes dart down to the cobbles.

"You're blushing, you remember! Anyway, you thinking what I'm thinking? I'm coming back to yours tonight for round two? Birthday treat?"

I almost spit my food out.

"That is quite the suggestion."

"Good lad. I've packed a change of shirt," he replies, thumping me on the back.

Oh Christ. Do I like Jam in that way? Am I really okay with overruling Saz's advice? Yes? No? Potentially? He is funny and familiar, if nothing else. I found the kisses with him embarrassing, but arguably that was because of my own behaviour – sloppy, slurred, unsophisticated – rather than him. My brain goes into overdrive: imagining him naked, wondering whether he'd be silly or serious during sex. Wondering whether he really would keep his tie on, whether he would charge per orgasm.

I change the subject. "Well, anyway, happy birthday. Twenty-four. Got your bus pass yet?"

Jam smiles and looks me dead in the eyes. "Behave. An older man is sexy, right?"

I laugh.

"When you two have stopped flirting, I'll have a Malibu Coke. A strong one," says Saz from my right.

"Sorry, drinks on the birthday boy tonight, are they?" Jam asks, turning to face Saz.

She shrugs. "My thank-you for putting up with you for so long."

"Oh, mate, if you're gonna be like this you can leave."

"What, leave this public area, mate?"

It's about to turn nasty so I interject, offering to buy fresh drinks for Jam, Saz and three others who are lingering nearby. Unfortunately, they take me up on my offer. I trudge into the Lamb Tavern and back out twenty minutes later, forty-six pounds down but clutching six different alcoholic drinks. The people to whom they belong have dispersed, so I weave through the crowd to find them, a reluctant waitress.

My evening continues in a similar vein, a dance through the different attendees. I apologise to Vaping Pete for my behaviour at Saz's party. He manages to answer me exclusively in monosyllables, an achievement I find as impressive as I do rude. I check whether Saz is okay, but her answers are as short as Pete's, so I give her a squeeze and move on sharpish. And, of course, I speak to Jam. He touches me whenever I'm near him: a subtle hand on my waist, his thumb against my thigh.

Eventually, the crowd begins to thin.

Jam's lips are by my ear. "I'm gonna say my goodbyes. Give it five and you do the same. I'll wait in Bank station."

"Sorry, Jam, not in the mood."

He guffaws. "Jenson, Jenson, Jenson. I'll give Bob a talking-to. I'll show you the time of your life. What's not to like?"

"The Bob bit, mainly." I've come round to the idea of intimacy with Jam, but Bob's omnipresence remains a significant stumbling block.

"I live ages away; you'd have to sit on a rail replacement bus for about a million years – does that work out better?"

I roll my eyes. "Or we could just n—"

"Plus, I think you're gorgeous. You know I've fancied you for months, right?"

My face grows hot. I bat my fringe away, trying to cool my forehead. Jam continues, "Do you think I hang around with everyone I recruit?"

I look around the gathering and clock plenty of people who have indeed been recruited by Jam. For some reason I don't bring this up, instead I sort of simper and say, "Well, maybe . . ."

"Good lad," Jam replies, "see you in five."

He squeezes my waist and then moves away.

"Right, lads, thanks for showing your faces tonight. Everyone who bought me a drink – thank you. Everyone who asked me to buy them a drink – fuck you, I won't forget when it's your birthday." Jam pauses to look pointedly at a scowling Saz. "I'm a boring old man now, so I'm heading off."

There are objections, of course, and taunts about Jam being past it, a lightweight. But he's not a celebrity, he's not that in demand; the protestations subside and he's free to walk away, disappearing into the dark. I sip at my drink and wait. I play with the ice cubes, trying to hook them onto my straw and escort them into my mouth, or else drink directly from the glass, trying to usher them all into my mouth at once.

When there are no more ice cubes left and my tongue is numb, I decide it's time to make my exit.

"I'm going to head too, guys," I say, putting my empty glass down on a table.

"Oh yeah? I'll come with," says Saz, hastily slurping up the last of her drink. Fuck. Fucking fuck fuck.

"Not really your direction, is it?" I say.

"I can go from Bank."

Ahh. I dither. If I'm actually going to go through with this, I'd rather Saz didn't know. I remember too keenly how stern she was when advising me not to get involved with him. It would disappoint her, I'm certain of it. She knows he's no good for me – heck, *I* know he's no good for me – and still, here I am, going along with him . . . I think about literally running away from Saz. Too weird. I think about telling her a mad lie, but I can't even come up with a mediocre fib, never mind an outlandish one.

"Err . . ."

"Don't you want me coming with you?" she asks, raising an eyebrow, as if she knows. She *can't* know.

I'm saved by her phone, which starts vibrating in her handbag. Saz takes it out and answers.

"Hey, yeah, right now," Saz says into the phone. She moves away to continue the conversation.

"Right, gotta go, bye," I say, seizing my opportunity to leave unaccompanied. I speed-walk out of Leadenhall Market and along Cornhill.

"Took your time," Jam says when I eventually meet him outside the Underground.

"I'm more popular than you are, there was more resistance to me leaving."

He laughs, and we head into the brightly lit station. Everything seems a little uglier down here: me, him, the situation. I fill the ugly silence with apologies: an apology for my wobbly single bed, for my weird landlord, for the fact I don't have anything to feed him for breakfast tomorrow. Jam comments on each as we board the Waterloo and City tube, as we climb out the other end, as we find seats on the train heading towards Barnes. "One of your beds is wobbly? Fuck me, Jen, you know I like my sleep stable." "Behave – you've got a twenty-stone landlord and he might be up for a threesome? Best birthday *ever*." "You've not got food in? You can hack off one of your arms and cook that up for me then, you tight little northerner." A bark of laughter escapes my lips at the same time as a burp. Jam raises his eyebrows and then laughs too.

"What am I going home with?"

"Sorry."

"Nah, nah, nah, don't apologise."

He presses his body harder into the dirty red fabric of the train seat. Our bodies are close but not touching. We sink further into our respective seats, seats thick with dead skin cells and human hair, seats that have been occupied by tens of thousands of Londoners before us. Jam looks at me with his big, brown eyes, and then he pushes himself away from the back of his seat, removes himself from the ghosts of commuters past. His face is soft, slightly out of focus. I'm drunk, just a little bit, and reminded of the last time I was drunk – how good it felt, kissing someone so warm and welcoming.

Jam smiles and then leans towards me. We kiss non-stop for three minutes. The time it takes to get from Clapham Junction to Wandsworth Town.

Beyond kissing, physical touch is limited. We don't hold hands on the walk from the station to the flat, and, when we're in my room, he doesn't make moves to undress me. This is something we do for ourselves. Once we're in nothing but our underwear, we get onto the stable single bed and sit as close as possible without touching.

I move to touch Jam and then pause. My eyes skim his body: doughy, smooth, near hairless. I'm not friends with Jam's naked flesh, it's not a part of him I know. I'm friends with his smart suits and colourful ties and the joke-cracking head which perches above them. Being like this with him is odd, but eventually I take the plunge and place my hand just below his neck.

We lie together companionably for an hour or so after having sex. Physical touch remains limited, but I don't mind at all. Easy chatter fills my room, as we swap tales about caravan holidays, about the best burgers in London, about some dumb new reality show Jam promises contains the most sensationally attractive contestants.

I laugh until I hear movement from below. Bob. I hadn't realised he was in. I hoist myself up, shushing Jam and straining my ears.

"What is it, your landlord? Please don't say you're worried about him finding me here, Jenson," says Jam whilst scrolling through his phone, on the search for the hottest reality television contestants he can find.

"I think he's a bit weird about me having visitors."

"If banning visitors wasn't in your contract there's fuck all he can do about it. Relax."

"Yeah, I know," I say. "Maybe he just wants that threesome now."

My joke prompts a small chuckle from Jam.

"I mean, I am irresistible . . . *Shit*."

Jam has moved his phone screen to within inches of his face.

"What?" I ask.

"Weird text. Really weird text."

"Oh yeah, from who?"

He doesn't answer, he just sighs and taps the phone against his forehead. He closes his eyes.

"I should go, Jenson. Sorry about this."

He's up and pulling on his trousers before I have time to make any kind of objection. He dashes about my room gathering up his socks, his tie, his wallet. He buttons up his shirt and avoids eye contact. He's not being completely honest, and it irks me. We just did the most intimate thing possible together, yet I'm not even owed a proper explanation for his departure. Nailed and bailed – a classic. Just not something I thought I was going to experience from a mate. I should have listened to Saz, my actual friend.

I bite my tongue, instead asking whether everything is okay.

"Yeah. Or . . . nothing for you to worry about, anyway." He slips me a small smile which falters near immediately.

"Okay. Well, let me know if I can do anything."

"Sure will. Alright, see you, Jenson, this was fun," Jam says when he has finished buttoning up his shirt and stuffed everything into his pockets.

"Mmm. It was something. Well, I guess good luck with the better offer you've just had. And try to leave quietly, please."

He doesn't leave quietly. He gallops down the first flight of stairs, and Bob's door opens just as Jam reaches the second. I'm hanging over the banister, watching, so I see Bob look down at Jam, and then up at me.

"Jen, what the . . . ? Who is this? Why do you look upset?"

"Oh piss off, weirdo," shouts Jam.

My eyes and Bob's eyes widen in shock. And then Bob charges from his room. I dash back through my door and over to my window.

I watch as Jam scuttles out of the front door and races across the road and into the night, on the hunt for whoever messaged him. And Bob jogs out ten seconds later, shouting at his retreating back.

CHAPTER EIGHTEEN

Wednesday 12th October

I plan on giving Jam the silent treatment. The problem with this, however, is that he doesn't contact me. Silent treatment doesn't work so well when both parties are doing it, and I have approximately no willpower, so I crumble and send him a message. My message goes unanswered.

"He's ghosting me!" I tell Saz as we're logging off our computers one Wednesday afternoon. "Jam, of all people, is ghosting me. This is a new low."

I almost wish I'd told her that we hooked up, just so she'd appreciate the extent of his rudeness. But I don't think I'd be able to handle her inevitable "told you so" attitude. Besides, turns out that, even without this additional knowledge, Saz is adequately incensed from the get-go.

"Jam's a little shit," she says, with more fervour than I was anticipating. "He has been for years. He's the worst."

"I mean, right now, yes. Normally he's a good guy, though."

Saz snorts. "Good isn't a word I'd use to describe him. Case in point – he's been replying to my messages. He deserves everything that comes his way."

"Oh." I pause to zip up my bag. "It is quite rude he'd reply to you but not me."

"Why are you so desperate for a response from him, anyway?"

I unzip my bag and rummage around in it, attempting to give myself time to think up a lie. The lift pings open, but I keep my head bowed, needing to put full concentration into my fib. "Uhm, I asked him a question about Seb."

"Seb?" says Saz, voice once again more enthusiastic than I was expecting. "Seb's right here, you can ask him now."

"What?"

I look up and, sure enough, Sebastian Matthews is striding towards the reception desk, mouth set in a bashful smile. Saz winks at me, pulls on her coat and then dashes into the lift Seb just exited.

I stutter as he comes to a stop in front of me, not entirely sure what to say to him, and bitterly wishing I'd bothered to straighten my hair this morning. I run a finger through the mousey mess.

"Oh, Seb, hi. Long time, no see. I think most of the underwriters have left the office, you might be a bit late if you were trying to catch them."

He ignores me. "You have a question for me, Jen? Or was I hearing things when I stepped out the lift?"

How the hell do I repeatedly trap myself in a web of white lies? I push my fringe back from my forehead, which is growing sweatier by the second.

"It's okay." Seb grins, putting me out of my misery. "I have a question for you, actually. That's why I'm here. Well, that and a meeting with Freya."

"Oh. Right." My heart leaps. I try to keep it under control, try to stay realistic. He'll be here to ask me about booking a meeting room. Something boring and decidedly unromantic.

"What are you doing on Friday the 28th?"

"What am . . . *I* doing?" I give him a chance to correct himself, to tell me he actually intended to enquire about the plans of a senior manager, rather than little old me.

"Yes, what are *you* doing, Jen Beeny?"

"Oh. I don't know. Nothing, I don't think."

"There's a Halloween party in Putney. It's bound to be lame, but I'm going with a few mates – ironically, of course. It would be nice to bump into you. Bring a friend, the loud blonde one, perhaps?"

"Oh. Oh, right."

"Do you need to plug it into a probability tree before you can give me an answer?"

"No," I say, feeling my face flush. "No, I can come."

"Wonderful. See you soon, then." He leans across the desk and kisses me on the cheek, lingering that bit longer than necessary again. And then he waltzes away, down the corridor and towards the meeting rooms.

I send Saz a text on my way home:

> So the Seb chat went well! He's invited me on, well . . . Not a date as such, but the opportunity to be in the same space as him. Halloween party in Putney on the 28th. Want to come and watch me fail to pull him for the umpteenth time?

She replies just as the train pulls into Barnes station.

> Lol, how romantic of him. But sure, I wouldn't want to miss out on that kind of entertainment. I'll ask Jam, too – give him a chance to stop being rude.

Even the thought of Jam coming along isn't enough to kill my good mood. I grin all the way along Rocks Lane, watching amber leaves swirl on either side of me, and – for once – not panicking when someone raises their phone, or I catch sight of a poster flapping about on the floor. My grin is wiped from my face within two seconds of entering the flat, though. Because Bob is waiting for me in the hallway.

"Err, hi," I say. There's really not room for both of us in the corridor. His body takes up two thirds of the space; I have to contort myself in order to shut the door, take my boots off and hang my coat up.

"Jen. Hi."

I get one foot on the stairs when I feel his hand on my shoulder. There's no force to his touch, nothing too alarming about it. But still, I shudder, feeling as though a damp tentacle has attached itself to my flesh. I shrug him off and step back down into the hallway, wanting to get whatever this is over with as quickly as possible.

"You okay?" he asks. "Haven't had a chance to check on you since that man was round."

No shit: I spend far too much time and energy desperately trying to avoid him. Still, it's sweet-ish of Bob to check on me. I don't tell him any of this, of course. I say, "Yeah, I'm fine."

"That man who was in the flat, he harmed you?"

"No."

"Upset you?"

I pause, unfortunately giving Bob enough time to say, "I thought so. He upset me, anyway! I'm putting a visitors' book by the front door," he says, holding up a tatty black notepad. "You need to fill it in whenever you have anyone over. And guests on a weekend only."

My mouth opens and closes. Bob isn't being sweet after all; he's being controlling. Is this normal in London? It doesn't feel normal. But then, nothing about this godawful living situation has ever been normal. I think about objecting, telling him to drop my rent if he's going to insist on such Draconian rules. Asking him why on earth he chose a twenty-something-year-old to be his lodger, rather than an octogenarian hermit, if he was going to be so pernickety about visitors. But I can't. I'm trapped here with the man; the last thing I want is an argument with the very person it's near impossible for me to get away from.

"Right. Okay." I have no intention of ever writing a sentence in the stupid book. But I smile sweetly, turn on my heel and walk up the stairs.

I feel his eyes on the back of my neck the whole way up.

Friday 28th October

Mist hangs in the air on Friday evening, the perfect accompaniment for a Halloween weekend. I press through it, approaching a cluster of ghoulishly dressed adults gathered outside the entrance of Le Fez, an unassuming nightclub on the corner of busy Putney High Street. Saz is amongst them, dressed as a snake with all the trimmings. She's wearing a scaly green bodysuit, and any visible areas of flesh have been decorated in a scale pattern with glitter and paint. Her hair is slicked back and dyed gold.

"Oh classic – you're a cat," she says, when she spots me. "But you hate cats."

"Yes, I hate cats. But black clothes and some drawn-on whiskers and you're good to go. It's easy."

"I mean, people normally look easy in it, yeah. You're actually a very modest cat, to be fair."

"Thanks," I reply. Not exactly the reaction I wanted before my Seb ambush.

We head into the bowels of the building, eager for alcohol. The nightclub has been dressed according to what seems to be the tacky, un-official law of Halloween: plastic props in the corners, cobwebs and lanterns dangling from the ceiling, green and orange strobe lights and "Thriller" blasting through the speakers.

We head over to the bar and order cocktails.

"Seb's here," says Saz, as a smoking, orange drink is handed to her.

"Oh, where?" I ask, attempting to feign nonchalance.

"Straight ahead."

He's on the other side of the bar, in the quieter half of the nightclub, which is full of plush booths rather than a pounding dancefloor. He's half hidden by vodka bottles and he's got hollow cheeks and blood running down his neck, but it's him. He looks exquisite with fangs and bags under his eyes. Once again, I wish I'd opted for a slightly sexier cat outfit.

"Go see him," says Saz.

"I can't leave you by yourself."

"I'm good, honestly. It's why I'm here!"

My feet remain stuck to the ground, so she continues, "Go on, off you fuck. Let's face it, there's more of a chance of me pulling without you – some hot man will probably take pity and sweep me off my feet."

I take hold of my drink (which seems to contain more plastic spiders than it does booze) and sidle round the bar, where I have a view of the booth area. Seb is wearing a long velvet cape and white shirt, and I scope out his companions: a werewolf, a Frankenstein, the Joker and a half-arsed pirate. No girls. Well, no girls apart from a scantily clad group who are not so subtly eyeing Seb from the other side of the bar. I'm struck by such a pang of possessiveness I'm almost embarrassed. Almost.

He invited *me*, but marching straight up to him isn't going to cut it. I need a plan.

Step one: down my cocktail for max Dutch courage. Step two:

head to the bathrooms (via the dancefloor side, can't have him see me yet). Step three: dial up sex appeal (brush hair, check for plastic spiders between teeth, push bra up and pull top down). Step four: re-emerge from the bathroom a veritable goddess, stride past Seb and his friends without looking. Step five: order self a new drink at the bar, glance back until we both make scorching eye contact.

My plan works like a dream. He's looking the first time I turn around. He smiles and looks away when we make eye contact. I turn back around to face the bar and soon enough I sense him behind me. He arrives just in time to pay for my drink. Smooth.

"Thanks," I say, turning to give him my full attention. "Didn't expect to see you here."

"You . . . what? Oh. Oh, I get the sarcasm." He's a little awkward and I love it.

"So you're a gargoyle, right?" I tease.

He falls for it. "No!"

"Oh yeah, silly me – ghost. Obviously."

"What?! Oh, ahh, very funny. You're a mouse, right?"

"Go one higher up the food chain."

"You're never a cat? With the pointy ears and six whiskers? I've never seen something so creative."

"Ha ha," I say, preparing myself for more grief about my costume. I look at Seb as he dishes it out, trying to memorise his face for future enjoyment. The gentle slope of his nose. The exact pink of his lips. The location of each of his moles. The man who ordinarily seems so tantalisingly out of reach feels closer than ever.

"You must be at least 203 years old, vampire boy. Want to take the weight off your limbs?" I ask when he's stopped mocking the quality of my feather boa tail.

He nods, so we relocate to a booth tucked away at the back of the club. Seb starts kissing me almost immediately, his lips on mine – rather than my cheek – for the first time in months. We drink and kiss and make awkward, giddy conversation. He smells of vanilla and whisky and he's still got those lovely crinkles around his eyes when he smiles. I must be dreaming. Nothing this good ever happens in real life.

"Shall we head off?" Seb asks once we've finished our drinks.

"I need to check on my friend, but sure, maybe."

Seb follows me out of the booth and onto the dancefloor. I can't see Saz amongst the ghoulish clubbers, so we head upstairs and outside. Saz is on the phone, standing near the smoking area. She still looks immaculate, covered in glittery scales.

"Oh, Jen." She hangs up as I approach her. "I think I'm gonna call it a night."

"Oh really? Is Jam not coming? We can go back and dance and things if you want?" I say, suddenly guilty that I made her come all the way to Putney from North London.

"We're heading off actually," Seb interrupts, placing his hand on my waist. "Back to Jen's."

I frown at him. "Oh we are, are we?"

"Yep, I'll order a cab."

"I've got a weird landlord."

"And I've got my brothers staying so mine is naaaht an option."

I'm about to disagree when Saz squeezes my shoulder and leans in close. "Go and have sex with Seb so that I can look forward to hearing all about it on Monday," she whispers, almost winking one of her fake eyelashes off.

She leaves, so I stand shivering on the pavement with Seb, waiting for a cab. He says things and I struggle to understand him, struggle to unscramble him. I'm drunker than I realised, perhaps, or maybe Saz was right all those months ago when she said he was too posh to be understood. I rub my cheeks. Look at my fingertips, smudged black from my whiskers.

"Cab's here," says Seb. He takes my palm and pulls me into the back of it, and soon we're speeding along Upper Richmond Road. He puts an arm around me and pulls me close, so that my right side is resting against his cape. There's a vibration from within his cape, and I drag my body upright, allowing him to take out his phone.

He answers, and I can hear screeching from the other end of the phone.

"How *dare* you get into a cab with another girl!? How *dare* you!"

My eyes widen, and so do Seb's. He stutters down the phone, "Who? Who is this? I don't know who you are."

"I'm your *girlfriend*, Seb! Or did you conveniently forget that, *again*?!"

I open my mouth in shock. My organs seem to drop in unison. I feel sick.

"You have a girlfriend?" I ask. I don't know why I bother asking, though. Of course he has a bloody girlfriend.

"No – I honestly, honestly don't know who this is. I don't recognise this number," he says to me, before shouting down the phone, "I don't know you!"

"Seb Matthews, you're lying!" the voice screeches back. "I hope whoever you're with can hear this, can hear how much of an evil, manipulative, gaslighting—"

Seb hangs up. He opens his mouth to say something to me, but the cab jolts to a stop outside Bob's flat. I lurch forward, feeling as though I might vomit my cocktails back up.

I exit the cab pronto, coming to a standstill under Bob's porch. Seb has followed but I don't want to look at him, so I look everywhere else instead: Bob's rusted knocker, his off-white doorbell, a flashing red light perched just above the doorframe. Eventually, I take a breath and turn to face Seb.

"Jen, I have no idea what that was, I don't have a girlfriend," he says.

"Right, it's just . . ."

"Just what?"

I think of all the women who constantly watch him. I think of Jam's warning to me, his insistence that Seb doesn't give a fuck about any of them. About anyone. The flame of arousal I had for him flickers. I suddenly realise what an idiot I've been.

"It's just that I don't believe you."

Seb slaps his palm against his forehead, a cartoon character.

"Jen, please, come on. I've been looking forward to seeing you."

I rummage in my bag and – mercifully – find my keys straight away. I insert them into the lock but pause before opening the door. Turning back to Seb, I say, "I just don't feel good about this situation anymore. Go and see your girlfriend, if you're so desperate for sex."

I yank the door open and slip inside before he can reply. As I'm locking up, I hear his body slide down the front door. I imagine him crouched on Bob's step, holding his head between his hands. A wave of sympathy washes over me, but I ignore it. I feel more sorry for myself. He's got a girlfriend. I was only ever his bit on the side. Probably not even that – more likely his emergency bit on the side, if the four bits before me all happened to be busy.

I slam Bob's stupid book shut – I certainly won't be needing *that* tonight – and then I clamber up the stairs and into bed.

Sleep doesn't come for me immediately. Instead, I drift for a while, hearing sounds which are either the start of a dream, or the end of my night, it's impossible tell. A car screeches to a stop. A conversation takes place on the kerb, I think, just outside of Bob's front door. I hear Seb's voice, I'm certain. I hear Seb laughing, even.

Classic – even in my dreams, he's a fuckboy.

CHAPTER NINETEEN

Wednesday 2nd November

The weather takes a turn, from mild to miserable. Winter wraps its fingers around London, and a definite chill accompanies me on my train ride home from the office. The tracks run closest to the river as the train approaches Vauxhall, and I turn my head away, not wanting to glimpse water reflecting the grim November weather. Not that looking away stops me thinking about Daniel and Liam. But I'm so used to these thoughts now I barely even register them. I snuggle deeper into Dad's old coat. Eventually, I alight at Barnes and start trundling up Rocks Lane.

My phone buzzes. I check it quickly, near certain that the texter is Seb, finally apologising for the whole girlfriend fiasco after days of silence. But it's not Seb. It's not even Jam. It's Scarlet.

"What?" A surprised smile stretches across my face. How random. I lean against an oak tree and read her message.

> Hey Jen! Sorry that things sort of fizzled between us – life, ay? You said earlier you wanted to catch up? I just grabbed a coffee in Barnes and remember you saying you live around there. You free to meet at Barnes Common? No worries if not xx

On one hand, it's fucking freezing. On the other hand, today I finally perfected winged eyeliner; I owe it to myself to showcase this achievement to as many people as possible. Plus, Scarlet's really hot. And I'll finally make it to two dates with a girl. I definitely didn't tell her I wanted to catch up, though . . .

But at the moment, I'll take any kind of distraction. I text back a reply:

> Hey, no worries, that would be fun. I can be at Barnes Common in about five minutes? Xx

Scarlet responds quickly:

> Fab, see you super soon xxx

I shrug and reverse myself back up the path, in the direction of the Common. The sun has long since set, and, away from the road and station, there's little in the way of light. My boots crunch over frosted grass as I walk across the cricket pitch. A delightful spot in summer; I've spent many a lazy afternoon lounging here with my notepad and pencils. But on a winter evening? Not so much. The pitch is surrounded by densely planted trees, between which anything could be lingering. What an odd place for a catch-up.

I continue walking, listening out for anything which isn't the distant rumble of a train, or the hooting of an owl. With each step further into Barnes Common, the temperature seems to drop. My fingers grow numb, and I pull my coat sleeves over them.

"Scarlet?"

Predicting potentially hours of fruitless wandering around the Common, I send her a message asking her to pin her location. No response. I keep walking, shivering. Fuck, it really is cold. Another message. Two more messages. I ring her. Nothing.

I'm in the trees now, in near complete darkness. Something brushes against my coat and I jump, spinning around. Just a branch. Just one of many branches, reaching towards me. I cough, pull my coat closer.

"This is ridiculous," I mutter.

It takes a while for me to find my way out of the Common. I trip over roots, jump at every rustle and take half a dozen wrong turns. I'm shaking by the time I make it back to Bob's flat. From fear or the cold, I'm not entirely sure. Regardless, I'm desperate for my bed. I do all my tasks in double quick time, and then I crawl under the covers.

I'm woken by Bob's footsteps on the stairs. It's still dark, so impossible to ascertain the time, but my guess would be early.

Really early or really late. They're interchangeable, aren't they? I roll over, sniffling.

Bob enters the bathroom. The walls in the flat are thin, so I hear the tap when he turns it on, the uneven splash of water against bowl as he wets his hands. This goes on for ten seconds. Another ten. Thirty seconds. A minute. He washes his hands for an unprecedented amount of time, though I bet they still stink of fish.

Eventually, the tap switches off, but he doesn't head downstairs. Minutes pass and I haul myself out of bed and over to my bedroom door. I push it open a couple of inches. Bob is standing on the landing, and in his hands is one of my bras, which I had hung over the banister to dry.

"Hey!" I say, opening my door wider and stepping out onto the landing. Bob jumps and turns to face me. His eyes widen and his mouth opens in shock.

"Jen. Sorry, it had fallen, just picking it up." He places my bra back on the banister, alongside the remainder of my drying clothes, and then dashes downstairs. I gather my clothes and find ways of spreading them out in my room.

I can still hear him moving around downstairs – huffing and puffing and dragging objects around and clattering in the kitchen – so I move my dresser in front of my door. I lean against it, sweaty and breathless. Wipe snot from my nose. Run my fingers through damp hair.

I climb back into bed, but I can't sleep; Bob is still rattling around, and my throat is dry, breathing is difficult. I turn my phone on, gripping the cool object tight in my clammy hand. There are far too few hours between now and needing to be up for work. I sniff. Maybe not. A sick day wouldn't go amiss.

I scroll through Twitter, LinkedIn, Instagram. I try to watch TV, but nothing holds my attention. With my phone in my hand and nothing to distract me, I start typing 'Tala Garcia' into Instagram's search box. I pause before clicking on her profile. For my own sanity, I've not been keeping up with the investigations into Liam and Daniel's deaths. The investigations had appeared to die down, and I managed to wean myself off checking for updates.

I move my thumb closer, and then further away. I click onto her profile, thumb shaking, a knot in my stomach. I simultaneously want and don't want to see what's been happening. There are more images of Liam, of course, almost all with the words HELP US GET JUSTICE transposed over the top. There are a couple of images of Tala, too, seemingly attempting to get on with her life – at a restaurant, in a rowing boat, at an art gallery.

There's something not right about the art gallery photo. The quality is poor. The angle is funny. I click onto the photo, and I realise what the weirdest thing about the photo is. Because it's not Tala. No. The girl in the photo is *me*.

The picture is a CCTV still of Liam and me at the Tate Modern. We're staring at an oil painting of a long-necked woman, I distinctly remember Liam saying was 'wack'. Half of my face is concealed, but I recognise my white blouse, currently in a heap on my bedroom floor, and I recognise my fringe, damp from the snow outside. I recognise the expression on my face, too: disappointment. I'm staring at Liam, and there's real malice in my countenance.

There's a caption in the top right-hand corner of the photo: *Request for Information.* Tala has added a caption too, of course.

> PLEASE READ – NEW INFO. Liam had been dating the girl in this photo in the weeks before his death. I think she might know something. She MUST know something. PLEASE SHARE AND HELP ME FIND THIS GIRL! The police won't look into it but I know she must be linked.

I don't know anything. I don't . . . I don't know anything. I don't. I don't. I don't. There are comments under the photo, and I move so fast to click on them that my sweaty thumb slips. I tap-tap-tap again, until the comments are revealed.

> OMG, you think she had something to do with his murder?

> Tala, ur so strong, sending love and prayers and so much love, love Aimee

That bitch looks like the murdering type for sure

I'm sure I've seen her

Yah, I recognise her

100% she looks like a murderer

#FINDTHISWOMAN

I almost throw up, dry heaving over the side of my bed. My throat burns. This can't be real. This can't be happening. I need to . . . To get my head back below the parapet, to bury it in the sand and, or to hide, to get away, out of London or just hide, hide, pretend this isn't happening. It's not happening, it's not.

My eyes scan over the rest of the comments. One of them catches my attention, as it is notably less hysterical than the others:

Check out my page

The username of the commenter is @justiceforDanielBrown. I know what I'm going to see before I click the link, but that doesn't dull the feeling of horror that overcomes me when I'm faced with the profile. It claims to be seeking the culprit behind his death, and showcases tens of pictures of Daniel. But there are also at least two or three pictures of *me*. They're similar to the picture used on the poster: me wandering around London with that bright, awful bouquet of flowers. The pictures are slightly blurry, thank God – as though someone took them from a distance and then zoomed in.

But it's the captions on the photos of me that make me want to scream:

Flowers Daniel gave to his girlfriend just before his death. Despite being his girlfriend, the woman in the pictures hasn't approached the police or his family. Suspicious? Almost certainly.

Fuck it, I don't just want to scream, I *do* scream, stuffing my pillow into my mouth and shrieking.

I turn my phone off and push it under my bed. Pull the duvet over my face, press hard against my eyes with my fists, until all I can see is black.

CHAPTER TWENTY

Monday 7th November

Over the next few days I barely sleep, which means I seldom forget. The police catch up with the internet sleuths, of course. And reality catches up with me. No more avoiding what's happened – no matter how much I want to. On Saturday afternoon, I'm interviewed by Inspector Grantham and DC Powell – the two police officers who visited the office in connection with Daniel's death. They tell me what I already know: that Liam and Daniel are dead. But they tell me something I don't know, too: that Jam, Seb and Scarlet have disappeared. Numbness. Terror. Shock. Confusion. Guilt. These emotions wash over me. And lies too, lies pour out of me. I'm not truthful about the days on which I last saw the missing. I tell the police I had no clue about the deaths of Daniel and Liam. Lies. So many lies. Lies that felt like the only way of saving my own skin.

The police interview becomes all I can think about. Over the weekend (between forcing down Lemsip and coughing into tissues) I analyse the answers I gave to DC Powell and Inspector Grantham meticulously, certain I slipped up somewhere, certain an expression I pulled was wrong, or that I answered in a guilty tone of voice. Whatever the fuck that might sound like.

Jam's disappearance takes a while to hit me. The reality of it takes a day to sink into my cells, to saturate my organs, until it feels like my heart and stomach are polluted – shrivelled and blackened by the news. Jam. My friend, Jam. Missing. The thought of not seeing his mischievous grin again makes my heart thump quicker. He was able to mock and reassure me in the same breath, and I suddenly realise how gutted I'd be to lose a presence so simultaneously cutting and comforting. He'll be found. Surely he'll be found.

By Monday, my cold has all but disappeared, the only remnant being the flaky skin around my nostrils. I've gone from being runny and leaky to dry and puffy. I could probably get away with calling in sick again, but I decide to head into work; Sunday was spent googling police interview procedures and the cost of bail. The police will probably seize my phone at some point and all my research will be completely damning.

So I head to the office – not so much from ambition, but as a distraction, to avoid doing anything further which might raise police suspicions.

Saz tries to hug me as soon as I'm out of the lift. I push her off me, extracting myself from her curls, which were halfway up my nostrils.

"We'll talk about it at lunch," I tell her, already regretting the fact I called her after the interview.

She presses a plastic water bottle into my hand. The liquid in it has a pale-yellow hue, quite obviously white wine.

"Defo gotta keep yourself hydrated, Jen."

An uncomfortable half-bark of laughter escapes my lips. It's as though she's just found out I've got a terminal illness, and she's being aggressively nice. I should find it sweet, but I'm more uncomfortable than ever.

Still, I sip throughout the morning. Half a litre of wine down by midday on a Monday, holy shit, I am becoming my mother. Speaking of, she keeps calling me. My call attempt on Saturday night evidently worried her; she knows something's up. I'll reply when neither of us is drunk. Fuck knows when that might be.

Desperate to keep busy, I throw myself into tasks: answering emails, chaperoning clients, booking meeting rooms, creating guest passes. But what I discovered in the police interview keeps coming back into my brain. All of it. The twisted fates of Liam and Daniel and Jam and Seb and Scarlet. Liam and Daniel and Jam and Seb and . . .

Saz is only able to hold her tongue for so long; within the hour she's hissing about Jam, dabbing the damp corners of her eyes and sending him voice notes I fear will go unanswered forever. But I can't talk about Jam right now. I feel horribly guilty that I've been so wrapped up in myself I didn't even realise he was missing. That I was actually pissed off about not hearing from him, rather than worried. If I talk about any of this, I fear I'll have a breakdown, right here in the middle of the office.

So I ask Saz to tell me about her latest holiday plans. She's reluctant to switch topics, but soon enough she's into it, rabbiting on about Malta, or maybe Marbella, or perhaps Malaga. A lottery win, which would allow her to see Australia. Two weeks in California to coincide with Coachella. See celebrities. Flight prices, potential costs. The hostels she's googled. Who she'd go with. Which country has the fittest boys. I think of Liam and Daniel and Jam and—

"Wanna go?" she asks.

"To Marbella?"

"I wish. Still waiting on that lottery win. But lunch?"

"Oh, yeah. Sure."

I empty the last drops of wine onto my tongue and pull my coat on.

We leave the lime green and grey of OnIt Insurance for the muted, natural colours of The Folly, a restaurant thirty seconds down the road. We nab our favourite spot, by the window, two comfy high-backed chairs and a little round table half-hidden by flowers and an ivy trellis.

"I feel sick, Jen. I've felt sick since you called me on Saturday. I don't know what to say. I don't know where to begin," Saz says as she sits down.

"Yep, the feeling's mutual."

"Honestly, just OMG. Just what the fuck?"

"Yep."

"You've got a cursed crotch. A voodoo vagina."

"This isn't a fucking joke, Saz."

I try to force a menu under her nose, but she's too busy scrolling through her phone.

"OMG – Liam's got a sister called Tala and she's been sharing pictures of him asking for help for like, ever," she tells me after a minute of screen staring.

"Oh. Really?" I ask, pretending that I haven't spent many hours agonising over the pictures on Tala's account, sick with the sadness I know she must be feeling.

"Yeah! Look!" Saz tries to shove her phone in my face, but I bat it away.

"I'm good."

"How can you not be interested, seriously . . ."

After a couple more minutes of scrolling, Saz finally puts her phone down and picks up a menu. She starts tapping it against the table whilst staring into the distance.

"I'm sorry, I know I'm being a bit over the top," Saz says. "It's just the shock of it all. Like, I guessed there was something going on between you and Jam, despite me telling you not to go there . . ." She pauses to roll her eyes at me. "But I didn't know you were an actual item. And the thought of not seeing him again . . . I've been crying all weekend."

"Jam and I were never an item," I say.

"Thought that the police said you were?"

I'm about to reply when I'm interrupted by a waitress, who asks to take our order. Saz seems to request near every variety of cheese and potato going: a Camembert, cheese garlic bread, two portions of chips and halloumi fries.

"Christ, Saz, I think that's enough."

"Okay, just that and two glasses of rosé. Large."

The waitress nods, collects our menus and walks away quickly, her heels click-clacking off the wooden floor. Saz turns her attention back to me.

"You must know something. You must be able to take a guess as to what's going on? Any links between the dates?"

"Nope." I shake my head and shrug my coat off my shoulders. "Honestly, I don't know anything. I mean, are they even linked? I wasn't really romantically involved with any of them. And besides – Liam and Daniel are both dead and have been for a while. Jam, Seb and Scarlet are just missing." Although I doubt "just missing" is any comfort to their families.

"True. Although Daniel and Liam were both missing for a bit before they were found dead."

"Nice, Saz," I snap. Put like that, it seems only a matter of time before Jam, Seb and Scarlet's bodies are washed up on the banks of the Thames. It sounds selfish, but I'm not sure I can go through reading about that three more times. I'm not sure Mum can.

"Maybe you actually aren't involved," says Saz, starting a line of conversation I much prefer. "Maybe they were all into drugs and had the same dealer? And all got on the wrong side of him, somehow?"

"I don't know, that seems far-fetched."

"Everything about this situation is far-fetched!"

No answers are going to come from this lunch, that's the only certainty. I shift my attention to the floor-length window in front of us, to the people rushing past with their bags of shopping, and the smokers braving the cold for their nicotine hit.

"Or maybe you've got an admirer?" says Saz. "Someone who's obsessed with you and taking out the competition?"

I drag my attention back to her just as our drinks arrive. We both take a generous, slightly jittery gulp.

"Much as I like your theories, I'm not convinced. I could do with figuring it out though, couldn't I?" I say, putting down my glass. "Before the police decide I'm guilty."

"Or the murderer comes for you, too."

"Fuck me, Saz, that's not helpful," I snap. I glance around. The hairs on the back of my neck rise. Even when I read about Liam and Daniel's deaths, I never truly thought that the same fate could await me. The posters and social media campaigns made me fear for my reputation, not so much my life. But with all five of my so-called flings missing or dead . . . that seems different. More than just coincidence. Almost as though there's a target on my back. I shiver. Jesus, the last thing I need is to go around worrying that someone is going to grab me at any given point.

"Nah, you'll be alright," Saz concedes. "Probably worst-case scenario is just jail."

"Just jail. Perfect."

I take another sip and scowl out the window. My eyes burn deep into a smoker who's wearing a startlingly orange jacket. My attention only returns to the restaurant once our food arrives. I dip a halloumi fry into the Camembert, and I'm just reaching for a second when my phone rings. I take it out of my bag, expecting to see Mum's name flash up. It's not her. It's a number I don't recognise.

"I'd better take this," I tell Saz. Her mouth is bursting with fries, so she just nods. I stand and walk away, out of the restaurant and towards the smokers gathered by the window. I stop next to the woman in the hideous orange jacket and answer my phone.

"Hello?"

"Hello, is this Jennifer Beeny?" asks an unfamiliar male voice.

"It is."

"Hello, Jennifer, I'm PC Wood."

Another policeman. Shit, this can't be good. A small, nervous whine escapes me.

"Are you the daughter of Leah Beeny?" PC Wood continues.

Oh my God. Oh my God, oh my God, oh my God. For the first time, I understand what people mean when they say their hearts are in their throats. But it's more than this, it seems to become a thrusting, scrambled organ – squeezing, dropping to the pit of my stomach and finding its way into my mouth all at the same time. My chest squeezes tighter and tighter and I can't breathe. Can't breathe at all. My hands are shaking so the phone knocks against my ear. My knees buckle, and I slide down the window.

"Jennifer? Are you the daughter of Leah Beeny?"

"Mmm. Yes."

A pause. A pause in which I feel bile rise in my throat.

"Are you in London, Jennifer? Your mum's been arrested."

I come to a stop on the concrete. She's not dead. She hasn't drowned in a pool of her own vomit. It's still not great news, though.

I press my phone harder against my ear and straighten up.

"I'm in London, yeah. Where's my mum?" I ask PC Wood.

"We've got her here in Holborn Police Station. You need to come collect her."

Holborn? How the hell did she get all the way to Holborn? She should be at home, 250 miles away. I glance back inside at

Saz. She's finished one portion of the fries and eaten most of the Camembert.

"Yeah, I'll be right there," I say. "Why did you arrest her?"

"She was spotted intoxicated outside King's Cross, wandering into the road and shouting. We brought her in to sober up, we just need a guardian to take her home safely."

"Okay. Yeah, I can do that," I say. I'm disappointed but not surprised – that classic line used by mothers to scold their children. Except in my circumstances, it's the wrong way around.

"Perfect. Ask for me when you arrive," says PC Wood.

"Okay, thanks for looking after her."

I hang up and shake my head. Then I return to The Folly and Saz, tell her I haven't recovered from my cold and that I need to go home. Attempting to look as frail as possible, I grab a handful of lukewarm halloumi fries and head for the nearest tube station.

When I meet Mum half an hour later, she won't look at me. She keeps her head bowed, her knotted grey hair covering most of her face. She keeps her hands busy, fiddling with her pendant necklace. The smile I used to love so much has been replaced by a sad little grimace. "Turn that frown upside down," is what I want to say to her. It's not that simple. I hug her, squishing her bony shoulders between my arms. She smells of wine and citrus, as if she's tried to hide the stench of her addiction by dousing herself in bathroom spray. Eventually she acknowledges my presence, laying her head against my chest.

"Let's get out of here," I say. After Saturday afternoon with Inspector Grantham and DC Powell, I have no desire to spend any more time in police stations. I feel her head nod.

I sign paperwork and apologise to the officers, and eventually we're free to leave. I want to sit by the Thames with her, but it's too far away, so we occupy a bench in St George's Gardens and pull our coats tight. Her head remains bowed, but her right hand travels onto the brown wool of my coat.

"He never used to take that off," she says to our laps.

"I know," I say. "I like to think it still smells of him."

"It does. Burnt toast and cigars."

I snuggle deeper into the wool. I look at the trees in the gardens and watch as the last of their leaves fall to the ground, leaving skeleton branches behind.

"Two years next week. Maybe we should talk about him, Jen."

I stare straight ahead, eyes burning into the withered trees. Falling leaves, frost on the ground, Christmas lights being hung up – all enough of a reminder without having to have some kind of official, unhelpful conversation with Mum. We don't talk about him. And that's the best thing for both of us. Talking about him just ends up in an argument. Case in point: my spur-of-the-moment relocation. I pull a clump of wool from my coat.

"Why are you in London?" I eventually ask.

"You rang me on . . . on Saturday . . . Saturday night. And I missed it and so I kept trying . . . I tried to call you back and you wouldn't answer, and I got sc—I got scared. So I haven't been eating and had one drink this morning, and decided to come try find you. And one more drink on the train."

This is a lie. Partly a lie. Two drinks today total is bullshit. Unless by one drink she means one bottle. Even then, I suspect it may have been more.

I don't say this to her. I just say, "I'm sorry."

"What happened on Saturday?"

Ahh, Saturday. Where to begin? How much to tell her? I stare hard at the bony, lifeless trees. I swallow, and opt for the truth.

"Five people have either died or disappeared in the past seven months. I was sort of romantically involved with all of them. The police wanted to see if I knew anything."

"Oh, Jen," Mum says, sounding shocked and horrified. Her head snaps up and she looks at me for the first time all day. "You're not a hooker, are you?"

"No! Oh my God, no! I couldn't even get most of them to sleep with me for free, never mind at a price!"

Mum nods. "Do the police know what's going on?"

"No. The timings of the disappearances are random. A couple knew each other, but most of them didn't. All I can think is they were involved in a gang I don't know about. Or they had some kind of pact. Or maybe I scared them out of London, maybe Seb, Jam and Scarlet have run away, whilst Liam and Daniel died trying."

A glance at Mum, to see if she recognises Daniel's name – she saw the news story, after all. But her expression doesn't change, and I feel grateful that she was probably too drunk to remember. And then I feel guilty for feeling grateful about this, of course. I sniffle, the ghost of my cold still with me.

"Well," Mum says, squeezing my hand. "You and I both know that the police aren't always the best people for the job. Have you looked into it?"

"Looked into it? Have I looked into it? This isn't like trying to figure out who finished off the biscuits – it's not something just anyone can look into," I laugh. But Mum is serious and stays silent, so I continue talking, if only to give her what she wants. "I mean, I guess I know some things."

I pause and rub my thumb over her knuckle. I know roughly when each person disappeared. And I know that I am uncomfortably closely linked to each occasion. Both Jam and Seb more or less went missing after coming back to mine, for God's sake. If I had a probability tree, I'm sure the odds of this happening and me being innocent would be tiny. I sigh, and feel Mum's eyes searching my face, as if she's trying to understand what I'm thinking. I squeeze her hand harder. She's too frail, I can feel the bones of her hand in mine. I get nervous when I hold Mum too hard.

Eventually, her hand wriggles out from beneath mine, and she strokes the silver pendant around her neck, the pendant in which a picture of Dad lives. She closes her eyes, as though she's thinking hard. I wait for her next sentence with bated breath.

"Shall we get something to eat?"

I laugh and exhale. Not the words I was expecting to slip from her lips. Good words, regardless.

"Yep."

We eat together at a cheap Chinese opposite King's Cross. I don't even object when she orders wine with her food. Tipsy Mum is more agreeable, and I manage to persuade her to get a train back up north. I come to the platform with her.

"You've got a good brain, Jen, use it," she says.

I give her a hug and an affectionate eyeroll. "Sure."

"I mean it. Without you, we might never have found your dad."

CHAPTER TWENTY-ONE

Monday 7th November

I don't go straight home. No. Instead I crouch down against the station wall and scribble into my notepad. Nothing helpful, of course: just spirals and crosses. I press so hard I almost rip the paper. I stick my tongue between my teeth and pull another clump of wool from my coat.

Mum has far too much faith in me. Unsurprisingly, no matter how hard I will myself to come up with some magical solution, it doesn't happen. The true crime podcasts I listen to on my commute have failed to turn me into a master detective. Inconvenient. I head into the Underground, flopping down against a grimy Piccadilly Line seat. I rest my chin between my hands, dreaming of my bed, getting lost in a book and pretending none of this is happening for a few precious hours.

I watch the stations as we pass through them: Holborn, Covent Garden, Green Park. I take my phone out and, from habit more than anything, click onto Instagram. Connection down here comes and goes with the platforms, but I can see that I have a message – from an old school friend I haven't spoken to in years. One of the ones who disappeared around the time Dad died. Is she finally checking up on me? Does she think enough time has passed, that I might have finished grieving, that 'fun' Jen might have returned? Surprised, I click into it:

Is this true lol?

She's sent me a picture from a page called @findScarletSmith. It's me. It's me again. My WhatsApp profile picture – just a boring old selfie, and not even one of my best. The caption underneath reads as follows:

> Scarlet dated this girl back in July. It didn't work out, but the girl WOULD NOT let it go. Scarlet was getting super freaked out, saying she felt like she was being stalked. And then, guess what? Scarlet goes missing. I'm her bestie and I'm worried sick. Someone must know this girl – tag her so I can tell the police and get her locked up PLS xx

"Bullshit."

The photograph has almost a *thousand* likes. The page has almost *ten thousand* followers. The police must have released the news of Scarlet's disappearance. And it's causing more of a splash than Daniel's or Liam's ever did. My phone slips between my fingers, clattering onto the dirty floor. I'm too panic-stricken to reach for it immediately.

"This is fucking ridiculous!" I snap. Commuters tut and glare at me over their newspapers, but I don't care. Someone is out to get me. Some weirdo troll has launched a fucking lying, stalking campaign of hate against me. Who does that? Who has so little going on in their life that they would actually bother? It's bullshit. Absolute bullshit. My life is spiralling, it's not in my control anymore and I, I start to hyperventilate, breathing becomes difficult, and I—

I pick my phone up, swearing, fingers slipping in their haste to do too many things at once: report the picture, block the profile, delete my account. The tube lurches to a stop and my phone once again slips from my fingers. Feeling dizzy, I claw it from the ground once more. And then I look up. We're at Gloucester Road.

Fuck it. Now isn't the time to curl up with a book and try to forget the shitshow happening around me. Now's the time to act, to figure this all out and keep myself out of jail. I dash off the tube just as the doors are shutting, clattering onto the platform, three stops earlier than I'm supposed to get off.

Seb's flat on King's Road isn't far from here. I'm not sure what I'm hoping to achieve, but I can't sit back and do nothing. Not now the walls feel like they're closing in.

I dash down Chelsea's pretty backstreets, between gorgeous white terraced houses and gated gardens. Orange leaves crunch beneath my feet, and the smell of dinner preparations drift up my nose. An alternate reality. One that I'm reluctant to leave.

Seb lives in the flat above a cocktail bar, and it takes me a while to find it – weaving between pedestrians, feet pounding from the pavement, growing more and more breathless. But eventually I do, and I stand staring at the innocuous blue front door he shares with the two or three other flats in this building.

What was I expecting? Signs of a forced entry? A note signed by the mastermind behind all of this? A trail of blood leading to Seb's body? This is London, for God's sake; any clues will be long gone, washed away in the tide of people who pass up and down this street day in, day out.

Still, I walk towards his front door. One step, two steps, closer and closer without having any kind of plan.

There are three buzzers next to the blue door: one buzzer for L. Zhang on the first floor, one buzzer for S. Matthews on the second floor, and a final buzzer for N. Jones on the third floor. I glance up at the windows above me – out of reach and all the more tantalising because of this.

I should go home. What are the chances of me finding something to clear my name here? What are the chances of me even getting in?

CLACK.

The blue door opens. Out steps a middle-aged woman, bundled up in coats and scarves, clutching two wriggling Chihuahuas and speaking into a mobile, which is precariously balanced between her scarf and ear.

"Down, Peanut, shhh, no – sorry, Kai, that was the dog. Peanut, shush. Shush. You going in?"

It takes a second to realise that the question is aimed at me.

"Uhm. Uh, yeah," I say.

The woman nods, hardly glancing at me, and holds the door open with her shoe. I grab the handle, mutter my thanks and watch as she continues on her way, still shushing the dogs and chattering into her mobile.

I step inside and pull the door closed behind me. The hallway is cramped, but not unpleasant. The giddy rush that comes from doing something ill-advised spurs me onwards. I stride up a flight of stairs and along the corridor, coming to a stop outside of Seb's door. I'd misremembered the door to his flat as being sexy: upholstered in leather, or entirely metal or something, but it's not, of course. It's just a plain old, slightly chipped, wooden door. A wooden door which looks remarkably difficult to open.

My first port of call is his doormat. I lift it up but, alas, there's no hidden key. So I take a hair-slide from my bun and attempt to wedge it into the keyhole. Despite furious wiggling, the hair-slide does sweet fuck all to open the door. Final option: my debit card.

I open my purse, pull the shiny piece of plastic out, and crouch down. I attempt to wedge it between the door and the doorframe, sweeping it up and down, feeling steadily more unhinged as seconds tick by.

Footsteps, on the stairs leading up to this floor. I freeze. Seb? Is *Seb* returning to his flat? Surely not, and yet . . . what if, what if disappeared doesn't mean gone? What if Seb's still here – a master puppeteer, lurking in the shadows somewhere and engineering all the disappearances himself? No, a crazy thought. It'll be a neighbour or a relative or, or . . . someone who's going to be livid when they find me attempting to break in. The debit card nearly slips from my fingers.

"What the . . . ?" says a voice from behind me.

There's no time for me to run. There's nowhere for me to hide. My frozen limbs seem to melt, and I turn around to find DC Powell staring at me from the other end of the corridor. She's wearing jeans and a navy jacket, her braids cascading over her shoulders. I hold my hands up, useless debit card still pincered between my thumb and index finger.

"Jennifer Beeny?"

Briefly, I think about lying. Madness.

"Yep."

"You can put your hands down, this isn't America."

I lower my shaking arms.

"This looks really bad, doesn't it?" I say.

"Yes."

"Are you going to arrest me?"

"Probably not."

Relief, oh God, the relief. I stutter out an answer, too shocked by her response to be articulate. "Oh. Oh right, nice. Great. What are you doing here?"

"My job. What are *you* doing here?"

I cringe. I look at her chin and then the bridge of her nose. As ever, I'm tempted to lie. But there's something reassuring about DC Powell's calm demeanour, which prompts me to say, "I'm trying to solve this, I guess. Trying to clear my name."

She looks at me appraisingly. "I get you. But you should leave that up to the police."

I nod. She can't be much older than me, but I feel as though I've been scolded by someone three decades my senior. DC Powell continues, after I've nodded my head eight or nine times, "And please don't tell me you were trying to break in with a debit card?"

"Um, yeah. It's really misleading that films make it seem like an option."

She rolls her eyes. "You'd have needed a screwdriver, at least. Shall we get out of here? There's a café down the road."

"Oh. Didn't expect you to say that."

"Don't misinterpret the invite, I need to talk to you, make sure you drop your private detective work before a more sceptical police officer finds you and you're really up the shitter."

"Okay."

"And you can pay – as a thanks for me not arresting you."

A nervous laugh escapes my lips. We head downstairs and out of the apartment building, back onto the busy street. A two-minute walk takes us to a cosy café, snug and inviting in comparison to the frosty night.

DC Powell opens the door for me. "I'll have a mint tea. And a cake."

"What kind of cake?"

"Surprise me."

I get her the most surprising cake on offer: a lumpy green and brown Aero extravaganza thing. I take this and two cups of tea to the table in the corner DC Powell has settled herself into. It's odd, being in this kind of setting with the woman who interviewed me two days ago. The woman I watched stride around the office, investigating Daniel's murder a couple of months ago. It's like meeting a celebrity. I blush and look away from her dark, intense eyes. I take a drink of my tea. Boiling.

I glance back up and she's still looking at me, a chunk of cake hovering three inches from her lips.

"Do you think I did it?" I ask.

She eats before answering, chewing thoughtfully, never shifting her gaze from me.

"No," she answers, running her tongue over her lips. "No, I don't."

"Oh. Good. Cos, I didn't." I try to twist my expression into something that screams *INNOCENT*. Wide eyes. Lips set in a frown. I sniff.

"You'd say that regardless," DC Powell replies. "No. You went on unsuccessful dates with them all so you have some motive – sure."

I find myself nodding. Catch myself. Start shaking my head. Try sipping my tea again but recoil; it's still fucking boiling.

"But for just one girl to take advantage of all those men? I don't buy it."

I open my mouth. There are ways of ending people's lives, making them disappear, if you really want to. Slipping something into their drink. Catching them by surprise.

"What do you think happened?" I ask.

"Honestly? Not a clue. I didn't even think they were linked, until we started receiving a variety of anonymous tip-offs, telling us to check the security footage of certain places at certain times."

"Anonymous tip-offs from *who*?" I demand.

"*Anonymous* tip-offs from *anonymous* people," DC Powell says, and I'm once again treated to an eyeroll. "Anyway, as discussed in your interview, we found security footage of you on a date with each of them. The one person linking a string of deaths and disappearances across the city. You can see why we brought you in for questioning, I hope."

"Because of some anonymous shit-stirrers," I mutter. I think about telling DC Powell that I'm being framed, but she's looking at me with such scepticism that I'm certain that, like every police officer before, she won't believe me.

"Yes," she continues. "But it might just be coincidence. You might just be unlucky."

"Typical me."

She slips more cake between her lips and pushes one of her braids back.

"I've been following the deaths and disappearances for a number of months," she says. "And the only other similarity between the five people – besides you, of course – is that they rubbed people up the wrong way. Liam was selfish, he could be nasty and bitter. Had a bit of a habit of trying to get revenge on anyone who pissed him off. Not everyone believed that, of course – his family still think he's a saint. But enough people disliked him. Daniel had a reputation as a sleaze, as getting a little too up close and personal on occasion. Pushy. Intense. Maybe even forceful."

"And Jam?" I ask. I force tea down my throat.

"Jamal has a sense of humour which some people find offensive, plus he's a bit of a ladies' man – always seems to keep a couple of women hanging around, hoping he'll commit. Seb is similar: leaves a trail of heartbroken women in his wake. He also has a reputation for being ruthless at work. And Scarlet has work-related issues too: she caused a real scene when she was fired last year. But take all this with a pinch of salt. It's just what we've gleaned from the people who knew them."

"Mmm." I keep my expression passive. Take another sip of tea. I must look worried because DC Powell lays her hand atop mine. It's soft. Her nails are chipped.

"Regardless, you need to let us do our job. Stay out of this. For your own sake."

She squeezes my hand. She keeps it there for the remainder of the time we spend in the café, whilst she eats her cake and we each drink our teas. We leave when the owner closes, back out into the night. It's hailing, so DC Powell gives me a lift home, over Putney Bridge and along Lower Richmond Road. She pulls over in the bus stop opposite Bob's flat, and I climb out.

"Bye, DC Powell," I say before I close the door. "And thanks for not arresting me."

"It's Aayla," she says, with a small smile. "Try stay out of trouble. But if you *do* get into any . . ." She takes out a pen and writes down her number on a scrap of paper, which she hands to me.

"Thanks."

"Hopefully I won't see you around, Beeny," she says, shooting me another, slightly wider smile. "Oh, and good choice of cake."

And with that, she pulls away. I watch her drive out of sight and then I look up. Bob's face is at the kitchen window. He looks from the road to me, and then back to the road. And then he disappears, behind the net curtain.

CHAPTER TWENTY-TWO

Tuesday 8th November

Saz spends most of the working day stalking my so-called exes. She lets me deal with clients and paperwork whilst she keeps her eyes fixed on her computer screen. She finds Facebook pages, Jamal Shaw Missing, Justice for Liam Garcia, and hashtags #SebastianMatthewsHELP, #haveyouseenScarletSmith. I open my mouth and shake my head whenever Saz tells me about them, pretending I haven't already looked at each dozens of times.

"Adult disappearances don't get the same kind of attention kid disappearances do," she says, whilst looking at a picture of Jam's face.

"I don't know. Scarlet seems to be getting plenty of attention."

"Yeah, I suppose her pages have a few more likes than the men's. But still not even close to a million. Still not national news."

My stomach lurches at the thought that *a million* people might end up seeing the lies being spread about me.

Saz continues, "If there's nothing suspicious, people just think adults have upped sticks and left. Quit their job or moved house, or fallen out with everyone, or gone to live in the wild."

"Yeah," I say, "I can't see any of them doing that, though. Especially Jam."

"Oh defo. Jam wouldn't last a day off-grid. And besides, there *is* something suspicious: the fact that Jam, Seb and Scarlet are linked to Liam and Daniel, and they didn't exactly return safe and healthy."

"*Possibly* linked. The five people are *possibly* linked," I say.

Saz doesn't agree with me. I tap my pen against my notepad. I've been drawing spirals and stickmen and little crosses. I squeeze the pen hard between my fingers.

"I tried to break into Seb's flat last night," I eventually say.

Saz turns away from her computer in slow motion, her eyes wide.

"Are you mad?" She raises her eyebrows – dramatic as always.

"Yeah, I dunno. I got freaked out, thinking I was destined for jail, and I was sort of passing his flat and felt like I had to do something. Mental, I know."

"Properly mental. Wow, didn't know you had it in you. Did Detective Inspector Jen manage to find anything the police had overlooked?" Saz asks.

"No. I didn't even make it past the communal corridor. And besides, I don't know what I was looking for. But I can't sit around and wait until the police decide I'm guilty."

"If you're not guilty they won't come to that conclusion."

"No, I just . . ." I don't say anything more. I close my notepad and stuff it back into my bag.

I'm just about to leave the office when a teenager clatters out of the stairwell. At first, I'm too shocked to react; no one climbs the stairs, no one under twenty ever sets foot in here, and there's never so much . . . energy. She seems to bounce across the floor, looking around and shouting, her long dark hair flipping back and forth.

Saz has already gone home, so I'm alone in the reception area with her. I run back to the desk in order to call security, and that's when I feel something crack on the side of my neck. Slime drips underneath my collar and I bat at it, finding egg nestled in my hood. I've barely scooped the egg out when another hits my jacket, smashing and smearing yolk across the brown fluff.

"Hey!" I spin around to face the girl, who has come to a standstill opposite the lifts. She responds with a jeer, and I'm met with two more eggs, which splatter onto the front of my jacket, smashing and smearing yolk across the brown fluff.

"Murderer! You're a fucking bitch!"

She pauses to take another egg from her bag, before shouting, "Confess to killing Liam!"

Oh my God. I glance at the glass doors to my left, beyond which my co-workers are just starting to pack their things away. A couple of heads turn in my direction, and I want to self-combust.

"Freak!" she yells, and I finally recognise her. It's Tala Garcia, of course. There's so much I want to say to her – that I understand what she's going through, that I wish I could do something to alleviate her pain – but I don't get a chance before she paws away her tears and then yells at me again.

I'm stuck, frozen to the spot, blinking and not really hearing any of her other insults. There's a ringing in my ears, and the edge of my vision blurs. More people join us: security guards, and office workers in suits. There are apologies, security guards telling me that she jumped the barriers, that they should have reacted quicker. Tala is taken away, and there are hands on me – reassuring, I think, asking whether I'm okay, I think. I nod, grab my bag and bail. My ears are still ringing, and I can't see properly: traffic blurs into one bright light, commuters are indistinguishable from one another. All the train destinations merge into one, so I do things on autopilot: onto the tube, off the tube, walk to platform twenty-two, wait and hope I'm getting on the right train. I sit upright and still against the seat, and then I alight twenty minutes later, walk along Rocks Lane and let myself into the flat.

And then, when I'm in my room, I break down. I'm quiet – no snuffles or wails or hysterics – but tears stream down my face and I take off my dad's coat. I mop at the egg with tissues but it's no good, the yolk has dried deep within the fluff. I haven't taken good enough care of it. I've been picking at this coat all year, picking *him* out, and now I've gotten it all covered in egg and even if I wash it the egg might not come out, or more of the fluff might disintegrate or and I, or—

"Jen, you're crying," says Bob from outside my bedroom door. I jump and place the coat down.

"I . . . I'm not."

"You are. Are you okay?"

How the hell does he know? The walls in this flat are thin, but I've been careful to barely make a sound.

"Has someone upset you? Another boy?"

I paw the tears from my face and stand up. I open the door and he's standing close, far too close; I get a high-definition view of his slightly sweaty skin. I take a step back.

"No boys. I'm okay."

He nods. He looks into my room, at my clock, and then he refocuses his gaze on me – or more accurately, the translucent white blouse that covers my chest. For fuck's sake – it didn't work with my dates, but it's lured in my middle-aged landlord.

"I'm good, honestly. Thanks for checking. Bye."

I close the door just as Bob reaches out his arm, inches from touching me.

CHAPTER TWENTY-THREE

Monday 14th November

I'm advised not to return to the office. My manager calls me and tells me that, what with everything going on, it's best I stay home for a little bit. She doesn't define "everything" which infuriates me, for some reason; I want to scream, "WHAT? You mean me being pelted with eggs? Two people I knew dying and three more disappearing? Me being accused of murder every time I look online? The police dragging me in for interviews? What? *What*? WHAT?"

I don't say any of this, of course. I just mumble in agreement. My manager tells me to let her know if I need to talk, and I know she doesn't mean it. She tells me I'll be more comfortable at home. She doesn't have a clue. My London home contains Bob. My northern home contains Mum. Neither are conducive to a comfortable existence.

So I stay in my room, mainly, staring up at the yellow ceiling and rolling between the stable single bed and the wobbly single bed. I've deleted all my social media apps apart from WhatsApp, which is what Saz uses to send me near hourly updates about what she discovers online, despite me specifically asking her not to.

> OMG – Seb's family have put out a million-pound reward for info leading to his safe return! Any news from the police?

Nothing, I reply. I don't know whether their lack of contact is a good or a bad thing.

> Apparently Scarlet had been feeling paranoid for a couple of months leading up to her disappearance. She thought

> someone was obsessed with her and wouldn't take the hint she wasn't interested!

I swallow. Shake my head. Scarlet was deluded; I barely even thought about her after our date. I wasn't close to being obsessed. If anyone was able to get hold of my messages to Seb, though . . .

As the hours tick by, my room starts to feel more and more like a cell. Bob, as ever, is in the kitchen – humming, muttering, cooking and barking out answers to the quiz shows he has on loop. So I head outside to get lunch. The hum of London is a relief – louder than Bob, but less irritating, and thus easier to ignore. I pull my scarf tight around my throat and head north, up Rocks Lane and towards the river, stopping to pick up a cheese toastie on my way. I continue towards the Thames and take a seat at one of the benches looking across it. It's beautiful. And ugly. And deadly, especially on a day like today, a cold day.

I unwrap my toastie and take a bite. Hot melted cheese dribbles down my chin. I sink lower into the bench and watch the few other workers who've ventured outside tuck into their respective lunches.

My phone vibrates in my pocket. Before reaching for it, I finish my toastie, scrunching up the wrapping, wiping my chin and savouring the last cheesy mouthful.

Finally taking out my phone, I stare at the message. And I nearly drop it.

Hands trembling, I fumble. Blink and blink again. Unlock my phone and stare at the screen in disbelief.

The message says:

> I can't stop thinking about you, Jen. Can I take you on an actual date? 7pm tonight at Chiswick Boathouse? How does that throw off the probability tree? 😉

The message is from a man who supposedly disappeared two weeks ago.

Seb.

"Impossible," I whisper.

Time seems to slow as I stare at the message. The words merge into one another. I blink and the words separate, time speeds back up.

I leap up and stride back and forth, along the river path, pacing like a mad woman. My mind races. This is mad. I need to tell someone.

I force myself to a standstill, screenshot the message and send it to Saz. She calls me almost immediately.

"Oh my God, Jen." Her words are mumbled, as if she's chomping down a sandwich. I hear her swallow. "Oh my God."

"Have you read it?" I ask.

"Yeah. Fuck me. This is absolutely mental. Seb? He can't stop thinking about you? Wants to take you on an actual date? What's a probability tree?"

"It's maths, it – it really doesn't matter . . . it can't, it doesn't, I don't underst—I don't." I run my fingers through my fringe. "He's been missing for two weeks. He never even used to text me when he *wasn't* missing."

Saz doesn't reply for five or six seconds. And then she says, "You gonna go?"

"No, no. Don't be mental. I need to tell the police."

"I wouldn't trust the police."

"What do you mean?"

"Just my personal experience. My . . . my . . . someone I know was a victim of revenge porn. And the police didn't give a shit."

"Christ, that's awful. And they really didn't care?"

"Horrific. And no, they didn't. I don't trust them – but that's just me."

Saz's words resonate, for I don't exactly trust the police, either.

"But also," she continues, "Seb has invited you specifically. You've literally been desperate for this all year."

"Yeah – *before* he went missing. I'm not thinking about getting with him, I'm thinking about clearing my name." This is mostly true.

"You have no idea why he's disappeared though – what if he's in trouble and gone into hiding? Half a dozen officers turning up might push him over the edge. You could save him, Jen."

I nod. If he's struggling, I need to help. I let one man down. This is an opportunity to right that wrong.

"I want to, but I can't," I say. "I've been warned to stay out of this. I'm one wrong move from the police charging me for the disappearances."

"But you're going to find him! The literal reverse of making him disappear."

I squeeze my eyes shut and grit my teeth.

"Fuck. Fuck fuck fuck."

I'm scared about being arrested and I'm scared about being murdered in a fucking boathouse but most of all I'm enamoured by the thought of saving Seb, of clearing my name. My stomach churns.

I open my eyes and I send one word to him:

Okay

Meeting Seb is all I can think about for the remainder of the afternoon. Making myself look attractive for a meeting with a missing man is ridiculous but, regardless, I get ready carefully: straightening my hair, dousing myself in perfume and applying fresh makeup. I choose an outfit (*not* the fucking white blouse) and text Saz asking her to call the police if she doesn't hear from me by eight o'clock.

Then I step out, into the night.

Google tells me that the quickest way to the boathouse is on foot, so I march along the path which cuts through Barnes Common. I'm almost entirely surrounded by trees, a rarity in London. It's eerie. I'm alone apart from a dog walker a hundred feet ahead, and the only real light comes from dingy, well-spaced streetlamps. The trees are taking over the path; bare branches brush and scrape against my arms, sending a shiver down my spine.

I twist my head from side to side, convinced that bodies lurk behind the trees. My heart beats that bit faster, my breathing quickens.

It slows only when I see the Thames. I follow the river path round, pausing when I reach Chiswick Bridge. The boathouse is just over the other side. When I cross the bridge, it becomes real. I don't know whether to check my hair or fashion a weapon.

I climb the bridge one shaking step at a time. As I cross, I look down to my right: more bare branches dominate the area. On the shore of the river, enclosed by trees, is the boathouse. The lights are off, but Seb is waiting there, I'm certain. I feel sick, simultaneously worried about meeting him in such a place, and giddy about the possibility of clearing my name.

I descend the bridge and follow the path back towards the river. It's deathly, eerily silent. The river is in front of me, and allotments, a golf course and football fields are behind. I stop walking. The Thames is all but lapping at my feet, and the boathouse is mere metres to my left. And it's . . . incredibly run down. Paint is peeling, the metal door is rusty and one of the windows has been smashed. An odd place for a date. I try to convince myself that Seb is trying to keep a low profile for some reason, but it's still downright creepy.

I take my phone out and check the time: 7.06 p.m. I read Seb's message once more, allow my eyes to linger on the part where he says he can't stop thinking about me. Then I walk towards the rusty metal door. I reach for the handle but pause just before gripping it.

My heart says yes but my head says no. Every sensible fibre in my body is begging me not to step inside. For once I listen, retracting my hand and glancing around.

"Seb?"

Maybe he's late. But he's *missing*; he surely doesn't have anything more pressing to do. The hooting of an owl makes me jump, and I can suddenly taste the cheese toastie once more, as if it's churning in my stomach, readying itself to make a reappearance. Ugh. I cough and compose myself. The last thing I need is for Seb to finally arrive and for me to vomit at his feet.

I shouldn't be so scared. I reach my hand towards the handle once more.

CRACK.

The snapping of a branch, from somewhere behind me.

My stomach flips, with the feeling you get when you're on a rollercoaster and it drops.

"Seb?"

He doesn't answer, but there's someone here, I'm absolutely certain. I can feel eyes on me, making each hair on my body raise. He's here, but he's hiding. Why?

"Oh God, oh God."

Fuck fuck fuckety fuck. All the bad thoughts return: when Jam warned me away from Seb, when Saz suggested that I might disappear too, the fact that Liam was found dead after Seb escorted him out of the bar. I've been stupid. Really fucking stupid.

I stumble backwards, not sure where to go, where someone might be hiding.

"Hey?" I say into the near darkness, my voice abrasively loud.

I swing around and my movements are clumsy, desperate.

"Please don't . . . Please don't hurt me."

I am every horror cliché in the book. I've watched so many films and thought so little of the protagonists, that they're stupid, that I would handle the situation better, and yet here I am, isolated in this dark corner of London and talking to whoever is hiding in the trees.

I should have fashioned that weapon. Taken a kitchen knife. Pepper spray. A rape alarm. Fucking anything.

Branches rustle, and I'm certain I hear breathing. Fuck this. I leg it, hoping blind luck will prevent me from running into the arms of the enemy. I run like I've never run before, through the trees and over the bridge, gasping with fear and exhaustion.

I run all the way back home, and even though I get further and further away from the boathouse, there's a feeling I can't run away from. It's the feeling that someone is watching me.

CHAPTER TWENTY-FOUR

Monday 14th November

I call DC Powell as soon as I get home. She answers on the third ring.

"Hello?"

"Uh, hi, it's Jen Beeny, is that DC Powell?"

"Aayla. Hi, Beeny, I thought I said I hoped *not* to hear from you?"

"Aha, I mean I'd hoped not to have to ring you." My voice shakes as I lose my cool. "But something weird just happened."

"Where are you?"

"At my flat. Bob's flat."

"I'm ten minutes' drive away so I'll drop in."

She hangs up before I get the chance to ask whether this is standard police procedure. Doubtful. But I don't care; I need her.

Bob has finally vacated the kitchen, and I hear no sounds of life from behind his door when I let Aayla in a few minutes later. Still, I lead her to my bedroom, not wanting to risk being disturbed by fishy meal prep or an impromptu quiz show binge. She raises her eyebrows but doesn't say anything.

"Sorry, it's just more private. Don't misinterpret the invite," I say, copying her previous gag and feeling like I'm joking with a teacher. I needn't have worried – Aayla laughs. She's clearly off duty, wearing jeans and a brightly patterned shirt with a silk bandana around her braids. It suits her – she looks younger, more relaxed. She perches on the edge of the stable single bed whilst I position myself on the end of the wobbly single.

"What happened, then?" she asks.

"I think Seb has something to do with it," I say, feeling more confident about this than ever. Seb escorted Liam away on the night he went missing, for Christ's sake. If Seb was innocent, surely he'd have seen the news and sent me a shocked text. Granted, he never texts me, but he'd surely have made an exception for actual murder. Was he hoping to keep it all on the downlow?

Aayla's eyebrows raise again, so high they almost meet her bandana.

"Seb Matthews? *Missing* Seb Matthews?"

"Yeah, except I don't think he's actually missing. I think he's . . . I don't know . . . Maybe hiding, or something."

"Wow. Maybe we should . . ." Her eyes dance around my piles of books and scruffy doodles and haphazard clothes, as though she's fighting the urge to move this conversation to a more professional location.

"I feel more comfortable talking about it here," I say quickly. "Besides, it's a bit late to go to the police station."

"Police stations don't have closing times, Beeny."

"Uh, no, I guess not." I shuffle myself further onto my bed. "But yeah, anyway, it's going to sound daft or crazy or something but . . ." I pause, floundering, suddenly feeling as though I've been hit by a bus. As if two years' worth of stress and turmoil has finally caught up with me, run me over.

Aayla lays her left hand atop my right. "Breathe, Beeny."

But I can't. I open my mouth, gasping at my stale bedroom air, but none of it seems to fill my lungs. The panic I feel is silly; I'm on land, I'm not drowning, and yet I keep gasping, fear building within me. Hot, frustrated tears spill from my eyes.

Aayla pulls me close. The buttons from her shirt dig into my body, but it's comforting: six tiny pinpricks which act as confirmation – someone is here for me. Slowly, I relax each of my muscles, let her hold me. Allow her warm hands to melt away the chill which has hung over me for weeks.

A door slams downstairs.

"Shit," I mumble, straightening up and inching away from Aayla. It's just Bob. Just Bob clattering around below us. His presence shouldn't make me this nervous, and yet I've *always* been nervous around him.

Aayla squeezes my hand and I look down at our palms, pressed together. I'm reminded of that first terrifying police interview. Of watching her eat cake in a Chelsea café. I look up at her eyes, two pools of chocolate.

Her phone rings. She holds my gaze until the fifth peal, at which point she says, "It's work, I should . . ."

She moves away from me but leaves one hand lingering on my waist, a stray affectionate limb. She takes her mobile from her jeans and answers.

"Hello? Oh. Now? Really? Okay . . . Okay wow yeah . . . Okay I'll be right there."

"You have to go?" I ask when she hangs up.

Aayla squeezes my waist. "You're a good guesser. Maybe I was overzealous in my banning you from detective work."

My lips curl themselves into a small, sad smile. "So you're leaving now?"

"Sorry, Beeny. Something urgent has happened. They didn't say what, but urgent enough that I have to haul myself over to the station. I told you – it never closes."

I nod. She stands up and smooths her shirt.

"I should—" I'm interrupted by my own phone, which has just received a message. I pick it up immediately, expecting the message to be from Seb. It's not from Seb. It's from Bob.

No visitors on weekdays

"Shit." I drop my phone. I glance up to see the surprise in Aayla's expression. Surprise and . . . concern, I guess. Who reacts to a message like that? Crazy people. Crazy, deluded people, who lie about what happened to their exes. I'm paranoid, and my thoughts are spiralling, I *know* my thoughts are spiralling, and yet there's nothing I can do to stop them.

"Who messaged you?" she asks.

"Just my landlord."

"Uh-huh." She nods and then moves towards my bedroom door. She leaves too quickly for me to be able to warn her about Bob.

Turns out it doesn't matter; he only exits his room when Aayla has left the flat. I peer over the banister, looking down at him, whilst he moves his gaze upwards. Bob starts speaking before I can.

"Don't have guests in my flat without asking me and writing it in the book. We discussed this."

I splutter, wanting to reply with a million different things. I finally settle on, "Don't text me like that – it's so creepy."

"Don't . . . ? Creepy . . . ? Creepier having strangers over, isn't it?"

"They're not strangers, they're my guests. I live here too. I *thought* I'd be living here alone. I didn't realise you'd be bloody sleeping in the living room." The volume of my response decreases with every word spoken, something which backfires on me because Bob makes his way up the stairs to hear me. I move under my doorway, clutching at the handle, ready to slam the door in his face should he get too close.

He reaches the top of the stairs, panting slightly.

"Jen, it's no good, no people over without my permission. Dangerous for you. Dangerous for me."

I shake my head. What the fuck is this?

"Why are you so obsessed with me?" I ask. It comes out as a meek mumble. I cough, irritated.

"What?"

"You need to leave me alone."

"Don't say that, Jen."

"You're such a creep."

I push past him and clatter down the stairs, pausing by the plastic table. I spin around, run my fingers through my hair and pull the sweaty strands tight.

Bob comes huffing down the stairs after me, and it's as if my resolve has finally crumbled; I can't bear the thought of being in the same space as him for a second longer.

"I need to leave," I say.

"Jen, please."

I shake my head and sprint from the kitchen and along the landing, just missing Bob as he descends the final step. I tear down the flight of stairs which leads to the hallway. I grab my jacket, thanking my own laziness that a tonne of random shit lives permanently in its pockets: three Vaselines and tens of used tissues and three rogue earbuds and my notepad and – most importantly – my purse and keys. I haul it over my shoulders, slip trainers on and let myself out the front door just as Bob reaches the hallway.

"Jen! Stop!"

I don't stop. I slam the door in his face and sprint along the dark road towards the station. I can't hear anything over the din of my feet slamming from the pavement and my own erratic breathing, so I keep glancing back, checking he hasn't followed. I look to my left too, at inky black Barnes Common. I'm certain someone – Seb or Bob or Jam maybe – is going to fling themselves from the trees.

"Shit." I trip over a loose lace and go flying. I drag myself to my feet, wiping mud from my hands. I take a breath, take another look around, and then I continue my journey, pounding up and down the steps which lead into Barnes station.

I catch the last train heading into central. It's deserted but I can't sit, instead I stand with my back against a window, blinking around at the ugly red seats in the carriage. The light keeps flickering. Dull and bright. My hands find a home in my jacket, picking at the dried mud and egg amongst the tufts. My breath catches in my throat every time we pull into a station and the doors open. Putney. Wandsworth Town. Clapham Junction. No one alights at any of the stations, and I remain alone, inside the carriage.

I get off at Queenstown Road, rush over to Battersea Park and catch another train to Victoria station. It's far too late for the trains out of London to be running, but I should be able to get an overnight coach from Victoria. Out of this damn city. I moved here to escape one ghost, and instead I'm haunted by five more. I text Aayla as the train pulls into Victoria:

I'm catching a coach home.

There's a coach leaving for Middlesbrough at quarter to twelve, thank God. I don't even stop to get snacks, I merely buy a ticket and dash to the coach, glancing around the near deserted, dimly lit station as I go. I sit right at the back and duck down behind the seat in front of me, my fingers wrapped around the headrest.

Breathe. I squash the navy material beneath my fingertips hard. Rest my head against the back of the chair. Squeeze my eyes shut.

The coach leaves in eight minutes. I'll be on my way out of this haunted city in a matter of heartbeats.

There's a noise from the front of the coach. At first, I think it's the driver getting on, or another passenger, but it's too loud, too frantic. Someone – no, some *people* – are rushing onto the coach. And I am absolutely trapped. Duck down? Look up? Break a window?

"Jennifer Beeny?"

Not the voice of Bob. Not even Seb's voice. No. It's Inspector Grantham. I poke my head over the seat, only to see the gangly police officer, flanked by three other men. My fingers squeeze the headrest harder. I can't decide whether I should be relieved or more worried, whether breaking the window is a good option, whether they've seen me, whether—

"Jennifer Beeny," Inspector Grantham says again as he strides down the aisle. "You're under arrest. You have the right to remain silent. Should you, however, refuse this right, anything you say can and will be used against you in a court of law."

He says more but my ears are ringing, brain is fuzzy, eyes are foggy. Can't breathe. What? What, what, what, what? I open my mouth to say something, but no sound comes out. I gulp at the air, a fish out of water. What? What, what, what, what, how? What?

I'm pulled to my feet and my hands are cuffed behind my back. I'm dragged from my dream of escape and back to the reality of London, just minutes before the coach was due to depart.

I'm taken to Hammersmith Police Station, a place I hoped I'd never visit again. I don't know what to say, so my emotions seem to leak out instead: sweat from my skin, a tear or two from the corners of my eyes. My nose starts running, despite the fact I got rid of my cold a week ago. I keep saying *what* in my head, over and over, an idiot parrot. Something new has happened for them to arrest me. They've found something new. But what, what, *what*?

Briefly, I think that perhaps Aayla has told them how jittery and scared I am, that they're arresting me for my own good. But it's not possible; they wouldn't be treating me like this if they didn't think *I* had done something wrong.

I'm led along the cold corridor, aggressively bright in contrast to the dark night. I snap my head from side to side, looking for Aayla, but she's nowhere to be found. Instead, Inspector Grantham stalks ahead of me and opens the door to a small, grey room. He slams a photograph onto the table in the centre of my room. And in this photograph, is the answer to my—*what?*

Her roots have grown out, revealing an inch of mousey hair above the ginger. Her cheeks are hollow, as if she's lost weight. There are big purple bags under her eyes. Her eyes. Sad, scared, starving.

My mouth hangs open in total bewilderment.

"Scarlet came back," says Inspector Grantham. "And she's claiming you kidnapped her."

CHAPTER TWENTY-FIVE

Tuesday 15th November

And so it begins. The shit which is fun to watch on television but fucking terrifying to live through. I'm arrested on suspicion of kidnapping Scarlet Smith. They parade me around the police station like a zoo animal. Everything is taken from me. My phone, my purse, my dignity. A chubby man sticks his fingers in my mouth and swabs the inside of my cheek. My photograph is taken in front of a blank white wall. Famous mugshots flood my mind: Ted Bundy, Myra Hindley, even Justin Bieber, for fuck's sake. I join them. This surely isn't real.

"Miss Beeny, do you want a solicitor?" asks someone. Yes? No? Maybe? I shake my head. I don't need a solicitor. Asking for a solicitor will just make me look guilty, won't it? I'm innocent, is that not obvious? How can anyone believe I kidnapped a girl I hardly know?

"Mmm-kay. Do you want us to inform someone about your arrest? A parent or partner, perhaps?"

At this I nod. Mum needs to know. It's what – two in the morning? Three in the morning? Perhaps she'll just be sobering up from her standard evening binge, maybe even sober enough to comprehend what they tell her. I picture her coming to my rescue, a knight in wine-stained armour.

I see Aayla only once, across the corridor as I'm led from one room to another. She's back in nondescript clothing, and any connection I thought I felt to her has vanished with her bright shirt and comfy jeans. She told the police officers where I was. Had I not messaged her, I'd be halfway up the A1 by now. She ducks her head when I look in her direction. At least she feels guilty.

I'm interviewed by Inspector Grantham and an older guy with

a lisp and an air of importance so great he's able to pull it off. I'm filmed, this time. And the room is different: off-white walls, grey laminate flooring, cold plastic chairs and a black plastic table. I'm trapped in a plastic nightmare. And this time, there's a mirror. I blink at my own reflection: pale, clammy, confused. Inspector Grantham's reflection locks eyes with me and I flinch. I drag my gaze from reflection to reality.

"You understand what's happened here, Miss Beeny?" says the older guy. "Scarlet Smith has been missing for almost two weeks. She stumbled into a police station a few hours ago—"

"Dehydrated and near delirious," Inspector Grantham adds, Adam's apple vibrating furiously.

"Yes, dehydrated and delirious. Anyway, she claims she met with you on Barnes Common. That you slipped something in her drink, took her back somewhere – not a house she says, somewhere dark, somewhere near the river – she can't remember right now—"

"Dehydrated and delirious, like I said."

"Yes, thank you, Inspector Grantham, she's in a bit of a state. Anyway, you tied her up, had plans to drown her, she thinks—"

"To . . . to . . . drown her in the river?" It's me who interrupts this time. My head is heavy. With a concentrated effort, I stop it lolling onto the plastic table. I'm dizzy. I'm the one who's drowning. "I'd never push someone in the river."

"No. That may very well be true. After all, we can't lock someone up and throw away the key just because they're accused of a kidnap. Otherwise, every Tom, Dick and Harry would bugger off on a week-long jaunt and return claiming whoever they disliked had held them against their will."

"But we *are* taking Scarlet's claims *very* seriously," adds Inspector Grantham, raising his tufty eyebrows.

Mad. Madness. It's late, so late. I'm underwater, or in a dream or . . . or . . . None of this feels like it's happening to me. If any of this felt as though it was real, was happening to me, it would be terrifying. But I . . . I'm disconnected, drowning, listening to them spin a tale about something fantastical, disgusting, horrifying. My chin nods onto my chest.

"Miss Beeny, when did you last see Scarlet Smith?" asks the older guy, his voice with a little more ice in it. I picture the Thames, freezing over slowly. I snap my head up.

"Uhh, July. I can't remember the date exactly. Sorry. Towards the beginning. I'm sorry I can't remember exactly."

An easy question, yet I feel certain I'm answering wrong. My brain is fuzzy, my tongue lethargic. I keep glancing at the mirror, wondering who is on the other side, how many people are watching me. How many people think I'm lying.

"Where were you on the day she disappeared? On Wednesday 2nd November?"

"At work. I felt a bit under the weather. And then, as I was heading home . . ." I pause, unsure about whether to tell them the next bit. "When I was heading home, I received a message from Scarlet. Asking me to meet her."

"Interesting. You didn't tell us that in your first interview," Inspector Grantham says. His tone – if possible – is even more accusatory. Shit. I'm about to respond, when he continues, "So you lied about the last time you saw her? It wasn't July?"

"No. That was true – I haven't seen her since July. In November, I went to where she asked me to meet, but she didn't show. So I went home and spent the rest of the evening in bed."

"You sure about that?"

"Yes."

"Do you have a witness to verify that?"

"Uh, my landlord Bob. I'm pretty sure he could." Uncertainty seems to drip from my every word. I glance once more at the mirror. Someone grey and sweaty stares back at me. It takes five or six seconds to realise that it's me.

"Okay. And you're certain you didn't see Scarlet that day in November?"

I'm a mouse getting dragged by its tail into a mangle. I squeak out an answer.

"Nope."

The older guy clicks his tongue. Inspector Grantham drums away on his clipboard with his pen.

"Very well," says Inspector Grantham, still tapping his pen. "Can you think of any reason she'd have to claim you kidnapped her?"

"No. Not a clue."

"There's no bad blood between the two of you?"

The tapping of his pen builds to a crescendo.

"Nothing."

He stops tapping his pen. The room is silent, completely silent. I cough. Take another glance at the mirror.

"Alrighty. And you know very well what we discussed last time you were questioned. That, over the course of the past year, the bodies of two men have been found under suspicious circumstances, and two more men have disappeared. And the only connection they all shared is you. You dated them all. Correct?"

"Yes. Kind of."

"And how did these dates end? Badly?" The older guy jumps back into the conversation, hissing his way through the word *dates*.

"Well . . ." I pause. My spine feels sticky. "I didn't really think of all of them as dates. But certainly none of the encounters came to anything, romantically."

"Evidently," he says. "And did you have any ill feelings towards these men? Ever think about hurting them?"

Time seems to stagnate, roll to an uncomfortable stop as I try to ignore all the resentment I did feel for the men. Liam, for being so rude and controlling. Daniel, for pestering me into going on a date with him. Jam, for leaving without explanation. Seb, for stringing me along whilst he had a girlfriend. Opportunity was there, motivation was present. But actually hurting any of them? I would never.

"I did not think about hurting the men," I say. I don't sound innocent enough.

"Very well."

"I don't want to hurt anybody. I didn't hurt anybody. I never would," I say. Better.

"Uh-huh. And you're absolutely certain you didn't see Scarlet on Wednesday 2nd November?"

"I didn't see her."

Inspector Grantham gives me a strained, fake smile. "Just her word against yours, then."

"I honestly, *honestly* didn't see her. She's delusional, you said so yourself."

They ask about me seeing Scarlet on the 2nd of November again and again, slipping it in when I least expect it, when my brain is growing sluggish and my tongue getting tired. But I'm certain. I'm certain I didn't meet her. I'm certain, I'm certain, I'm certain. Until I'm not.

Inspector Grantham closes his notepad and leans back in his chair, running his fingers up and down his long, bumpy neck. My muscles relax ever so slightly, anticipating the end.

It's not.

"Your dad died two years ago," he says.

I tense up – my chest and stomach and throat.

"Mmm."

"He drowned, correct?"

"Yes. I don't see what that has to do with anything." I can't help but snap. This conversation needs shutting down.

"No. Suppose I just thought it was funny, what with what Scarlet said about you planning on drowning her. And the way in which Liam and Daniel's bodies were found. The connection there."

"Yes. Ha-ha. Hilarious," I say, voice stony.

"You could find some sort of satisfaction in that, I might guess – ending other people's lives in the same way that your dad's ended."

"Nothing could ever be satisfying about my dad's death."

Inspector Grantham leans forward, so I get a high-definition view of his stupid, pathetic moustache.

"Your dad died, and your mum turned to alcohol," the lips beneath the stupid moustache say.

"My mum has always had alcohol issues."

"Okay. But they worsened, correct? I checked her records: she never had any public charges before he died, but after? Ten public order offences in the last two years. Your mum turned to alcohol and you turned to—"

"Nigel, that's enough," says the old guy.

Inspector Grantham opens his mouth as though he's going to say more. Three seconds pass, and then he seals his lips shut. My fists are balled up. I release them, noting the nail-shaped indents left behind in my palms.

"It's late, we can wrap this up for now."

I'm led to a cell, stumbling like a zombie, dizzy from fatigue and fury. I force myself to think of Scarlet rather than my dad, the little I remember of her. She was passionate but seemed sane. Our date was arguably the most normal I experienced all year. So I can't fathom why she would have told her friends I was obsessed with her, let alone why she would accuse me of kidnapping her. The only plausible answer is that she's unhinged. Or perhaps she ran away of her own accord and has come back wanting attention. But that doesn't answer why she would accuse *me* of kidnapping her. It also opens up the possibility that, unlike Daniel and Liam, Seb and Jam will turn up alive. Visions of the pair of them returning, malnourished and accusatory, haunt me as I stagger onwards.

I see them everywhere I look in the little rectangular room. Liam's damp remains slumped on the end of my thin blue mattress. Daniel's swollen body lying by the door, water dripping off him and into the cracks in the floor tiles. Jam laughing and shaking his head, saying the word *Jenson* over and over.

Eventually, I lie back on the mattress, willing sleep to take me. I close my eyes and imagine Seb, climbing in beside me. I shiver.

CHAPTER TWENTY-SIX

Tuesday 15th November

I'm allowed a phone call. I daren't risk ringing Mum and wasting it on slurred words and tales about rats. I phone Saz instead. She answers quickly.

"Hello?"

"Hey, it's Jen."

"OMG hi, how did things go with Seb? What did he say? Please tell me you're calling from *his* phone?"

Christ, Seb. Going to look for him feels as though it happened days ago, rather than last night.

"Of course things didn't bloody go well with Seb, he obviously wasn't there," I say, with a little too much venom in my voice. I take a breath. "Sorry. It's good to talk to you."

I mean it. The relief I feel upon hearing Saz shocks me. It's like receiving a warm hug on a cold day.

"It's good to speak to you, too, but what's going on?"

I glance around. I'm in the main custody area. It's larger than my cell or the interview room, but of the same plastic composition: a red plastic floor and black plastic chairs, one of which I'm sitting on. A policeman is standing across the room. I lower my voice to a whisper.

"I'm in Hammersmith Police station. And . . . I probably shouldn't tell you this . . . but Scarlet came back last night."

"Shut up."

"Yeah."

"OMG that's insane. *Scarlet* Scarlet? *Missing* Scarlet?"

"Yeah. And she's accused me of kidnapping her."

"Shut up."

"I wish I could." It's a joke, but my voice wobbles as though I might cry.

Saz laughs once, hollow. She doesn't say anything.

"You still there?" I eventually ask.

Another pause, even longer this time.

"Were you . . . Were you involved?"

"What? No!"

A feeling of claustrophobia, of being trapped with no way out, overcomes me. The off-white walls seem to shift a foot closer. There's an all too familiar acid taste on my tongue. I take a breath and try to compose myself.

"Sorry, Jen, of course I don't think you had anything to do with the disappearances. Just sort of have to ask, y'know?"

I shake my head. I don't know.

"Mmm."

"I mean, of course you didn't have any involvement. It's just . . ."

"Just what?"

"The police seem to think you did it, Jen. And basically all of Twitter."

"The police are wrong. So are the internet crazies," I say. There's a lump in my throat. I swallow, trying to force it down. Acidic.

"Oh, a hundred per cent. I'm super, super certain you're innocent, I mean, I *know* you, but just . . . just things."

"What things?"

"Well, mainly how pissed off you were at them all. Scarlet for ghosting you, especially. And I completely understand you – it's shitty behaviour."

"Please don't tell me you believe the Scarlet crap that's online? The only person I was actually into was Seb, I was too indifferent to the others to be properly pissed off. And Jam is my friend, I'd never, ever have hurt him." The off-white walls seem to edge another foot closer to me. I swallow hard, but the lump remains lodged in my throat.

"You're right. Guess I've just been spending too much time on social media. Kinda spooked, I guess," says Saz. She pauses and then continues, "Let me know if I can do anything, though? Like, I dunno – ring your mum? Order you a Nando's?"

My cheeks are wet. Tears are streaming down my face, and I've only just realised. I let out a watery laugh and wipe them away. "Do Nando's deliver to police stations?"

"Worth a try, isn't it? Have you progressed to Medium or are you still on Lemon and Herb?"

Another weak chuckle. "Still on Lemon and Herb. I think my phone time is up but hey, thanks for answering."

"No problem. Keep me updated," she says, before hanging up.

Wednesday 16th November

"Jennifer, come with me," says Aayla.

She's in my cell early. I drag myself off the bed. My skull is heavy, brain thick and woozy from the crying I did last night. Tears at midnight, 3 a.m. and 5 a.m. The hysterical kind – tears that turn into ugly sobs and hiccups. My eyes feel swollen.

I try to shake some life into my body and follow Aayla out of the cell and into an interview room. I sit in a plastic chair, not sure I can handle another hour of questions. And not sure how to interact with Aayla, either; it's the first time I've been this close since she was comforting me on my bed.

"How did you sleep?" she asks, settling into the chair opposite me.

I look up without speaking, and I can tell from her sympathetic exhalation of breath that my puffy face has given her all the answers she needs.

"You told them where I was," I say bluntly.

She sighs. "I had to. My job comes before everything. We needed to question you."

"Right," I mumble, wishing I was snug in Mum's living room rather than in this cold, hard police station.

"I'm sorry, Jennifer. But I do have something new to tell you."

"Uh-huh?"

My thick brain shakes itself from its stupor. It's instinctive, almost, I'm on high alert. New news can't be good. It's never good. Another missing person, or another accusation. My head snaps around, as if I'm expecting Jam or Seb to burst into the room, waggling their finger and shouting at me. I rub my eyes and try to breathe normally.

"Yes. The CPS don't believe we have enough evidence to charge you."

"So? I'm . . . ? Sorry, what?"

"You're being released. But we do ask that you stay in your place of residence in Barnes as the investigation is ongoing."

"So, you believe me?"

"As I said, the investigation is ongoing."

"But I'm – but do you still believe me?"

"The CPS seem to. Won't even grant my boss a warrant. He's pretty furious."

Aayla doesn't look at me. I want to leap across the table and slap her or kiss her or just – just *something* to elicit a reaction. To shock her out of this robotic, emotionless state.

"I really trusted you," I continue.

She reaches out and then pauses, as if going for my hand and then thinking better of it.

"You can still trust me, Jennifer. You've still got my number. But it was wrong of me to make it so . . . personal."

"Yeah – there are apps for that kind of thing. Though, believe me, it doesn't always work out."

A small smile flashes across her face.

"No. But, look – the headline is that Scarlet's accusations alone aren't currently enough for us to charge you. You can grab your things and leave. Now."

"Right now?"

"Right now. But, Jen, no more detective work, okay?"

I nod. Hope and shock. My hands shake against the table. She says more, things about the media, about the law, my confidentiality, but the details seem to disintegrate before they reach my brain. I rub my eyes, double checking I'm not dreaming.

I nearly cry upon reaching the outdoors. London is as grey and miserable as ever, but I couldn't be more grateful to be out in it. I try to pull as much fresh air into my lungs as possible. I open my mouth wide, wider. That's when I spot her.

She's waiting for me across the road. My mouth remains open.

Mum.

I dash through the traffic in a flurry of beeps and screeching tyres. Mum hugs me hard, and I hug back harder.

"What are you . . . How are you here?" I ask once the embrace finishes.

"The police called. DC Powell, I think? I was on the first train down," she says. There's a fullness and steel to her voice that I haven't heard in a while. It's a voice of clarity. Her hazel eyes are bright, and today they're the master of the wrinkles that surround them, pulling them into one expression after another, expert puppeteers.

"I'm glad," I say.

We walk down to the river and sit on a bench overlooking the steely water and naked trees. I shiver, and Mum puts her scarf around me. For once, for just this one brief moment in time, I am in need and she is my saviour.

"So, they arrested you. Why?" Mum eventually asks.

"Scarlet came back. I dated her in July, she disappeared a couple of weeks ago. Anyway, she claims I kidnapped her." My voice gets louder and more shrill as my anger and disbelief increase. Once again, lies are being spread about me. I can't figure out why, and I can't figure out how to stop them.

Mum looks away from me. She seems to deflate; breath rushes from between her lips and she sinks an inch or two down the bench.

"Insane," she whispers.

"Yeah."

"Insane."

"Mmm. Uh-huh. But they're only allowed to hold me for twenty-four hours, or thirty-six with an extension or something, so . . . here I am. For now."

"You won't be arrested again, I promise."

These are empty words, but they're comforting, nevertheless. I picture Mum throwing herself between me and the police station and almost giggle. I sink into the bench, so that my shoulders are level with hers. I need to get in touch with Scarlet, somehow. I need to convince her that she's got things wrong, or beg her to stop lying about me. I'm not sure how closely she's being monitored by the police, but there must be a way of contacting her. I've got no other options.

"You know what day it is?" Mum asks, pulling me from thoughts about Scarlet.

"Of course I know what day it is."

Two years today since Dad died. Two years since he walked to the river Tees, stuffed stones in his pockets and drowned himself. I stare ahead, at the river rushing past me now. Imagine his big, lovely body being submerged. Imagine running forwards and grabbing him, begging him not to leave me. I blink away the tears forming in my eyes.

"It still hurts so much," I say. Funny, admitting that, finally. I've suppressed it for so long. Buried my feelings. Drowned them. Tears spill from my eyes and Mum pulls me in close, wraps a thin arm around my shoulder.

"I know. But he loved you, Jen. You made him so, *so* happy."

"I didn't. I was a brat." I pause, remembering the argument that had pushed me into leaving for London. Mum had been drunk, of course. She'd been crying about Dad. I take a breath. "That . . . When you . . . you said I'd added to his pressure, his stress. You think I made him do what he did."

"Oh God, Jen, never!" Mum says this with such conviction, her skinny body jumps a couple of inches off the bench. "Christ, I'm so, so sorry I made you feel like that. I've never thought that. Never."

"But that . . . what you said about me adding to his stress. I've spent the past year thinking you blame me for his death."

Mum's face droops in a fashion which would be comedic in any other scenario. It's as if the pull of gravity around her mouth is double its usual strength. The corners of her lips become almost vertical.

"Never, Jen."

"What you said . . . made me question everything. My relationship with him. My relationship with you," I say. I'm sad that what I'm saying is the truth. But I'm relieved to finally get the truth off my chest.

Mum shakes her head. "I blame me for his death. I blame work for his death. I blame the government for his death. I blame him for his death. I blame . . . God, anything and everything for his death, depending on the time of day. Depending on how much I've had to drink. But I've never, ever blamed you," she says. I'm overcome by such an unexpected wave of relief, I almost burst into tears. "Jen, I shouldn't have said that. I'm so sorry I said that. All I'd have meant by that was money. The extra money needed. Look." She squeezes my hand tight. "You were never a brat. You were brilliant. You are brilliant. You were the reason he managed to stay with us for as long as he did. You're the reason I'm still here."

I nod, trying to let her words sink in. I cling on to her tighter.

"I'm sorry I left you," I say.

"No. I'm sorry I tried to hold you back. It was selfish of me not to encourage you to go to university, or to travel, or to move to a new city."

I shift forward. Paw the tears from my cheeks. I let myself think about Dad. *Properly* think about Dad. He'd worked at the steelworks for decades, before being laid off seven years ago. We struggled on as a family, scraping together money, but Mum started drinking too much. Dad was jovial, initially. Or at least, he appeared to be. He tried his hand at every job going: working in the arcade, cooking fry-ups in the Stray Café, behind the tills at Aldi. And he doodled, of course, gripped by a deluded certainty that he could draw his way out of his problems. Sell his work to a newspaper or an art collector. I used to complain about dumb shit – not being able to go on school trips, having a brick for a phone. Getting my prom dress from a charity shop. I must have made him feel awful. And none of it mattered, anyway. I'd trade every material possession I own to bring him back.

He'd never describe himself as depressed. Instead, he'd reference "the black dog", as if this was a less traumatic way of describing the misery he was enduring. The river wasn't his first suicide attempt, it was just the one that worked. The police had returned him late one night a month earlier, merely telling Mum and I that he'd been causing a nuisance, loitering by the train tracks. When he did disappear for good, they didn't even bother looking, despite our begging. I spent four days cycling around Middlesbrough, until eventually I found his body washed up on the banks of the Tees.

A memory that haunts me, flashing up whenever I close my eyes.

"You can love him, but you can also let him go," says Mum.

I breathe in. For the first time in the longest time, it's as though my chest has expanded to the right size, as though I can finally get enough air in.

We sit in silence for a few more minutes, and then Mum says to me, "I'm staying at a hostel. It's not glamorous, but you're welcome to join me."

"I wish I could. But I have to stay in Barnes. With Bob. Police orders." The thought of doing so makes me shudder. I forget how observant Mum is when sober. She catches on to my discomfort quickly.

"You don't seem happy about that?"

I shrug. "Yeah . . . it's the Bob part."

"Thought you said he was just over-friendly?"

I almost laugh. Over-friendly. The kind of bullshit description you give to a parent when you don't want them to have to worry about just how big of a creep you're dealing with.

"No, he's odd. Odd in loads of little ways which have built up over time. It's like he's obsessed with me. He monitors who I have over and who I'm with obsessively. I think he even followed me to a date once. He knew I was reading *American Psycho* and, in retrospect, I definitely never left that lying around in the kitchen. In fact, he just knows what I'm doing in my room full stop, and I have no idea how – unless he climbs up and looks through my window, or has a spy-hole, or a . . ."

My bottom lip drops, and I squeeze Mum's hand tighter.

"Fuck." I'm shaking, and she's asking me what's going on, what I'm thinking, but I can't answer. She thought I was good at figuring things out, that some stroke of genius had allowed me to find Dad's body. That wasn't the case; it was sheer persistence. Cycling for days, searching relentlessly. I wasn't a genius then, and I'm sure as hell not now. Because Bob's been hiding in plain sight all year.

I stand up.

"I need to go," I say to Mum.

"You've . . . You've thought of something new? Are you going to the police?"

I almost laugh – between Aayla giving away my location and Inspector Grantham bringing up Dad, they're the last people I'd ask for help.

"No. Somewhere else."

I leave before she can object or tell me to be careful two dozen times. I'm gripped by the urge to do everything at breakneck speed, so I run to the closest bus stop. The bus journey from Hammersmith to Barnes doesn't take long, but I'm impatient throughout, banging my fingers against the windows and the seats, tapping my foot on the floor. When I'm finally off the bus, I sprint from the stand to the flat door.

And I look up, finally seeing what's been glaringly obvious since I moved in. The blinking red light above the doorframe. I unlock the door and step inside, giving myself a tour, like the one Bob gave me a year ago. Except this time the wool is no longer over my eyes, and I can see the half-a-dozen blinking cameras which populate the flat. They're in the clocks, in plant pots and on top of doorframes, even in my fucking bedroom.

It blows my mind that someone would do this. And if he's capable of this, then what else? I try to keep calm, try to stay focused on the task in hand, but I allow myself some release, booting the kitchen wall.

"Creepy shitty little bastard."

I scrunch my hands into fists. The cameras are disgusting, but now I know they're here there's a chance they're also going to save me. The porch camera should have captured that Seb never came in on the final night I saw him, and the ones in my room will show that I spent the whole night in bed, alone. A solid gold alibi from the total weirdo I live with. I just need to get my hands on that footage.

The flat is deadly silent, no gameshow questions or heavy breathing. It doesn't mean that Bob's room is unoccupied, of course. I move over to the permanently locked living room door and lay my ear against the wood, straining to hear movement from inside. I wait five seconds. Ten. Nothing.

"Uh, Bob?" I say.

Still nothing.

Good. Good and bad. There'll be no asking nicely, not that he'd have said yes anyway. Instead, I'm going to have to steal it. Harder, possibly. But I'm relieved that I won't have to come into contact with him. The irritation I've felt about him all year is no more. Now it's just disgust.

I turn his door handle. Locked, of course. I turn harder, fighting against physics and logic, certain that I've turned into the Incredible Hulk and can simply force my way into things. Obviously not. Goddammit. Doors look so tantalisingly breakable.

I push my fringe to one side. Force gears to turn in my brain – and preferably not towards a debit card shaped solution.

I recall what Aayla said when she found me trying to get into Seb's flat. Something about needing a screwdriver, at the very least. Bob being Bob, his toolkit is kept in the kitchen cupboards, so this is where I head, yanking out all the screwdrivers I can find, and dashing back to the door.

I crouch down and start prodding at the screws, until I finally find a screwdriver that fits. I turn and turn, breath bated, hardly daring to believe that this might actually work. I must turn each screw a dozen times, and I grow nervous, sneaking glances at the plastic chairs – a backup option if I need to smash through the door. But finally, the doorknob comes off. Hardly believing my luck, I remove the plate, pull on the locking mechanism and let myself into Bob's room. The little I know about it stands: off-white bed sheets, yellow walls. He sleeps on a mattress on the floor. The room is cluttered. Model figurines of warlocks and dragons, fancy old-lady plates and bundles of clothes cover every available surface. The room smells of mould rather than fish. I'm not sure which is worse.

I start rummaging through his drawers, on the hunt for his laptop and trying to ignore the doubts in the back of my mind. He's out of the flat and his laptop is with him. He deletes the videos after watching them. My chances of proving my innocence are gone. Long gone. Not helpful. I keep looking – under his pillows, behind the curtains, under the piles of clothes. I don't find a laptop.

I don't find anything that the hidden camera videos might have been sent to. And I jump at every sound, sometimes imagining it's Bob's car, sometimes imagining it's the front door. Every noise seems amplified.

Time is running out; he's never normally out of the flat for too long. And the possibility that he'll freak out on his return is very, very real. After all, the evidence of my innocence also proves that he's a bona fide stalker.

Outside, a car engine backfires and my hand shakes so much I almost drop the china plate I'm holding. I steady myself and prepare to move over to his bed, when something catches my eye. It's a photograph of a slightly younger-looking Bob, and a middle-aged woman. His arm is around her waist and she's smiling. It's a sweet photo, and I realise I've never seen Bob look so content. There's a scrap of newspaper tucked in the corner of the photo, which I pull out. It's a crossword clue: *Depression of jet setter. Five, three.* Beside this, Bob has written the answer, and a sad face: *Black Dog*. My stomach lurches, and a wave of sympathy, of *recognition*, even, overwhelms me. But I catch myself. Can't be thinking like this – can't be getting all empathetic. There's probably more to the photograph than meets the eye.

I move over to his bed and look under the pillows again. I take hold of the end of the duvet and give it a shake. I'm overwhelmed by the smell of musk and sweat. I almost choke and . . . and there's a shiny silver square in the middle of the sheet. His laptop.

I claw for it and dash from Bob's room, slamming his door behind me. I take the laptop into my room and sit against my door. A shaking finger finds its way onto the power button. Slowly, agonisingly slowly, Bob's laptop comes to life. And it's password protected, of course, but I know the password. Or I know the first three letters, at least, and I'm certain that I can guess the rest.

J – E – N – N – I – F – E – R – B – E – E – N – Y

I hit enter. And I'm met with a red cross and an 'incorrect password' message. Irritating. But not unexpected. I try again.

J – E – N – A – N – D – B – O – B

That doesn't work either. I try a variety of different combinations, hissing as I go.

"Jenny Beeny – nope. Jennifer 23 – nope. Nope. Shit. Shit."

The red cross appears time and again. I hit my head against the laptop lid, exasperated. I need the password. If it's written down anywhere, it'll be in Bob's room.

I stuff the laptop into a satchel, which I sling over my shoulder. Then I thunder back down the stairs and into Bob's room. What are the chances of the password being written down somewhere? He's pretty old, but surely *no one* physically writes passwords down anymore? Regardless, I tear through his drawers and rifle through any notepads I can find. I find bills and receipts from years ago and even the contract I signed, all the way back on the 4th of January. It's been kept neatly in a purple envelope. For a second, I think about tearing it up, before shaking my head and moving on.

There's a distant jangling – metal on metal, keys or a chain or something. I throw down the notepad I'm holding and move over to his bookshelf. I start pulling books out at random – cookbooks and a Scrabble Dictionary and *Who's Who in the Movies* from two decades ago – and shake them, praying a tiny scrap of paper will fall out. Nothing. Nothing.

No, not nothing. There are footsteps on the stairs. I drop the cookbook. My whole body is shaking. And I try to do too many things at once – try to think up an escape route, try to listen for Bob's rasping breath, try to hold the satchel steady. I scan Bob's room, feeling sweat on my brow. The footsteps continue, slow and then quick. And then they stop.

"How the . . . ?" says Bob, from right outside his open door. And then he pokes his head around the frame. His glasses nearly slip from his nose.

"Don't come any closer!" I shout, because it's the only thing I can think of. "I've got a knife. And pepper spray!"

Bob seems unable to form sentences, he just gulps at the air and moves forward slowly. I move back, in time with his steps, until my arse hits the windowpane.

"Don't come any closer!" I shriek again, so high-pitched I'm barely audible.

"Jen, what are you doing?"

"You've been filming me all year," I say. I want to sound enraged, but I can't; this statement comes out as a sad little whimper. Bob doesn't react, he just keeps moving towards me, and it's impossible for me to move any further back. I try to read the expression on his face, but he's blank, completely blank.

"Just for our safety."

"Why do you need cameras in my room for your safety?"

He's level with the mattress. A couple of metres from me. He's blank, still unpredictable. And he's close. Too close. Fuck. I turn slightly and use my left hand to tug at the windowpane. It won't budge. I check the sill for a key but can't see one.

I look back up. Bob is standing right in front of me.

It's only then that I realise how much danger I've put myself in. I don't know him at all. I don't know how he might react to accusations thrown his way. I don't know what he's done to people in the past, or what he might be capable of doing to me.

"You have my laptop?" he asks.

"I need the videos."

"I can't let you take it."

He's so much bigger than me. This is a stupid situation to be in, really, properly dangerous. The realisation seems to jolt through my body, and I tug harder at the windowpane, desperate to get away from him.

"Jen."

I yank the window open. I climb onto the ledge and—

And his hand closes on my satchel. I try to yank it away. I scratch and claw at his horrible paw, but he won't let go.

"Get off!" I try to pull it from him, and slip from the sill. My stomach drops, air rushes past my body, my coat scrapes down the bricks. I fall two metres onto the ground below. I land in a heap, gasping, body seized by shock and pain.

"Huh. Huh."

Hard to take air in. Gasping and red, all I can see is red.

"Huuh."

I blink and the red mist clears. The initial pain subsides, slightly. I look to my left: my satchel is ripped, but it's on the ground beside me. And the laptop is within it. Looking up, I see Bob closing his window, expression panic-stricken.

I take hold of the satchel and drag myself up. Nothing broken, as far as I can tell. One last look back at Bob's bedroom window. And then I grit my teeth and stagger away.

I take out my phone and google Unlock laptop near me.

Search results appear as I reach the woods. There's a small electronics store less than a mile away.

Okay, reachable. It will be an agonising journey, but I can make it. I shake my left leg, attempting to force pain from my ankle. I clutch my satchel tight.

And there's a grunt from behind me.

Bob has followed.

And amongst the adrenaline and the pain and the abject terror, it begins to click. I'm not the only person who links all the missing people together.

Bob does too.

CHAPTER TWENTY-SEVEN

Wednesday 16th November

Bob's weight and my injuries put us at about an equal pace, both moving at a sort of desperate, lolloping jog through the woods of Barnes Common. I keep glancing back, checking he's still fifty or so metres behind, rage and exhaustion twisting his features. Occasionally he disappears behind an oak or a particularly dense bush, and I'm gripped by a sickening mixture of hope and panic – wondering whether I've shaken him off, or whether he's about to pop up in front of me, arms open.

But he's not quick enough to trap me, and I'm not quick enough to shake him. We're embroiled in the world's most pathetic chase scene: taking place at a speed of approximately three miles per hour, with middle-class dog walkers and fallen branches our only obstacles.

I think about asking one of the dog walkers for help, but the thought of stopping, even for a second or two, of allowing his body to draw closer to mine, is untenable. He's the kidnapper. He must be. And, if I stop, I'll end up wherever Jam and Seb are.

So I keep shuffling, ignoring the pain in my left ankle, my swollen knee, my bruised arse cheeks. There's blood trickling under my jeans. Irrelevant. I have to keep moving.

Eventually, grass turns to concrete. On one side of the road are fancy houses overlooking the Common, across which Bob is still jogging. My footsteps echo obnoxiously loudly as I haul my aching body along the road, until a horrifying sight comes into view.

A level crossing. A level crossing whose lights have just started flashing.

"Fuck."

A train line in front of me, houses to one side and Bob on the other.

I can hear the train approaching.

The red lights of the crossing blur as my eyes fill with tears. Trapped. I'm going to get trapped on this side with him. I slow my pace and glance back: he's just forty, maybe even thirty metres from me. His lips twist into a crooked smile.

I could jump into the bushes, I could bang on someone's door, I could try doubling back, limping my way past him. My head snaps from side to side, as though I'm watching a horrifying tennis match, my shitty options disappearing with each passing second.

The level crossing beeps and the track shakes as the train gets nearer.

Fuck it. I sprint forwards. The barriers are closing, and half a dozen people are already standing patiently on one side, happy to wait for the train to pass, but I don't have that luxury. I daren't glance along the track, daren't see just how close the train is, instead I duck under the barriers. A yummy mummy with a pram gasps, as does a Lycra-clad man with an orange bike. Ignoring them, I race across the tracks, ducking under the barrier at the other side.

"You're a bloody idiot," is my greeting, from a well-dressed man clutching a newspaper.

I ignore him and glance back: Bob has reached the barriers. He's next to the pram and he's clearly torn, not sure whether to follow me, or to wait. For half a second, we lock eyes, and then his decision is made for him, as the train thunders past.

Seizing my opportunity, I go. I stumble along the pretty streets of Barnes and Mortlake, past fresh-faced kids and ruddy couples, whose lives are perfectly normal and uncomplicated, who seem more distant, more unlike me than ever. I hobble on for the sake of my freedom, for my life. My gaze alternates between the map on my phone, and the street behind, certain Bob's body is going to spring from the shadows.

It never does. I make it all the way to Sheen Lane, and a store called Eye Phone which is nestled halfway along it. The shop is cluttered with phone covers and sim cards and chargers, and a greasy-haired man leans across the plastic counter, scrolling through TikTok.

"Hi," I say, striding up to the counter.

The man keeps his gaze fixed on his phone, at a video of a teenager miming along to a song.

"Hey," I say again, and I'm met with the man's palm – surprisingly calloused for someone who works in a phone shop and, for all other intents and purposes, fits decidedly into the computer geek cliché.

I wipe sweat from my brow and glance beyond the phone cases, to the street outside. My coming to this shop is hardly a surprising move. There's every chance that Bob will guess at my intentions and drive himself over here. A sizeable man passes by the window and I jump.

"Hey." I turn back to the man and place my satchel on the counter, knocking his phone an inch or two to the left. I finally have his attention; he looks up at me with bored blue eyes.

"Hey," he replies, with a small, mocking head wobble. I'm in too much of a hurry to take offence.

"I know this is a phone place, but I really need you to look at my laptop. Can you do that?"

I take his shrugging as affirmation, and promptly whip out Bob's laptop.

"I've forgotten the password," I say.

"Uh-huh. And you're sure this is yours?" asks the guy, with a snide smirk.

"Ah, yeah, yep. I've just had a bit of a moment and forgotten the password."

"Oh yeah? Cos protocol and all, someone dashing in all panicked and sweaty with a fancy device they've just happened to forget the password to is normally a reason to ring the police."

All the colour must drain from my face because the guy cracks a smile for the first time since I set foot in the store.

"I'm shitting you. What do I care? I get paid eight quid an hour for this. Give it here. I'm sure I'll be able to get into your stolen goods."

Not feeling entirely comfortable, but with no other option, I hand over Bob's laptop. I lean against the counter and watch as the man's fingers dance back and forth across the keyboard. Another glance to my left, out of the window, tells me that Bob is yet to find me. But every passing shape makes me uneasy; I'm certain that, any second now, he'll come rushing into this little shop, where there's nowhere to hide, nowhere to escape to. I shuffle, resisting the temptation to run.

"No dice I'm afraid, the hard drive is encrypted."

I turn back to the shop worker, who pushes Bob's laptop back across the counter, and returns to his phone.

"What does that mean?" I ask.

"Means you need the password."

"What, you can't hack into it?"

The guy chuckles, eyes still fixed on his phone. "I'm flattered but who d'you think I am? An FBI agent?"

I nod, heart sinking. I rest my elbows atop the counter and place my head in my palms.

"Sorry, pal. Try to remember that password you supposedly forgot."

My head feels heavy, but I drag it up. Fingers shaking, I give the password one more attempt, thinking perhaps Bob spelt my name wrong.

J – E – N – I – F – E – R – B – E – E – N – Y

I'm wrong again. And I'm all out of ideas.

"Fuck."

I exit the phone shop but force my legs to keep moving; stopping seems too much like giving up. There's only one option left, really. It's the wrong thing to do, and it will probably cause me much more trouble in the long run, not least because the police explicitly told me not to. But it's all I have. And I'm desperate. I take out my phone and dial Scarlet's number.

CHAPTER TWENTY-EIGHT

Wednesday 16th November

She doesn't answer, of course. So I send her a message:

> Why are you doing this to me? I've got video evidence that proves it wasn't me. We need to talk.

I call her four more times, and am continuously met with her chirpy, irritating voicemail. My legs give up, and I collapse against a tree in Mortlake Green, holding my head in my hands, running my fingers through greasy hair. The park soundtrack of couples snogging, kids giggling and dogs barking only adds to my irritation; crying and gunshots would be far more apt. For once, I'm not even being dramatic.

My phone buzzes, and I jump. I reach for it, desperate for Scarlet's response.

But it's not Scarlet.

It's Seb.

Or at least someone pretending to be him.

Bob?

It has to be. How many other people can have it in for me?

> Come to the boathouse and I'll explain everything. If you're not here in the next thirty minutes, I'm killing Seb. I have a mole in the police, so if you tell them, I'll know, and I'll kill him.

So many swear words tumble from my lips that the children near me stop giggling, and their parents shoot me looks of disdain. But

I'm fucked, and I don't care who knows it. I don't have evidence – certainly not any I can access. I don't have anything that might clear my name. And I don't want to be responsible for Seb's death.

So I haul myself up. Because what other choice do I have?

I clearly can't contact the police but, in a last-ditch attempt to be responsible, I leave Saz a voice note telling her where I'm going. And then, for the second time, I make the journey along the Thames and over Chiswick Bridge. I take the steps down at a limping jog. Adrenaline is wearing off, and my various injuries seem to be catching up with me. Blood has seeped through my jeans, turning the light denim crimson.

The boathouse is just as run down as I remember, although there's a quaintness about it in the daylight. I do a lap of the building, looking for Bob, trying to do as many clever, survival-type things as I can: move quickly, keep my back against the wall.

Once again, no one's here. My phone receives a message just as I'm pulling it from my bag. It's from Seb's phone, of course:

Seb is inside.

In spite of myself, a worried noise escapes me. I feel sick. This message suggests that Bob can see me, but I can't see him. I'm on the back foot, and this fills me with dread. I reply:

Can't we meet out here?

A hand grabs me, and a rag covers my mouth and nose. I struggle – kicking and gagging – but, all too quickly, my world goes black.

I regain consciousness slowly, painfully. My brain seems to have swollen, pounding against my skull. And I still can't see anything. I can hear, though: someone is dashing about around me, whimpering and cursing. I can feel, too: something cold and metallic is wrapped around my right wrist, and a blindfold covers my eyes.

Shit. He's got me.

I can't fight the desperation to rid myself of the blindfold, so I reach up my shaking free hand and nudge it onto my forehead. My vision is still imperfect: hazy, and black in places. Water streams from my eyes, but I can just about make out the boathouse. Broken rowing machines, whiteboards covered in split times and empty bottles of water. There's a foul, rotten-egg odour, which I can only attribute to the mounds of unwashed kit in one corner.

And a body, hunched over and facing away from me. I blink tears from my eyes. The body isn't Bob's. I gasp, I can't help it.

And Scarlet Smith turns to face me. She looks as rough as she did in the police photo, but there's a desperation to her expression which unnerves me. Her curly hair is sticking out from a messy ponytail, and she clutches Bob's laptop tight in her hands.

"Wha . . . Where's Bob?" I ask.

"Who the fuck is Bob?"

Something halfway between spit and sick dribbles from between my lips. My head pounds. I feel fucking wretched. I drag my body up, so that I'm sitting against the wall.

"What do you . . . ?" It's a struggle to get words out. I paw away the dribble.

Scarlet ignores me. She sets the laptop down on her knees and starts hammering at the keyboard, a mirror image of my earlier actions. I watch as she sighs, shakes her head and pulls more hair from her ponytail. After thirty seconds, she puts the laptop down, and picks up a phone I recognise.

"Hey, is that—"

"Your phone, yes. And I need your password."

"What?"

"I need your password," she says, as she taps letters into my keypad. "Shit!"

"W-why?"

She pulls more hair from her ponytail, a great clump this time, and a tear dribbles down her cheek.

"Because you've got video evidence! You've got a video of me!"

My bottom lip opens – out of confusion, this time, rather than the urge to wretch. I look away from Scarlet, to my right. I'm handcuffed to a radiator. I tug, as if I'm expecting the cuffs to be a toy, to come loose as soon as pressure is applied. They don't of course.

"I don't have a video of you," I say, returning my gaze to Scarlet.

"Liar!" She throws down my phone and picks up the laptop. Puts down the laptop and picks up my phone again. And then she collapses forwards, scrunched up in a little ball of desperation.

"I have, I mean . . . There are videos. On the laptop. But not of you," I say.

Scarlet drags herself back up. She dries her eyes and re-ties her ponytail, taking deep, shaky breaths.

"How many people have you sent the video to?" she asks, her voice a little calmer than before. "The police? Have you sent it to the police?"

"I don't know what you're . . ." I scan the ground around Scarlet. Two more phones are by her knees. I recognise one of them. "Hey, is that Jam's—"

"What's the password for the laptop?"

The foul smell pushes itself up my nostrils, drowning me. I'm going to throw up again. I cough and attempt to compose myself. My head starts thudding as everything starts clunking into place.

"It was you?" I say, scarcely believing my own words.

"I need to see this video."

"There isn't a video," I say. "I lied." I try balling my right hand into a fist and shoving it through the handcuff. No such luck. If anything, I've just made my hand bigger.

"What? What do you mean you lied?" she says.

I try and sneak a look at my watch. It must have been almost an hour since I messaged Saz. Someone will be coming. Surely to God, someone is coming to save me. Maybe if I just keep Scarlet talking . . .

"Why have you done this? To them? To me?"

"Shut up."

Scarlet glances about the boathouse. She shakes her head, bites her lip, types in another attempt. "Shit!" she says, having been greeted by an "incorrect password" message I'm all too familiar with. "Tell me what it is."

"I'll tell you if you tell me why," I say desperately.

"What do you mean tell you why?"

"Why you killed them?" I cry, tears starting to dribble down my face. "They were innocent. *I'm* innocent."

Scarlets lets out a strangled laugh. She doesn't look much less tearful than me. She takes a steadying breath and says, "I can tell you that Liam Garcia was not innocent. He was a vindictive piece of shit. I dated him last year. When I broke up with him, he lost it. I had to block his number, delete my socials. So, he found a different way to get to me . . ." She pauses and looks up. Her face floods with emotion: eyes watering, the corners of her mouth pulled down, a pink flush in her cheeks. "He released a video of us having sex. I recognised my bedroom before I even played it. I recognised my tits, my tattoos, the expression on my face: pathetic. I watched the video and felt so much, more than I'd ever felt. Embarrassed and angry and hurt and appalled and humiliated and angry. So fucking angry."

I think of Bob's cameras, and a pang of sympathy hits me. I nod, and Scarlet continues, "Liam sent it everywhere. Ruined my life. I lost my job, lost my friends. I tried to get the police to press charges. Don't even think they looked into it. And now some other little jumped-up shit is trying to ruin my life with another fucking video."

"I'm, I'm . . ." I flail, not sure quite how to respond. I take a deep breath. "So you took things into your own hands? You killed Liam? How? How did you even know where he was? And we didn't even meet until after he'd died? What have I got to do with it?"

Scarlet opens her mouth to reply, but we both hear them at the same time. Footsteps. Someone is sprinting towards the boathouse. The police? Thank God. Despite my many reservations about them, they'll surely realise that it's Scarlet who's guilty, not me.

But it's not the police. Saz rushes through the door, sweaty and breathless.

"Saz, be careful, she's, she's the . . ." My warning trails off. Neither Saz nor Scarlet are looking at me. They're completely focused on one another.

"What are you doing here?" Scarlet asks her.

"What are *you* doing?" Saz retorts.

"Get out of here, Saz. Ring the police," I say, voice shaking. As pleased as I am to see her, I will never forgive myself if she gets hurt.

But Saz stands firm, frozen in fear and still staring at Scarlet. "Why's Jen tied up? What the fuck are you doing?"

"What I have to," Scarlet replies. She turns to me. "You were wondering how I knew where Liam was?"

My eyes water again. I nod. My head feels bowling-ball heavy. I look at Saz.

"Seriously, Saz, it's not safe. I'm so sorry."

But only Scarlet moves. She picks up Jam's phone and slides it across the floor to me.

"The password for Jam's phone is *Jam29092022*," Scarlet says, as the phone comes to a stop next to my feet.

"What?" I ask, caught off guard and confused.

"You heard me. It's *Jam29092022*. You might want to take a look."

I pick up the phone and enter the code with my uncuffed hand. I click straight into Jam's messages, because I know exactly what Scarlet is referring to. I know what she wants me to find. I remember all too well what prompted Jam to rush from my room on the day of his disappearance. There are hundreds of recent messages on Jam's phone, of course – every friend, relative and colleague under the sun seems to have messaged, desperate to know his whereabouts. The messages grow increasingly panicked, increasingly heart-wrenching. I scroll through them as fast as possible, to the 29th of September. One message sticks out. It's from a number that he doesn't have saved. Finger shaking, I click on it:

> Sorry, this is so random, but I think you're the only person who can save her. Please, I'm desperate – Saz is going to do something. I'm so scared. It's her stepsister, Scarlet. We're at Chiswick Boathouse. I'm scared she's going to hurt herself.

Heart pounding, I look up at Saz.

How else would Scarlet know so much?

Saz has been in on it the whole time.

CHAPTER TWENTY-NINE

Wednesday 16th November

They're not related, so they don't look alike, but I can see subtle similarities, evidence that they've rubbed off on one another. Both style their hair in striking curls, though Scarlet's hair is red, whilst Saz's is blonde. Saz wears monochrome whilst Scarlet wears earthy colours, but both are adorned in accessories – some of which match, most of which don't.

"*Why* have you tied Jen up? I thought we just needed her DNA near the bodies?" Saz asks her stepsister.

"She's got a video," Scarlet replies.

I stare at Saz, and it's like I'm looking at a stranger. My heart sinks as it processes the fact that my perception of Saz is all wrong. Has always been all wrong. God, I've been . . . what? Blind? Stupid? Ignorant? I've fucked myself over by trusting the wrong person; no one can help me now.

"No. No. This was not the plan," Saz says to her stepsister.

"Saz," I whisper, unwilling to give up hope that my friend will help me.

"What's happened, Scar?" Saz asks, careful not to look me in the eye.

"I'm taking care of it," Scarlet replies.

"What does that mean? You promised we wouldn't have to hurt anyone else." Saz sounds desperate and shrill.

I finally find my voice and shout over the pair of them. "Saz. Explain. Please."

"Get out of here, Saz. I don't have time for this," Scarlet hisses.

Saz's gaze shifts between me and Scarlet. I've never seen her look so miserable. Smudged mascara amplifies the desperation in her eyes. She keeps shaking her head at Scarlet, and then she turns to me.

"Saz," I whisper.

"You have to understand, Jen. We didn't plan any of this." Her words rush out of her. "When you brought Liam along to drinks, I recognised him and I couldn't believe it. I called Scarlet. How could I not? When she arrived we went to look for him. Only to confront him. Not to hurt him. We never meant to hurt him." Saz's eyes fill with tears. "He was trying to hurt her."

"Saz, please get out of here," Scarlet says. "This isn't helping."

"We just wanted an apology, some acknowledgement of how much he'd fucked her life up. But he just smirked and tried to shove her out of his way. And then I . . ." Saz covers her face and really begins sobbing. "I didn't mean to. It just happened. But we couldn't feel a pulse. And the river was right there. Less than a metre away."

Christ, the pair of them are a mess: two people who are in way over their heads and floundering. It would be tragic, if I wasn't stuck in the middle, my life on the line. I tug harder at the handcuffs, panic rising. But I can't afford to lose my head. "So you . . . that holiday you went on in April? Wasn't real? Cos it was straight after the night with Liam and . . ."

"No, it wasn't real. I was in bed crying and panicking and throwing up for two weeks."

"But . . . but why did you keep going, then? What happened with the others? They can't all have been accidents. What about Jam, Saz?" I ask, attempting to stall whatever their plan is. And also attempting to find out what the fuck has gone on over the past year.

"I—"

"We need to leave. We need to finish this and leave." Scarlet interrupts Saz. She composes herself, once again re-tying her hair and wiping away the last of her tears.

"Please, Saz, tell me. Tell me what happened," I implore, looking at her with what I hope are sympathetic eyes. Her own eyes are still ringed with makeup stains, as if she's been in a fight. They flicker between me and Scarlet. Eventually, she takes a deep breath and focuses on me.

"It was so fucked up. I felt horrific when Liam died, but I couldn't go to the police. I just couldn't do it. Couldn't face the thought of jail. And . . . and it's not like a confession would have brought him back . . . But then, that evening at The Ship, Daniel overheard my phone call to Scarlet when I found out that Liam's death was being treated as suspicious. I was really panicked, must have been talking loudly, saying that I was terrified that people were going to find out what we'd done to Liam. And turned around and Daniel was looking at me, smoking a cigarette and I just . . . I knew he'd heard what I'd said. And I hoped he'd think it was a joke, but then he told me at reception, that day you went for lunch with him. He was threatening me with what he knew. I was so scared, Jen. I didn't know what to do. Scar was just trying to protect me. She'd do anything for me."

"Saz, stop. We need to give her the pills and get out of here," Scarlet says.

"Pills?" Saz and I ask together. I watch in horror as Scarlet rifles in her bag and pulls a bottle of pills from her rucksack.

"No!" Saz cries.

"It's gone too far."

She's going to kill me. She's going to fucking kill me. Desperation and fear seize my body. If I wasn't handcuffed, I'd be sprinting away as fast as I could. Instead, my mouth motors into action, "Oh yeah, because a dead person chained to a radiator isn't going to look suspicious at *all*," I say, my voice much more level than my emotions, which are all over the fucking place.

Scarlet's head snaps up. "I'll need to unlock you after. Good point. And I need the passcode to your phone."

"Scarlet, please," Saz pleads.

"And what's your plan, Saz? How else am I going to keep us out of prison?"

"How is killing me going to keep you out of prison?" I ask.

"Well, it's going to look like a guilt-induced suicide, isn't it? That plus a confession text from your phone should be enough."

I clench my lips together that bit tighter, ready to resist.

"We can't, Scarlet," Saz sobs. "I can't do it again."

Despite the fact I've never been more scared in my life, a strange sense of calm washes over me. It's clear that, unless I keep Saz talking,

I'm in serious danger of death. I mean, I'm in serious danger of death regardless, but at least this way I'm able to hold on to a small thread of hope that I might be saved somehow.

"But what did you do to Daniel?"

A couple of seconds of silence. And then Saz answers my question. "Scarlet lured him into her car. Pretended she'd lost her dog. She drugged him. And then she made me dump his body in the river. It was her idea to frame you, I swear. I just wanted to forget."

"We would never have been able to forget everything," Scarlet says. "I knew that the police would eventually look into my revenge porn accusation. They would link me to Liam. I didn't want to give him the power to ruin my life again."

I take a deep breath, eyes fixed on Scarlet, who has started counting out pills. She pauses to wipe at the tears and snot which are once again streaming down her face, giving me further motivation for ensuring that those damp, deadly pills stay as far from my mouth as possible.

"When you asked about Daniel, I panicked," Saz says to me. "I texted Scarlet, but she'd already realised you could take the fall. She'd said she'd find a way to protect us, but I didn't know she was going to do that. I was so freaked out when those flowers were sent to you. She started following you, found a way to bump into you, to get your number. When I realised you were going on a date with her . . . I wanted to stop it, but I didn't know how."

This is and isn't surprising. It is and isn't horrifying. I've known for months now that I'm being framed. But for my closest friend to have been involved? It makes me want to scream. I shake my head, feeling stupid and gullible and embarrassed and most of all absolutely, irrevocably fucked.

Saz continues, "She used the date to . . . to try figure out whether you'd be easy to frame. And then she started creating posters and social media pages. I begged her to stop, but she wouldn't."

"You wanted me to stop, did you?" Scarlet asks, standing up, with a fistful of pills clutched in her hand. "Even when Jen kissed Jam? When she shagged him? I don't remember you telling me to stop then?"

Saz opens her mouth to reply, but she can't get words out. She blinks, and her cheeks redden. I gulp. My mind whirls, remembering Saz's references to a man she couldn't move on from, a man she was on and off with, who her stepsister didn't approve of. The extra effort she put into her appearance when she was around Jam. The simmering tension between the pair of them. She didn't want me dating him because *she* liked him. *Of course* she realised that Jam and I had kissed. *Of course* she realised we went home together. It was wishful thinking on my behalf to pretend she hadn't. God, I've been stupid. Wilfully naive.

"I made a mistake. I'm so sorry, Jen."

"Jam was a shit, he led Saz on for ages. Recruited her and then became her friend, and then started sleeping with her, promising her the world. Before dropping her for a new shiny thing, and then crawling back whenever he got bored of that," says Scarlet.

"That doesn't mean he deserved to die," I cry, utterly repulsed. I look around the boathouse, my gaze coming to a stop at a door which leads into a second room. The awful smell overwhelms me once more.

Saz inhales. Her breath is watery, wobbly. But when she speaks her voice is steely. "What we did to Jam was . . . I suppose . . . part revenge and part framing you more thoroughly – having him disappear after visiting you. Two birds, one stone, Scar described it at the time. But . . . I hate what I've done. It was never supposed to go this far. I-I don't know what I was thinking."

"And what about Seb? That was after Jam went missing. Do you know what you were thinking then? You must have told her where we were that night at the Halloween party?"

"I didn't know what else to do, Jen. I couldn't see a way out. I'd told her you were obsessed with him. She decided it would make sense if Seb disappeared too. You know, if everyone you'd dated since moving to London disappeared. Made you more obviously guilty. And you invited me to that party and it just sort of happened. She picked me up outside the club. She found Seb's number in Jam's phone and called him, shrieking about being his girlfriend. You left him outside, and we offered him a lift home a few minutes later."

"Why bother framing me for Scarlet too? Why bother having Scarlet disappear at all?"

"Made you an even more obvious link. Especially if she came back accusing you of her kidnap. We . . . she thought the police would take her word as gospel. Case closed. Wanky men dead, neither of us in jail. Didn't, don't want anyone in jail . . . especially not you . . . Didn't even really want anyone dead . . . but . . ."

My head pounds. I tug at the handcuffs again, wondering if I can break the radiator. Scarlet starts walking towards me slowly, fist full of pills and a sad but determined expression on her face. I scramble to my feet and tug harder, trying to use the full force of my legs to free myself.

"Okay, enough now, Saz. We need to get out of here."

"No!" Saz shrieks, pulling Scarlet back. She turns to me. "Jen, just show us the evidence and we'll delete it. Or we can just smash the laptop!"

"And we all leave here happy, right?" Scarlet says, pushing Saz away from her. "Impossible. She knows too much now. It's her or us."

I don't make it easy for Scarlet to get close, of course. I kick my legs out and use my free arm to throw whatever I can at her: marker pens, my trainers, an old book. Eventually, she pins me down, and I bite hard on her arm.

"Fuck!" she screams. "Saz. Help."

Saz is torn, I can see it. I shake my head at her, begging her to finally do the right thing.

"Saz, please. Please. You can stop this."

I snap my head left and right, attempting to avoid Scarlet's hand. She tugs at my hair and my head lurches back, but I manage to avoid opening my mouth – just. I'm sweaty. Sticky and sweaty and still nauseous, there's a pounding in my head. I'm exhausted, I have no idea how long I'll be able to fight.

And then Saz joins in. She presses one hand against my shoulder, but her other pushes its way into Scarlet's jean pocket. She takes out a key, and Scarlet doesn't realise what she's doing until it's too late.

"Hey! What the fuck?"

The handcuff unlocks and I drag my bruised wrist from it. And then, in a movement which is half punch and half slap, I force Scarlet's face away from me. She loses balance, and the pills scatter across the floor.

"Shit!" she cries, scrambling for the pills as I haul myself into a more upright position.

And then, amongst it all, there's the sound of a siren, in the distance. Everyone freezes. We look at each other, all wondering the same thing: *who called the police?*

"It'll just be passing," whispers Saz.

It's not, though. The siren sound grows louder and louder.

Scarlet shakes her head, gripped by panic and desperation once more. She clambers to her feet and sprints from the boathouse. Saz follows. My fall seems to have caught up with me – I can barely drag myself to my feet. I hobble forward, picking up Bob's laptop and Jam's phone as evidence. Surely the police will have ways of breaking into the laptop? The stupidity of not going to them in the first place hits me round the face like a slap. Why am I like this? Determined to do everything by myself, even when it's patently disadvantageous. Scarlet having a mole in the police was clearly a bluff, but I leapt at the chance not to get them involved. I leapt at the chance to not let go of the past. I shake my head and stumble over the rowing machines, following Saz and Scarlet out the door and into the chilly afternoon.

I'm anticipating . . . I don't know . . . apologies from the police? Appreciation? I get none of this. Scarlet has started sobbing. She collapses, wailing and pointing at me.

"She – she – tried to – hurt – me again." She chokes each word out, tears streaming down her face. Saz is frozen, but the officers act quickly. Inspector Grantham grabs me, once again telling me – with barely concealed pleasure in his voice – that I'm under arrest.

"No, you've got it wrong," I say, squirming against his grip. I wriggle round, so that I'm facing him. I fix my eyes on his, begging him to listen. "Scarlet confessed. Liam released revenge porn of her. She reported it, I'm sure – I'm *sure* – you can find her report. You can see I'm not lying. That's why they killed him, and then—"

"Jennifer Beeny, you're under arrest." His eyes are small, a watery blue colour, and utterly devoid of emotion.

"*Please*. Please. And they had to kill Daniel because he knew. And then killing Jam was revenge for how he treated Saz, and Seb was all a part of framing me—"

"Jennifer Beeny, I would advise you remain silent."

Inspector Grantham is forceful; he spins me round so that I'm facing away from him, and tries to pull Bob's laptop from under my armpit. I blink back tears of desperation, only to see a familiar face. Aayla. Her eyes are so different to his: big, brown, compassionate. She glances over at Scarlet – still in hysterics and being attended to by three officers – and then returns her gaze to me.

"Is what you just said true?" she asks.

I nod. "Yes. *Yes*. And I've got evidence."

"Let go of her," she says to Inspector Grantham.

"What?!"

"Let go of her."

Aayla and Inspector Grantham stare at each other, deadlocked. But she looks at him with such conviction, it's impossible not to take her request seriously.

He lets go of me, and I nearly fall forward. I steady myself and pull Jam's phone from my pocket. Maybe, just *maybe* the text luring Jam away will be enough. Probably not, but I have no way of getting into Bob's laptop, of getting hold of his videos. I type the password into Jam's phone: *Jam29092022*. What kind of sick bastard sets the password to the date of the abduction? Scarlet, evidently. And—

Oh fuck. Bob.

My move-in date. All the times he tried to celebrate it: with cheese and wine, with champagne. He knew the date that I moved in, the date that he *got* me, better than the back of his hand.

I drop Jam's phone and tear open the laptop. Inspector Grantham moves to grab me again, but restrains himself. With shaking fingers, I type:

J – E – N – 0 – 4 – 0 – 1 – 2 – 0 – 2 – 2

It's correct.

"Huh." A sound halfway between a whinny and a sigh escapes my lips. I click into Bob's folders and find one called *Videos*. There are more folders in here, and they're ordered by date.

"Now what's she doing? This is ridiculous, Powell, not protocol at all," Inspector Grantham grumbles, but I ignore him. I'm too absorbed by the screen in front of me. My heart is racing, my armpits are damp. I'm doing everything I can to hold myself together, to find the *29th October* folder. I press play on the porch video. More officers have joined without me realising. Like Aayla and Inspector Grantham, their eyes are glued to the laptop.

00:01 on Saturday the 29th of October. The road outside Bob's house is empty. The traffic lights flicker between red, amber and green, but there aren't any vehicles to stop or go. Seb appears in the frame, hauling himself up from Bob's doorstep, unaware of the fate that awaits him. He sways, slightly. I'm nowhere to be seen. I move my finger, about to click out of this video and into the one from my bedroom, when something else happens.

In the video, a car – the only one around – pulls up in front of Seb. One person exits the car, and then a second. Everyone around me inhales. They're all completely silent, I can't even hear Scarlet anymore. I blink back tears of exhaustion and hope.

It's dark in the video, but not dark enough to conceal the key details: both of the people are female, both have curly hair and one is wearing a snake costume. Saz and Scarlet. There's no sound, but I can see them saying things to Seb. Eventually, they lead him into their car.

An innocuous enough video to the untrained eye, but everyone around me knows this was the last thing Seb ever did. Christ. I really did have video evidence of Scarlet.

A tear rolls down my cheek. I look up and lock eyes with Aayla. She holds my gaze for a couple of seconds, and then she looks at the police officers.

"Fuck," she says, voice shaking with shock.

Everything seems to happen at double speed, after this. The officers rush away, yelling about arresting Saz and Scarlet, who screeches in protest. With fewer people around me, my legs almost buckle. I stumble but manage to stay upright. Aayla rests a supportive hand against my shoulder.

"How did you know we were all here?" I ask her.

"Your landlord, Bob, reported his laptop as missing. Said you'd been acting erratically, too. What with your situation, we knew we had to find you. Luckily, his laptop has a tracker."

"Bloody hell."

"Why the hell are you living with a middle-aged guy you don't even know? You really do have awful taste in men."

I gesture in the direction of Scarlet, who is still resisting the officers. "My taste in women isn't much better."

The officers are ignoring Scarlet's protests. They hold her still and read out her rights in voices that grow louder and louder. Only one police officer is next to Saz, who seems deflated, on the brink of collapse, as if all the life has been sucked from her. My heart drops; I'm overwhelmed by the urge to comfort her.

With an effort, Saz looks up and locks eyes with me. She mouths one word: "Sorry."

I nod. I try to think up the right reply but I'm too slow; the stepsisters are led into the back of one of the police cars. I stare after it, mouth hanging open. Gormless. Gobsmacked.

"Beeny?"

"Huh?"

I turn back to face Aayla.

"We're still going to need to ask you some more questions. But this is almost over for you. I promise."

"It was . . . it was complicated. With Liam, at least, I can kind of see how it happened. And Saz didn't really want to be involved."

"We'll get to the bottom of it," says Aayla, looking up at me from beneath her hat. "I trusted you. And you *can* trust me."

I nod and watch as the police car containing Scarlet and Saz exits the car park. The sun has almost set, and long shadows are cast from the trees, the two remaining police cars and the other officers.

"Jam and Seb are in the boathouse. In the back room, I think," I say, and the fact that there are two dead bodies metres away from me suddenly hits home. Two families will be devastated. Two families have already been devastated. Countless friends have had to mourn. Four lives have been snubbed out too soon. Did they deserve it? Does anyone ever deserve death? I close my eyes and it's not Dad walking away from me anymore. It's Jam and Seb and Liam and Daniel.

I shake this thought from my head.

"We know," says Aayla. "I need to get you out of here, okay? Your mum is at the station."

I stay stuck to the spot, watching as police officers enter the boathouse. The rotten smell seems to overwhelm me, even from all the way out here.

"Beeny?"

"Yeah. Okay. That sounds good. Thank you."

Aayla takes hold of my hand. Her skin is warm, soft. Her grip on me is loose but reassuring.

"I'm sorry I couldn't stop this," I say.

"Jen." She squeezes my palm. "None of this was yours to stop."

I nod. And then, with the boathouse to my right and the river to my left, she leads me to a police car. I get in, and we drive away from the men.

I try to loosen my jaw, relax my shoulders. My muscles ache, as if my emotional stress has manifested itself physically. I can learn from all of this, and I can ensure others learn from this too. I can honour the memories of the men – both good and bad – but I can also let them go.

I breathe out.

EPILOGUE

Ten Months Later

I can hear traffic and I can hear birds tweeting. The wonderful, horrible mishmash of city and nature, hustle and serenity that is London. The air is thick with the swell of an unusually warm September day. My eyes stream on and off, my nose is burnt and freckly and my fringe, long since grown out, is damp with sweat. An English woman in late summer. A nervous one.

I'm in one of the art studios at Goldsmiths, a bright space cluttered with other people's creations. Some are sublime, some are sinister. They're all thought-provoking, all eccentric, all wonderfully diverse, much like the city itself. In the middle of the studio, there are two easels. One for me, and one for her.

The door clicks open. And in she steps, eyes bright, hair pulled back into a plait and summer dress flapping about her ankles. I hug her and realise I needn't have been nervous. She feels strong and whole and happy.

Mum moves to one easel whilst I stand by the other.

"Right then, what whimsical thing are you making me draw today? Are we even drawing? Or are we gluing smashed plates to canvas? Or throwing balls of clay at paper?" she asks.

I laugh. Mum still lives up north, but she comes to London often. Since starting my art psychotherapy course, we've been creating together. She always pretends to begrudge this activity, but I see a smile spread across her face as soon as she has a brush or pencil in her hand.

"Oh please," I say. "I'd never make you do something as silly as throwing balls of clay at paper. They'd rip straight through."

"And you'd probably call that 'art.'"

"Someone would." I hand her a paintbrush and a palette, keeping my eyes trained on her face, waiting for the second she lights up. That first squirt of paint onto the palette. That's when I see it. That exact moment. I return to my easel. "Today we're just painting."

"Painting what?"

I gesture in front of us.

"There's nothing there."

"Exactly."

"Oh Jen, I can't be dealing with all this new-fangled stuff."

It's not long before she's painting, though. I join her, adding one colourful brush stroke at a time to my canvas, revelling in the simple pleasure of creating something from nothing.

"Flatmates still treating you well?" Mum asks.

"Yeah. They're really nice." I live in Lewisham now, a stone's throw away from Greenwich Park, with its breath-taking view out across Canary Wharf. I occupy the smallest room in a five-bed house share, with a cluster of twenty-somethings who irritate and thrill me in equal measure. Yes, they seem to order three million Amazon parcels a day, yes, the washing machine seems to be in constant use and yes, there are never any clean spoons. But they got me cake for my birthday. They include me in their weekly pub quizzes. They wash my mug if I ever leave it out. Little touches, which make me feel as though I belong.

Better than Bob, of course. Though credit where it's due – I'd perhaps exaggerated his awfulness. I found out later that his flat had been broken into not long before I moved in. His fiancée was injured in the process and it ultimately led to their breakup. The cameras were put up because of this, I suppose. Still, they were creepy as hell, and I'm glad he had to pay a hefty fine. But he did (albeit unknowingly) save my bacon. I sigh; we were probably just about square in the end.

"Alright?" asks Mum, clocking my sigh. I'm still not used to her being so alert, so present. "Job making you miserable?"

"No. No, not in the slightest." I work part-time at a café by the park. Putting all my earlier tea-making experience to good use.

"Well. Good. Cos they'll have you back at the—"

"—Stray Café. I know, I know," I interrupt, laughing.

Mum nods and sticks the end of her paintbrush between her teeth, like a proper artist.

"And how about that girl?"

"Saz?"

"Mmm."

"Sometimes I write to her. Sometimes she writes back."

"Well, just you be careful about that."

Unsurprisingly, Mum doesn't trust Saz. Perhaps I shouldn't either, but I miss her. I can empathise with what she did, to a certain degree. Saz and Scarlet are in jail, and rightly so, but sometimes I'll check in on Saz, or she'll check in on me. Justice has been carried out, as far as possible.

I dip my brush into blue paint and carry out my final stroke, before shifting back and smiling at my work. I turn to Mum.

"Come on then, time's almost up! Show me what you've painted," I say.

Mum grins. We flip our canvases round at the same time. And we're in sync. We're finally in the same place. A good place, a healthy place.

She's painted me, and I've painted her.

ACKNOWLEDGEMENTS

Huge thank-you to my lovely family, for their ongoing encouragement and support. Extra special thanks to my brothers for being a constant source of entertainment. For my gran, who encouraged an early love of reading, and would queue up at midnight with me to get the latest Harry Potter book. For my grandad, and his tales about sailing around the world in his youth. For my parents, who have always had an unwavering belief in me, and facilitated the printing addiction I developed over lockdown. I now have a healthy appreciation for the price of ink, and a stack of annotated drafts.

I'd also like to thank Paul Telfer, my English teacher, who encouraged my love of writing and has read far, far too many of my essays, my screenplays, and my abandoned novels. Hopefully this one will be a little more enjoyable.

The critters on Critique Circle, who commented on the chapters I posted on the forum. Your constructive criticism taught me so much, and your encouragement was completely invaluable.

And finally, a massive thank-you to my agent Amy St Johnston and editor Hannah Smith (and the wider teams at Aitken Alexander and Embla Books). Thank you for believing in this story and enabling it to get out into the world. This is a dream come true for me, and I feel incredibly lucky to have both of you in my life.

ABOUT THE AUTHOR

Charlotte Bigland grew up in Middlesbrough, before migrating to London for a more tropical climate, and to work as a terrorism insurance broker. When not telling anyone who will listen how warm it is, or the correct way to pronounce 'bath', she enjoys zhuzhing up the more mundane aspects of being a twenty-something-year-old by putting a fictitious, killer spin on them.

ABOUT EMBLA BOOKS

Embla Books is a digital-first publisher of standout commercial adult fiction. Passionate about storytelling, the team at Embla publish books that will make you 'laugh, love, look over your shoulder and lose sleep'. Launched by Bonnier Books UK in 2021, the imprint is named after the first woman from the creation myth in Norse mythology, who was carved by the gods from a tree trunk found on the seashore – an image of the kind of creative work and crafting that writers do, and a symbol of how stories shape our lives.

Find out about some of our other books and stay in touch:

Twitter, Facebook, Instagram: @emblabooks
Newsletter: https://bit.ly/emblanewsletter

Printed in Great Britain
by Amazon

86979563R00150